DATE DUE			
9/25			

THE RACE FOR
PARIS

Center Point
Large Print

Also by Meg Waite Clayton and available from Center Point Large Print:

The Wednesday Daughters

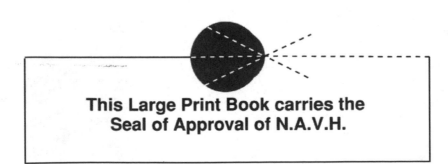

This Large Print Book carries the Seal of Approval of N.A.V.H.

THE RACE FOR
PARIS

MEG WAITE CLAYTON

CENTER POINT LARGE PRINT
THORNDIKE, MAINE

Library of Congress Cataloging-in-Publication Data

Names: Clayton, Meg Waite, author.
Title: The race for Paris / Meg Waite Clayton.
Description: Center Point Large Print edition. | Thorndike, Maine :
Center Point Large Print, 2016. | ©2015
Identifiers: LCCN 2016008238 | ISBN 9781628999525
    hardcover : alk. paper)
Subjects: LCSH: Large type books.
Classification: LCC PS3603.L45 R33 2016 | DDC 813/.6—dc23
LC record available at http://lccn.loc.gov/2016008238

For Mac,
pour toujours,
and for Marly and Claire

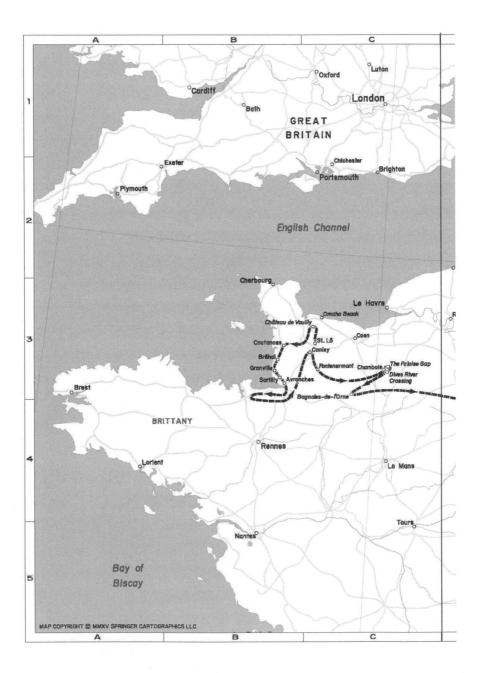

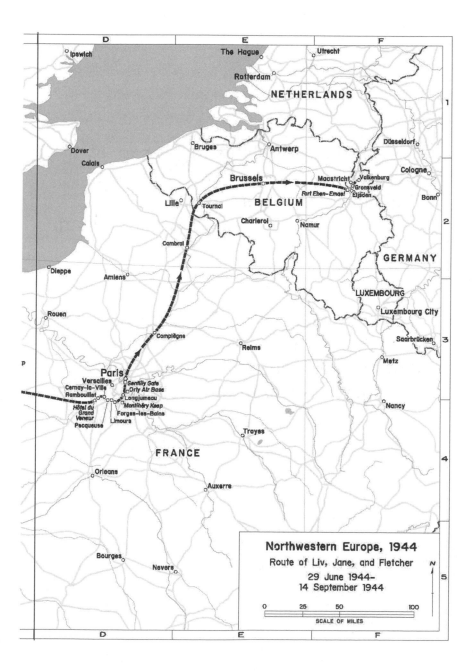

Northwestern Europe, 1944

Route of Liv, Jane, and Fletcher

29 June 1944–
14 September 1944

0   25   50   100

SCALE OF MILES

I would give anything to be part of the invasion and see Paris right at the beginning and watch the peace.
—Journalist Martha Gellhorn
in a December 13, 1943, letter

And yet love turns out to be the only part of us that is solid, as the world turns upside down and the screen goes black.
—Martin Amis, from *The Second Plane*

AUTHOR'S NOTE

This novel was inspired by the women who defied military regulations and gender barriers to cover World War II and the "race for Paris," vying to be among the first to report from the liberated city in the summer of 1944. They did so by stowing away in bathrooms of Channel-crossing boats, going AWOL from support positions to get to the front lines, climbing fences meant to contain them, struggling to get their photographs and stories out, and risking their lives. Despite being confronted with red tape and derision, denied access to jeeps and to the information and accommodations provided to their male colleagues at press camps, pursued by military police, and even arrested and stripped of credentials, women like Lee Carson, Helen Kirkpatrick, Sigrid Schultz, Iris Carpenter, Ruth Cowan, Lee Miller, Sonia Tomara, Catherine Coyne, Dot Avery, Virginia Irwin, Judy Barden, Tania Long, Barbara Wace, Margaret Bourke-White, and Martha Gellhorn proved that they could report the war, and opened the way for generations of women. Although this is a work of fiction, I've striven to make it historically accurate, and to that end have borrowed heavily from the facts of the lives of soldiers, support troops, journalists, and civilians involved in the war, and particularly from the experiences of these pioneering women.

HÔTEL DE VILLE, PARIS
◆
SATURDAY, AUGUST 20, 1994

Every image he sees, every photograph he takes, becomes in a sense a self-portrait.
—Photojournalist Dorothea Lange

The moon over the Hôtel de Ville hangs as round and golden as a C ration can to complete this fairy-tale setting: the clock in the tower striking the half hour; the stone flag bearers rising above slate roofs like egrets poised for flight; and the windows, of course, all those windows leaving guests trying to remember which one, exactly, de Gaulle addressed us from—those of us old enough to remember, anyway. Inside, tuxedoed men and sparkling women will be claiming flutes of champagne. They'll be toasting *Pushing Against the Fog*, an exhibit of Liv's photographs taken as she and Fletcher and I crossed Normandy fifty years ago, vying to be the first to report from a liberated Paris—a moment that could make a young journalist's career. That's what we were, Liv and I: young journalists. Before the war, I was a typist at the *Nashville Banner* and Liv was in school. Then Pearl Harbor was bombed and the

11

boys headed for war, leaving girls like us to step into vacated bylines. Women, I perhaps ought to say, but we were girls then in so many ways, as surely as the men who came back, or didn't, were boys when they left.

Britt, who was sent to collect me for this opening celebration, nods at the clock, to the left of the de Gaulle window. Yes, I do remember which one it was. With my good hand, I smooth a wrinkle in her red silk sheath (vintage, they call it now) as a tour boat passes behind us on the Seine.

"The gown fits you like a thick newspaper fits a Sunday morning, Britty," I say, although in truth I prefer her usual cargo pants and T-shirts, the vest she wears unless the devil himself is sweating in whatever godforsaken war zone she finds herself. On impulse, I unhook my necklace, a lonely emerald in a circle of diamonds. "You have the better neck for this," I say, "and I expect it will fit nicely in your field pack after tonight."

"That necklace wouldn't last one moment in my pack, nor would my life if I were carrying it!" she responds easily, kicking the possibility of her death high and wide. Does anyone in her twenties imagine herself mortal? In her twenties, as Liv and I were when we met, Liv barely twenty-one and me just a year older.

"Well, I'll wear it for you tonight," Britt concedes.

I say, "It's not too late. We could climb onto one of those tacky tour boats and make a getaway."

12

The look she gives me: *No, we can't; of course we can't.* Liv's photos will be here for a month, with crowds lining up (*queuing,* Britt would say) at the side entrance on Rue de Rivoli to see the exhibit and perhaps buy the "companion book," as if this exhibit came first and the book followed rather than the other way around. But tonight is for the book, which has been fifty years in the making, fifty years already made if you don't count finding a publisher and getting the censors to release their sweaty grip.

And it was so long ago—Fletcher and Liv and me. Maybe my guilt isn't really guilt. Maybe it's something else, or nothing at all.

My eyes haven't adjusted to the brighter light in the reception hall before the publicist hurries toward us with a gaggle of society reporters in tow. "This is Jane, of course," she tells them, leaving me no choice but to accept champagne and settle into the wrong side of the interview, answering questions rather than asking them. I pocket my discomfort like an after-dinner mint and try to sound clever for the journalists while "chatting casually" for the photographers, all of whom surely must be more interested in the movie stars and politicians scattered about the room, the computer kids in tuxedos and tennis shoes, the gray-haired Wall Street moguls in proper footwear escorting dates younger even than the computer kids. Copies of the book sit on podiums through-out the hall, not the cover photo I would have chosen but I do understand the choice. A sign points to the room where the photo exhibit begins. Its black lettering reminds me of that on the cave walls during the war, VERBLYF VOOR 5 PERSONEN. Everyone remains huddled out here in the reception hall, though, near the champagne.

A journalist puts a question to Britt about her gown, and she tilts her head to mine to give a better angle on our companion jewelry, her emerald necklace and my matching earrings. Yes, the photographers do like that. They will run us under some caption like "Old Journalism and New, in Gucci and Gems at the Hôtel de Ville" in the *Times* Sunday style section tomorrow. The *New York Times*, not the London papers. The London papers will already have been put to bed.

Britt negotiates our escape from the press and pulls me into the exhibit room, and there I am in the first photograph, taking aim with a pistol, Fletcher's arms wrapped around me as he teaches me to shoot.

Britt says, " 'For someone who so obviously loves the feel of a gun in your hand, it's sad that you're such a poor shot!' "

" 'Such a *bloody lousy* shot,' " I correct her, wanting suddenly to tell her about the day Liv took this photograph, about the German boy. But her attention has been caught by the book sitting like a Bible—in the beginning, God created Liv—on a pulpit below the bloody-lousy-with-a-gun photograph. Someone has left it back cover up so that we're looking not at the front but at a photograph Fletcher took: Liv in military fatigues, standing in that jeep with her Speed Graphic in her hands and her Leica hanging from a camera strap.

They surprise me, these photos do, or the girl I was in them surprises me, the girls Liv and I both were. I didn't have Liv's delicate prettiness: her short dark hair and long dark lashes, graceful dark brows, her narrow nose with that odd little bump going down to a fragile tip of chin, her boyish build. Liv's changeable eyes—the sturdy blue of my mother's Sunday milk pitcher on a clear morning and something greener and more varied in other light—leave me thinking even now that my own eyes are as plain brown as the trunk of a walnut tree. But in the photo my legs look graceful where I thought them gangly, and my arms, too, my square shoulders. The wave in my bottle-blond hair frames a face that is clear-skinned, that might have been downright attractive if I'd had Liv's confidence, or perhaps even was.

Britt rights the book and opens it. She flips past the half title page to the title page and the verso with its copyright information and disclaimers, its grateful acknowledgment of permissions to reprint. When she reaches the dedication, she stops turning pages.

"Renny—the Renny the book is dedicated to—isn't my mother," she says uncertainly, as if she wants to insist it must be.

I lean close to her, the smooth silk of her gown cooling against my ruined hand as I trace the letters with my good one—the *R* and the *e,* the *n, n, y*—trying to weave a reply from the threads of hurt: all the days and nights Liv and I shared, the things we did during the war and the things we ought to have; the lives Fletcher and Charles and even Liv knew before the war and my own more circumscribed past; the unspoken words in the years since, the griefs held back out of respect for other, greater griefs. Have we ever spoken the truth about what the war made of us, or who we might instead have become? *To Renny.* So simple, and not.

A FIELD HOSPITAL IN NORMANDY
◆
THURSDAY, JUNE 29, 1944

So you want to go to war? . . . You won't
be very comfortable. Things will happen
you won't like. Do you think you can take
it?

> —Chief of the War Department's
> bureau of public relations'
> war intelligence division, speaking
> to AP journalist Ruth Cowan

It was raining again, still raining, the morning
I first met Liv. I'd been at the Normandy field
hospital for a week, sharing the end tent in the
WAC stockade with Marie Page from *Ladies'
Home Journal*—a tent too close to the eight-holer
latrine, but we'd been offered no other. Marie and
I awoke in our bedrolls underneath our cots to
the lousy plunk of rain on the tent canvas, and Liv
entering through the door flap. Her poncho
streamed water onto the dirt floor that we worked
so hard to keep from turning to mud. Already,
Marie was scrambling from her bedroll, reaching
up to turn on the flashlight we'd strung from a
rope across the tent and offering to help Liv with

her rain gear, pulling Liv's poncho over her head as if she meant only to be hospitable. Underneath the poncho, a lanky tripod hung from a strap at Liv's shoulders, as did a large-format Speed Graphic camera and a 35mm Leica. The Leica's chrome was painted a dull black lest it reflect light and draw sniper fire.

"You must be the new girl," Marie said.

She held Liv's poncho under the door awning outside and shook off the rain as she introduced herself.

Liv tentatively touched the rope from which the flashlight hung. Like all correspondents, she wore a captain's uniform for credibility with the soldiers and to convince the Germans we weren't spies, hers with a *P* for "photographer" on her armband that replaced the original *WC* for "war correspondent" but also for "water closet"—the john, the bathroom, the loo; the Brits had a field day with that. She opened her Speed Graphic and accordioned out the bellows, locked the lens plate down, and took a photograph. Just that: the rope. Not even the flashlight.

"Olivia James Harper, with the Associated Press," she said. "I go by Liv."

I pulled my notepad from inside my bedroll and rolled out from beneath my cot, careful to avoid the tentacles of wet dirt left behind by Liv's poncho. Liv turned her camera to photograph me as I did so, capturing me with tent-floor dirt on my face, morning breath, and my helmet on. Even inside the tent, it was as cold as a slave merchant's heart.

Liv said, "You sleep underneath your cots?"

"Only when the Germans make night raids," Marie answered.

"Our sweet German lullaby," I said. It was surprising how quickly I'd gotten used to huddling in the slit trench behind the tent when the raids started, and sleeping under my bunk in my fancy four-pound helmet, taking baths out of the same helmet, washing my clothes in the water afterward and hanging them to dry from the tent ropes on the sunny side of the tent when there was sun, which there wasn't much.

"I'm Jane Tyler, with the *Nashville Banner*," I said, helping Liv ease off her rucksack and the smaller musette bag.

Liv unstrapped her bedroll and draped it across the cot assigned to her. Marie asked if she needed any help unpacking and, when Liv declined, began to lay out her uniform on her own cot the way she did each morning, as if preparing for a homecoming dance.

"You're sure you don't need help?" I asked Liv, but I was already settling cross-legged on top of my cot with my typewriter—a foldable Corona—in my lap. A lead for a story had come to mind as if ducking in with Liv, and the first words of a story are always the hardest to come by, and the most fleeting. I loaded the paper and carbon and tapped out several words, hit the carriage return, and typed the rest of the sentence and the blessed first period. The day was starting to look like a good one despite the rain.

Liv said, "I love the sign, by the way. '1st Tent.' "

"Don't encourage her," Marie said to Liv.

The sign I'd made from an empty bandage box and hung over our tent door was meant to be funny. At the press camps where our male colleagues were billeted, a "1st Tent" assignment was a mark of prestige. We weren't allowed at the press camps, though, even for the briefings. "No ladies' latrines, and we aren't about to start digging them now" was what we were told, although the press camps in Normandy were set up at swanky French country homes, with indoor plumbing and fireplaces, on-site censors and telephones and wireless transmission, and good whiskey on tap.

Liv said, "So how do I go about getting the commanding officer's permission to go to the front?"

"To the front?" Marie repeated.

I said, "You haven't even unpacked your nightie, Liv."

Liv eyed my long-handle GI underwear, the bedroll around my legs. I was still thinking of the press camps, wishing not so much for the whiskey

(I poured my own generous whiskey rations for the doctors and medics I interviewed) as for the ability to negotiate changes to my pieces with the on-site censors and to make sure my censored copy made sense. Marie's and my articles went by field messenger service to Price's gang in London, who wielded their hatchets, stuck the remaining bits back together, and left our names on what was often not quite the truth, and sometimes pure gibberish.

"We'll never be the first to report from Paris if we're not at the front," Liv said. "But if we approach the CO together? How can he say no to all three of us?"

Marie peered suspiciously into each of her boots, stuck a hand into one, and pulled out a snail—which she fussed at for coming in uninvited.

"My editor wants coverage of the field hospital and the boys here," she said to Liv.

Liv began pulling rolls of film and cut-film holders from her musette bag, the realization dawning: neither Marie nor I had been granted permission to cover the front, or had even asked for it.

"For pity's sake," Marie said as she stripped off her long johns and began dressing quickly in the cold. "Why would any decent woman *want* to photograph dead boys?"

Liv watched Marie clip her regulation cotton stockings to her garter belt and try to smooth out

21

the bagginess at her knees. And I watched Liv watch Marie; I watched Liv absorb Marie's implication of Liv's indecency, waiting for Liv's hurt to work its way into harsh words. She only popped open the Speed Graphic's back and focused on Marie, though, and handed the camera to me.

"Have a look through the ground glass, Jane," she said.

The leather, as I put my face to the camera's viewing tunnel, smelled of the Stahlmans' library back home: the leather chairs I was not to sit in and the leather-bound books Mama quietly slipped out for me to read, books I took up into the magnolia tree where no one would notice me, or into the garden shed where Old Cooper allowed me to read on rainy days.

Through Liv's camera lens, Marie appeared upside down—her baggy-stockinged legs feet upward.

"Her editors at *Ladies' Home Journal* would be appalled!" I said, realizing how silly I, too, must have looked upside down in my helmet and bedroll, underneath my cot.

Liv put her own face to the camera and moved right up to Marie's baggy-stockinged knees, saying, " 'If your photographs aren't good enough, you're not close enough!' " and even Marie giggled.

I suppose I started liking Liv in that moment,

with that first glimpse of her humor. Her humor and her mercy, letting Marie and me both off the hook for our cowardice, letting Marie's charge of indecency stand against her without a word.

"So where, exactly, am I?" Liv asked.

Outside, the rain had let up, the drip on the tent giving way to the chirp of magpies and the rolling whistle of wrens, the peewit of lapwings drawn to the marshes here, even in war.

"You're a few miles outside of Saint-Lô, the summer home of the German Eighty-fourth Corps," I said. "Captain Harper, welcome to France."

Liv went alone to the CO's office that morning and waited while he signed papers. She listened mutely when he began to speak, his voice full of the life-is-to-be-endured gruffness of small-town Vermont. She didn't care, really, that there would be no chitchat, that he didn't give a blink where she was from or why she was here; he just wanted to make sure she was well acquainted with the rules and wouldn't get in the way of his doctors. She nodded politely, waiting until he had clearly spoken his piece before she said, "If it's convenient, sir, I'd like permission to go to the front."

The CO sat back and crossed his arms, his shirt barely creasing as he stared over his reading glasses. "What's your assignment, Mrs. Harper?"

"I'm assigned to this field hospital, sir, but—"

"And you've been here how long? Two hours?"

The day's first ambulances were arriving outside, the hurried sputter of engines announcing the day's first wounded.

"In two hours, Mrs. Harper, you've covered everything at this field hospital? My doctors? My nurses? The boys who've had their legs sawed off or their eyes taken out, who are lucky enough to be on their way home to wives and mothers and kids who are going to back away from them like they're god-awful freaks?"

"Well, sir—"

"Can you get them all in the time you've got here? Twenty-one days and you go back to London. Your accreditation papers are very clear on that, Mrs. Harper, no matter who your husband is."

"I understand that, sir," Liv said, the creep of fear returning: that she would be left forever approaching this war, that it would end and she would never have gotten to photograph it, much less gotten to Paris. So many months spent arguing with the War Department, the Passport Office, her own husband, for goodness' sake. Margaret Bourke-White had already flown over Tunis in a lead bomber to photograph exploding landing strips while Liv couldn't even get a passport. She imagined Bourke-White already in Paris, flown there on a military plane with the six hundred pounds of luggage and three thousand peanut flashbulbs she'd taken to the bombing of

Moscow, men in uniform holding her lenses while military officers worked her extra cameras to get every angle of a shot. Although that wasn't true, and Liv knew it. Bourke-White had been denied even the three weeks in Normandy Liv was given ("too temperamental"), and no one was in Paris; the troops were not much beyond Charlie, Dog, Easy, and Fox—the code names of sections of the invasion beaches that stretched alphabetically across the French coastline, some sections further divided by color designation: Dog Green, Dog White, Dog Red. Everywhere the word "stale-mate" was spoken in hushed tones as Allied troops advanced only a hundred yards a day—progress the medics measured in morphine units dispensed, thirty-two grains per hedgerow.

The CO said, "And you want me to free up a jeep and driver, Mrs. Harper, to take you to a front already so covered up with the press that soldiers are tripping over them?"

"Sir," she said, thinking, *One jeep*. She didn't need a driver. She could drive herself perfectly well. Thinking the troops would never make Paris in three weeks. Thinking there were doctors and nurses and wounded enough to photograph at home.

"Sir," she repeated, "even General Eisenhower says public opinion wins wars."

"Is that why you're here, Mrs. Harper? To persuade the ladies back home to spend a little less time rolling their hair and a little more rolling bandages?" He reached for a document and began flipping pages. "Well, I'm sorry to disappoint you, Mrs. Harper, and I'm certainly sorry to disappoint General Eisenhower, but I can't spare a jeep today."

Outside, the ambulances—jeeps fitted with steel frames to carry two stretchers—were stacked three abreast and ten deep. Medics unbuckled the litters and gently unloaded them before the ambulances left again, to return an hour later with more mud on their wheels and more boys with gut or chest wounds, or without legs. Only the worst of the wounded were brought to the field hospitals, boys who might not survive the longer ride to an evacuation hospital farther back from the front, or even the wait for a full ambulance load.

That's where I found Liv later that morning, standing in front of her Speed Graphic mounted on her tripod, with what looked to be a telegram in her hand. She wasn't reading it, though. She was looking resolutely at the boys soaking their bandages on litters in the open field as exhausted nurses checked their tags for how much morphine they'd received at the front and gave them sulfa, plasma, antitetanus shots, and sympathetic if hurried smiles.

"Any luck with the CO?" I said, wanting to ask

about the telegram—which Liv folded and tucked into her pocket—but not wanting to pry. "I did warn you he's an old goat, didn't I?"

She loaded a cut-film holder—two shots—and focused on a wounded German. His knobby wrists extended beyond his outgrown uniform, and he was so rotten with the mud and sweat of having been too long at war that the nurse attending him held her breath.

"They treat Germans here, even before our boys?" Liv asked.

I took out a ration package of Lucky Strikes ("Lucky Strike Means Fine Tobacco") and offered her one, which she declined. "If they're closer to dying," I said.

She removed her dark slide and took the shot—the terrified boy watching the nurse prepare the morphine needle.

"He thinks it's poison, Liv," I explained. "Imagine if you were in a German camp."

Liv and I were working together that night in the "operating room"—a relatively well-lit if not much more sterile area set off by mosquito netting at one end of the surgical tent—when I registered the distant sound of the night's first shells.

One of the nurses I'd come to know, Annette Roberts from Asbury Park, New Jersey, said softly to a boy whose vein she was testing for an IV, "They're ours, Joey. Those shells are headed for the Germans. Now I need you to make a fist."

Her white surgical gown was ridiculous against her muddy boots, as was that of a surgeon who gazed at the tent top and said in a Dracula imitation oddly tinged with a Southern accent, " 'Listen to them. The children of the night. What music they make.' " The Count, I nicknamed him, although Mr. Lugosi was tempting, too.

"M3s," a boy on another stretcher said. One of the ways soldiers passed time in the foxholes was by identifying the shells by sound.

The Count said, "Y'all can swap out this soldier."

He smiled at Liv and me then, his eyes between his surgical mask and his helmet suggesting he didn't mind Liv's flash or my questions. Some of the surgeons did mind, of course. Some glared at us as if we ought to start administering morphine or step out of the damned way.

As the shelling continued, boys in various beds called out identifiers for each whoosh. A stretcher crew moved the Count's patient away, leaving the two sawhorses that formed his operating table to be filled by another wounded soldier's stretcher. And the rhythm of the room continued against the background percussion of the shells: the doctors asking for scalpels and suction, teams moving the wounded, nurses soothing the waiting.

It seemed the shelling was letting up when one of the boys cried out "A Great Gustaf!" his words barely out before a metallic shriek filled the tent.

The hospital staff hit the ground, Liv and me with them, and Annette, too, Annette holding the IV needle up so it didn't touch the ground.

A boom sounded and the ground trembled.

Almost before the sound dissipated, Annette was back on her feet, saying, "Don't worry, Joey. Our tent is marked with a red cross."

Liv and I stood, too, Liv pulling a fresh flash-bulb from her pocket—broken.

"Do you learn all the boys' names?" she asked Annette as she repositioned her camera to photograph the doctors removing their surgical gloves and putting on clean ones, the staff collecting instruments to be resterilized.

"The ones from home, at least," Annette said. "Joey here is from Toms River, aren't you, Joey?" She warned the boy that he would feel a stick, as if the IV needle could possibly cause him more pain than his leg, which no longer had a knee or calf or foot. "I think it makes them feel a little better to be taken care of by a girl from home," she said to Liv.

Another shell screamed overhead, and we again hit the ground, Annette saying, "Hold your arm still where the needle is, Joey. Hold still and you'll be fine."

The roar. The explosion. The lights flickering and then failing while earth pelted the tent walls as if the world outside had shattered. I was still on the ground when Annette's voice came from above me, calling into the darkness for someone to see about the electrical circuit.

"Good job, Joey," she said. "Now don't mind the dark. I'm right here."

A flashlight shone, and another, lighting the surgeons' hands as the surgical gloves and instruments were again changed for sterile ones. Liv was left without enough light by which to photograph well. We had that excuse to quit, and we did want to quit; we wanted to run for the relative safety of the slit trenches. But even as artillery fire flared in spots of light through the tent canvas and shrapnel from the antiaircraft guns rained down, the hospital staff continued working by flashlight, pausing only to tighten the straps of their combat helmets or to curse the German planes. And so we, too, carried on. Liv removed her flash attachment so as not to startle anyone in the darkness, and adjusted her shutter speed and aperture. I borrowed a flashlight to hold between my chin and neck while I jotted down notes.

I was watching the Count finger a patient's intestines for bullet holes and shell fragments in the beam of a flashlight when Liv whispered something about her father.

"Work like this might have saved him," she said with a longing in her voice that made me think of the telegram, perhaps news of her father. Was her father in this war?

"Might have saved him from what?" I asked, thinking she might want to talk about it now. War does that. The sense of your own mortality can make you want to be known by someone, just in case.

Liv turned her camera on its tripod to face the Count, flipped the dark slide over, reinserted the film holder, and adjusted the lens. She'd heard me, but didn't want to allow that she had.

The Count, with a nod at the intestines in his hand, said, "Like a moth through a mitten, this one," and Liv released the shutter, capturing the doctor's easy manner despite the wounded and the mud, the German fire, the late hour and the limited light. This was why she'd brought the Speed Graphic: its bellows structure made it bulkier and more cumbersome than the Leica and you had to change the cut-film holder for each shot, but the larger-format film captured more detail, especially in low light.

From behind us, Joey asked for ice cream.

"You hang on, Joey!" Annette answered. Then, "I need a doc here! I need a doc!" with an alarm in her voice that hadn't surfaced even in the worst of the shelling. "You hang on, Joey," she said more calmly. "We'll see about some ice cream after the doctor here fixes you up. What flavor do you want? You tell me. Strawberry? Chocolate? We have anything you want, Joey, you just tell me and I'll get it for you right now."

"Peach," the boy said weakly.

"In a cup or a cone, Joey?" Annette said, and it seemed for a moment that she really might get this boy his peach ice cream.

The boy said, "God, I'm so cold."

Annette started cooing in a frantic way then, saying, "Keep looking at me, Joey, keep looking at me, I'm going to get you peach ice cream and I'm going to get you back to Toms River." Someone shone a flashlight on them so Joey could see Annette's face, as close to him as a lover's. "You're going to have such a good life back in Toms River with your girl, Joey. You're going to have five kids and you're going to eat whole gallons of peach ice cream together every Saturday night if you just keep looking at me. Joey, keep looking at me. Keep looking at me."

Liv turned her tripod and took the shot, Annette's face and the boy's together in the single beam of the flashlight.

A doctor appeared at Joey's stretcher, barking orders: he was not going to lose this boy who was some poor mother's son. Liv shot photographs and I took notes as the team worked and worked.

Then they didn't. They stopped working, and a silence settled over Joey.

The team dispersed, leaving Annette to cover his face. She blinked moist eyes as she whispered, "You have all the ice cream you want now, Joey. You have a cone for me. I'll have peach, too."

With my right hand, my pen between my fingers, I made a small sign of the cross over my heart. I couldn't cry, I reminded myself. I was a war correspondent, a professional. I was to remain stoic lest any emotion I showed add pain to those whose lives I'd been sent to write about. If I couldn't take it, I was to let my editor know and he'd send someone to replace me.

As a stretcher crew came to move the dead boy out, Liv photographed the end of his stretcher: the single, lonely combat boot.

Back in our tent, Marie was rolled up in her bedroll under her cot but still awake, just returned from the muddy trench behind the tent. Liv and I climbed under our cots, too, as if that would provide any protection at all. I buried my notes from the operating room underneath me lest they be destroyed, and suggested Liv do the same with her film. We both tucked our clothes into our bedrolls, to keep them dry. And while in the distance German bombers droned and American ack-ack answered, Liv said, "I don't know anything about scalpels or morphine. All I know is shutter speeds, *f*-stops, angles of light."

I said, "Most of the soldiers who make it here from the front, they survive, Liv." But I, too, was having trouble shaking off the sound of the boy asking for peach ice cream, the inadequacy of what I could do even when I did my best. And the best of my words were no more likely to be published than were the best of Liv's photos. The filthy, stricken, raw, bloodred wounded were too stark a contrast to the fresh-faced American heroes the public imagined. They would never get past the censors, much less newspaper editors focused on sales.

"Charles feels it's the right thing to do, to stick with photos and stories that will go down well enough with the morning coffee," Liv said. Her husband was the editor in chief of the *New York Daily Press*; Liv, who'd gone to work for him after we joined the war, moved to the Associated Press after she became Mrs. Charles Harper. Charles's paper was in the AP consortium so he could still use her photos, and Liv would never have been accredited as a war photographer if she hadn't moved to AP.

Marie wondered aloud what her fiancé was doing—a boy to whom she'd gotten engaged just after Pearl Harbor. He'd gone off to enlist, and she'd been heartbroken, and he'd returned without a uniform and she could neither go through with the wedding nor call it off, and she'd fled; she supposed that's how she'd gotten to France. 4F. It meant only that her fiancé was disqualified from military service for medical reasons, but medical excuses were drummed up easily enough that 4F carried the stink of cowardice as surely as did Liv's husband remaining in New York.

"Charles was in Warsaw when the Germans

invaded," Liv said. "He and his photographer stayed even after the lines were cut and they couldn't get stories or photos out." She pulled her bedroll more tightly to her throat and shifted her head, awkward in her new steel helmet. "Even when the Polish government fled to Natęczów, Charles stayed to cover the invasion."

A clock tower in the next town marked three a.m., an echoing bong, bong, bong followed by silence, the absence of drone and ack-ack, which might last or might not.

"I brought a ball gown," Liv whispered into the blackness, that late hour when it's always easier to share the things we hold close.

"A gown?" Marie said just as I said, "Here? To France?"—our voices as soft as Liv's: a secret revealed, a secret received.

Liv had stuffed the silk sheath in with her gear at the last moment, and evening gloves, too—gloves of soft kid leather that went up over her elbows, dyed the red of the dress.

"The gown folds up to be just a tiny little thing," she said, and I imagined her gloved right hand in her editor in chief husband's left, the two of them twirling around a ballroom, drinking champagne and laughing as nobody had laughed since the war began while, just blocks away, a child slept in a crib in the room next to theirs.

I said, "Three children, two sons and a daughter—that's what I want someday."

"I want five," Marie said.

"A Renny and a Charles Jr.," Liv said, "after the war."

Liv said, " 'If your photographs aren't good enough, you're not close enough'—that's what Robert Capa says." Her voice wistful, lacking the force she'd been full of when she'd arrived that morning. "But I've been an ocean away. I'm still miles away from the front while Capa and Frank Scherschel and Ralph Morse are already on their way to Paris, making their way with the troops toward the city, to the Eiffel Tower and the Champs-Élysées and liberation, Allied troops marching in to throngs of crowds filling the streets, celebrating what will be the moment of the century. A moment that will make a photo-journalist's career."

"Make your career," Marie repeated under her breath, a reprimand. We were all supposed to be doing whatever we were meant to do to win the war. We were to follow orders. We were to set aside our discomfort. We were to do everything for the war effort, and nothing for ourselves.

"Well, for my part," I said, smoothing over Marie's censure and tucking away my own, "I figured I'd be an old maid by the time the boys returned home, so I thought I'd best come here to find a beau!" As if I'd skipped the whole routine of accreditation and vaccination, passport and visa and PX card, and gone directly to be

36

measured for my Saks Fifth Avenue uniform—which had been the idea of my publisher's wife, as had been my move from the typist pool to the books page, from journalist to foreign correspondent. Lord & Taylor had made Catherine Coyne's uniform to order for the *Boston Herald*; Savile Row had made Helen Kirkpatrick's; and when Patricia Lochridge went to the Pacific for *Woman's Home Companion*, Saks made hers, and Mrs. Stahlman insisted the *Banner*'s women readers would accept no less for their own "Intrepid Girl Reporter," whom she insisted they have. That was the truth of how I got to Europe: my mother washed Mrs. Stahlman's dishes and mopped her floors, and Mr. Stahlman owned the *Nashville Banner*, and Mrs. Stahlman—who wanted a lady war correspondent like the big-city papers—could imagine me in a role I'd never imagined for myself. I'd lived my whole life on the wrong side of Nashville and that was my future, and this was my one shot to change that.

None of our reasons for going to war made sense, and yet they all did.

The drone of planes sounded again, faint but present, and Liv and Marie and I started singing together, lying underneath our cots and waiting for morning to come around. We sang softly, barely over whispers, just because it felt good to sing. "The White Cliffs of Dover." "Always." "As Time Goes By." I closed my eyes to block out the shadow of canvas cot above me, the drone and the ack-ack, the sharp corner of my notepad pressing against my back. And I imagined I was a girl again, singing alongside Mama's high, sweet soprano voice, just the two of us in harmony as we washed Mrs. Stahlman's Wedgwood china in the big sink in the big kitchen at the Belle Meade mansion, where I used to imagine I might someday live.

THE U.S. FIRST ARMY PRESS CAMP AT CHÂTEAU DE VOUILLY, NORMANDY

◆

TUESDAY, JULY 11, 1944

If we really wanted to go to a battle, we simply showed up on the doorstep. The briefing officer would tell us where action would be that day. If we wanted to attend, we picked up a jeep and went. We might stay for two or three days, we might live in a foxhole or in a nearby farmhouse or go back to the base to file our stories.

—Walter Cronkite

Fletcher eased the jeep past a cluster of two dozen journalists' tents, the mess tent, and the wireless trucks improbably mingling with spotted cows in a field along the drive of the Château de Vouilly, the US First Army press camp in Normandy—for the time being, anyway. The air was fresh with the smell of dawn mist and cows and new-mown hay. No cordite. No death. The countryside was alive with such a delightful racket of chirps and trills and hoots, the quacks and honks of ducks and geese, that Fletcher might have left the world of the war behind entirely. And the stone home in the early light (not sunrise so much as a vague transition from starless black to gray haze) reminded him so much of his own family's country house back in England that he just sat there for a moment, thinking of the evacuee schoolgirls billeted in Trefoil Hall, and of his parents, and of Elizabeth Houck-Smythe. It was only half five; the morning briefing wouldn't start for hours. Half five on Tuesday, July 11. Edward's birthday. His brother would have been twenty-nine.

Fletcher climbed from the jeep and crossed the little moat, following signs to a door to the left of the arched front entry. It opened into a long, cool hall: limestone floor, white walls, and blue doors running along the front of the château's north wing. A dining room done in white with blue trim—now set up for the censors—was empty, as was a living room cleared of furniture and reloaded with rows of hard wooden chairs and small writing tables, with maps and charts hung on its walls. But at a table in the kitchen, a regal, white-haired woman chatted easily in French with an American corporal and several farmhands.

"*Bonjour! Je m'appelle Alexandrine Hamel*," she said, greeting Fletcher with an enthusiasm that suggested this was exactly what her home was intended for, to provide for foreign journalists and the occasional military photographer. She offered him a glass of milk still warm from the cow, and introduced one of the men at the table as her son. The man nodded but did not rise.

"*Et mon épouse,*" the son said, nodding to a younger woman, who was pregnant, at the sink.

"*Vous avez été à Saint-Lô, Monsieur Roebuck?*" Madame Hamel asked Fletcher.

"*Non, à Caen,*" he answered, not offering more because of the son, because this chap Hamel was safe in his château rather than in a German POW camp and that left Fletcher suspicious. Suspicion, he'd learned, served one well at war.

"*Vous aimeriez prendre un bain, j'imagine,*" Madame Hamel offered. "*La guerre prend un tres mauvais tour à Caen, oui?*"

Yes, Fletcher thought, a bath would be just the thing to wash away this bloody war, which was indeed going badly at Caen. He'd set off in his jeep with his gear, a sleeping bag, a change of clothes, five ten-in-one ration parcels (food enough for a month), and orders to trust his instincts, to return to the press camps or to England when he needed to return. He'd lasted a mere eleven days photographing the fighting at Caen, though—an objective meant to be taken on D-Day but still in German hands—before fear and exhaustion drove him here.

He glanced at the Hamel son's warm, open face. Fletcher supposed that if he were at Trefoil Hall and the Germans marched into Chichester, he'd do whatever he needed to do to stay alive, too.

He ought not to accept Madame Hamel's offer of a bath, he knew that. He ought not to impose. But he imagined his own mother in this position, and he heard voices in the hallway now, too—the censors arriving. So he accepted, asking only if he could get his film off first.

He asked the younger Madame Hamel when the baby was due, and when she said October, an image of Elizabeth pushing a pram through Hyde Park on a warm October day came unbidden, unwanted.

"*Félicitations*," he said, silently hoping for them that their child would be a daughter who would never be sent to war.

The American corporal offered to show him the way to the darkroom, but Fletcher assured him he'd manage himself. He headed not to the darkroom, then, but rather directly to the censors' room, where he found his contact. As he waited for the man to get settled, Fletcher looked out through the wavy windowpanes crosshatched with safety tape to three herons floating in the moat below the window, raindrops plinking on the murky water. The walled pasture beyond the moat, where at Trefoil there was a proper garden, hosted spotted cows like the one Fletcher had shot the day before, there being no bovine ambulance to help the poor wounded beast. Beyond the cows, a charming outbuilding set into

the stone pasture wall sprouted radio antennas—
Fletcher's excuse for this interlude from dead
cows and dead soldiers and the possibility of
dying himself. A booster rigged up here extended
the 75-mile transmitter to 190, allowing transmission to London.

"All right, then," the censor said, and Fletcher
handed him two rolls of film to be developed
and transmitted.

"Uncensored," Fletcher said. The rest, he said,
could be sent by courier.

"To British intelligence back in England—
undeveloped and uncensored," the censor confirmed.

Fletcher lowered his voice and asked about the
Hamel son.

"He fought in the French army and spent
some time imprisoned by the Germans," the
man answered as he marked the two rolls for
processing. "But he was no good to them because
of the leg."

"The leg?" Fletcher said, registering why the
son hadn't stood to greet him.

"The Germans released him in the *relève*, I
believe. French workers volunteering to work in
Germany in exchange for the release of prisoners.
But of course the Germans only released prisoners
they couldn't get work out of anyway. Monsieur
Hamel's good luck, the fact that he will never
walk well again. His ticket home."

• • •

By the time Fletcher bathed and stopped by the mail room to send off his letters (to his parents, to the evacuee schoolgirls, to Elizabeth), the mess tent in the pasture was filled with correspondents eating a full hot breakfast. Fletcher grabbed a cup of tea (bitter, oversteeped American stuff) and a plate of eggs and bacon and toast, and he joined Matt Halton and Charles Lynch at one end of the table. The two Canadians had brought a basket of carrier pigeons along on the D-Day invasion, meaning to use the birds to send their reports back across the Channel—birds that, when released, headed instead directly toward Germany.

"Too bad about those Nazi birds," Fletcher said by way of greeting.

"Traitors! Damn traitors!" Lynch replied, shaking his fist in the air as he had when the birds had flown the wrong way.

"Roebuck, you unsympathetic bum," Halton said. Then to the others, "Careful of this one. He looks like one of us, but he's a British spy."

Fletcher nodded in greeting to the others, saying, "AFPU, actually." The British Army Film and Photographic Unit. Fletcher had spent the first years of the war photographing bigwigs in England for the British military newspapers, a cushy position his father had arranged, that allowed the respect of a uniform without the danger—what Fletcher had wanted after Poland.

It wasn't until Edward died at Dieppe in August of 1942 that Fletcher had felt his own cowardice, and it was almost two years more before he joined the AFPU's new No. 5 section, which was being formed to support the Normandy invasion. Fletcher hadn't volunteered; he'd only agreed to the transfer. He was charged now with getting photographs revealing the positions from which the Germans best fought, to identify the vulnerabilities of their pillboxes and tanks and planes—photographs that could communicate in a moment's glance as much information as pages of military reports requiring hours to read, and with an accuracy that eyewitness reports could never match.

"I'm just a military photographer," he said.

Halton said, "And the difference between a spy and a military photographer is what?"

Fletcher said, "Maybe we should have asked those Nazi birds of yours?"

Fletcher listened to the resultant laughter, thinking if he had any guts at all, he'd at least use a movie camera; you couldn't wear a helmet while operating a movie camera because it banged the eyepiece. He'd gone to Poland without a helmet, certainly. But back then he couldn't quite believe war would actually break out, and he was too young to believe he was mortal even if it did.

The journalists, as they ate, gossiped about Ernest Hemingway's wife, Martha Gellhorn, a

Collier's reporter who had hidden in the loo of a hospital ship just after D-Day to become one of a very few correspondents—female or male—to go ashore for the assault on Omaha Beach. When she returned to London, she was stripped of her military accreditation, her travel papers, and her ration entitlements, and confined to a nurses' training camp. "She hopped the fence and hitched a ride to an airfield," someone said. "Left a note for Hemingway that she was off to Italy. Some RAF pilot flew her to Naples."

Gossip. It was the favorite pastime at the press camps.

More coffee, more tea. More off-color jokes. "It could be worse," someone said. "We could be in the Pacific, having our photos intentionally miscaptioned to leave the impression that General MacArthur is at the front when he's nowhere near it, or our articles censored out of existence if his military genius is brought into doubt." And more posturing about which correspondent would do what by when, most importantly who would be the first to report from Paris. Fletcher listened quietly, remembering when he'd been one of this club, when he'd walked away from Oxford with only his camera, in search of adventure.

"So you're Fletcher Roebuck," an American said, a cameraman by his armband, so Fletcher gave him some respect.

"'This crazy Brit who will stand up against

anything for the photo'—that's the way Charles Harper describes you," the chap said. "He likes to tell how prescient you were in Poland, although of course that story makes Charles Harper himself prescient, too."

Laughter again, this time at Charles's expense. The American cameraman laughed the loudest.

But Charles Harper had saved Fletcher's life on that street in Warsaw—or, if you believed Charles's account of the story, then it was Fletcher who'd done the saving, and Charles whose life had been at risk. It had been exciting, Poland had been, but you couldn't see how close to being killed you were until you arrived home and knew you had survived. And if you had any sense you found a nice girl and settled down to a normal life, like Charles had.

The cameraman said, "I guess the prospect of fatherhood is making Charles Harper soft, keeping him Stateside."

A *Stars and Stripes* journalist replied, "But I heard Olivia Harper is here, in France."

"You think Charles Harper's wife is his only chance for fatherhood?" the cameraman replied.

Fletcher frowned as the others again laughed. Even in Poland, Charles had girls, yes. A cameraman he and Charles had met in Warsaw—Julien Bryan—loved to joke with Charles's Polish girls that Charles could only put them in stories while Julien could put them in the movies. That was before Charles married, though, and it was one thing to risk getting a girl pregnant when you were free to make it right, and quite another when you had a wife.

"To Charles Harper, a hell of a reporter," Fletcher said.

"To hell with Harper," the cameraman said. "To Paris!" And they raised their cups to that.

In the château's living room, new maps and charts were swapped in for ones from the prior day, and journalists settling into the hard wooden chairs made plans to jeep together to the front or to meet back at the château that evening for a bit of hard cider from the tap in the kitchen or a neat whiskey, or two, or three. A. J. Liebling from *The New Yorker* was taking up a collection in hopes of acquiring a barrel of old Calvados from a neighboring farmer. The American cameraman from breakfast invited Fletcher to join in a poker game at the end of the day, but Fletcher claimed prior plans with Charles Harper; Fletcher couldn't say why he wanted to yank the shirty little American's chain, except that the chap slept in a dry bedroll in a tent and wore laundered uniforms, and came back to friendly poker games in the warmth of the correspondents' room fireplace every night.

A hush fell as Monk Dickson took the front of the room and smiled his shy smile. "Shall we talk about where you can find the war today, if you're so inclined?" he asked. He set to on the details: a million men, a half million tons of supplies, and two hundred thousand vehicles had landed on the beachhead, which was now seventy miles wide. The next objective was the city of Saint-Lô and the commanding ground encircling it.

"Isn't Paris in the other direction?" one of the correspondents called out.

Another answered, "I'll have a glass of champagne waiting for you when you get there," and everyone laughed.

A coordinated attack by three divisions through the hills protecting Saint-Lô originally scheduled for July 9 was going forward that morning, along a ten-mile front, Dickson explained. The Thirty-fifth Division was to take the right bank of the Vire, the elbow made by the river northwest of the city. The Second Division would make an assault against Hill 192. The Twenty-ninth would push toward the ridges along the Saint-Lô–Bayeux highway and Saint-Lô itself, to cut off the German reserves from the south and east.

Saint-Lô, Fletcher decided. If he had any guts, he'd still be with the soldiers at Caen rather than eating hot eggs in a press camp and casting suspicion on a Frenchman who had by some miracle survived a German camp. But Fletcher couldn't bear to return to Caen.

Monk Dickson had barely finished his

presentation before everyone piled into jeeps. Fletcher followed them down the rutted drive and along a sunken road through Saint-André-de-l'Epine, the journalists going slowly so as not to kick up dust, staying low as bullets flew overhead. Outside Saint-Lô, while the journalists left their jeeps at the point beyond which nonmilitary vehicular traffic was prohibited, Fletcher showed his British military identification and continued on. By noon, he was on foot, too, photographing engineers from the US Sixtieth Combat Battalion planting discarded casings of 105mm shells filled with TNT to blow through the hedgerows. He checked his pistol—a Webley Mk IV that had been his brother's—and gathered his nerve to follow a platoon of German soldiers long enough to see them sever the wire connecting the Second Battalion from its command. There was nothing he could do to stop them. He took the photos and slipped back to rejoin the exhausted Allied soldiers pressing on, replacements coming in, going out, getting killed. More replacements replacing them.

A FIELD HOSPITAL IN NORMANDY
♦
WEDNESDAY, JULY 5, 1944

Dearest Mrs. R; Thank you very much for letting me come down. The White House is certainly a fine rest cure place . . . I was a fool to come back from Europe and I knew it and was miserable about it; but it seemed necessary vis-à-vis Ernest. (It is quite a job being a woman, isn't it; you cannot do your work and simply get on with it because that is selfish, you have to be two things at once.)
> —Journalist Martha Gellhorn in
> an April 28, 1944, letter to
> First Lady Eleanor Roosevelt

The Normandy weather routinely went from bone-cold rain to yellow-dust heat with nothing in between, but on the rare fine days at the field hospital, Marie and I would pull a table and wooden folding chairs from the mess tent into the shade of an apple tree, and we'd set up our typewriters and smoke and talk and bang out our stories. Liv would join us when the mail came (thin paper, thin envelopes), and I would share my mother's letters, always reading them twice to myself first, choosing carefully and editing to make it seem that Mama sat, wool and needles in hand, in the drawing room with the Belle Meade ladies rather than coming around with the coffeepot and washing the china afterward. Liv and Marie loved Mama's colorful expressions— "every dog should have a few fleas" to excuse someone's shortcomings or "the bishop himself is kicking in the stained glass" when something irritated her. They loved, too, the snippets she sent from Eleanor Roosevelt's popular "My Day" columns. I'd just read one—" 'No creative work, it seems to me, can be accomplished unless people sometimes have quiet and peace around them. It is hard to find such peace in this war period.' "—and I was imagining the First Lady's secretary adding one of my pieces to the clippings of women's writing she compiled for her boss or even inviting me to attend Mrs. Roosevelt's weekly gathering of women journalists at the White House, when the CO's clerk came to find us.

As he approached, Liv whispered, "Why does he always look like he means to send us home to shoot fancy wedding copy for the society pages?"

Marie said under her breath, " 'Fancy wedding copy'—for pity's sake," her feelings hurt by Liv's easy dismissal of the kind of reporting Marie had done before the war, and which I imagined as the best I might hope for after the peace.

The clerk, though, had come with news that the CO had found a spare jeep for the next day. "Two seats, for Mrs. Harper and Miss Tyler," he said.

Several AP newspapers, including the *Chicago Daily News*, had run Liv's shots of the Count fingering the boys' intestines and of Joey and Annette—photos that were grainy and dark, the slight blur from the long exposures leaving the subjects ghostlike, evocative. "Operating Room by Flashlight," they were captioned. They'd run in the *Nashville Banner* along with the piece I'd written, too. And they were the reason the CO had found us a jeep.

After the clerk left, Liv shared a letter from her brother, the first she'd received from Geoffrey since she'd been in France, as far as I knew. He'd written from "somewhere in England," where he was training for a special mission, so she shouldn't worry if she didn't hear from him for weeks or even months. As I listened to her read— every word down to the "P.S. Do you remember that doll with the shoe that disappeared? I needed a fishing bobber. Sorry!"—I thought really the best way to get anyone to start worrying about a thing is to tell them not to. But Liv tucked her worry down under a good thick layer of how smart Geoffrey was, how he could do anything.

It was the fifth of July, that day was. We hadn't had fireworks or even a bonfire the day before because of the blackout, but we'd received no new wounded, the hospital emptying in preparation for leapfrogging forward, closer to the front. And I'd written a little skit the nurses and the mess tent staff had performed. A skit didn't have to be all that funny to make people laugh when they'd spent their day tending maimed boys—gallows humor was the way we let the steam off the boil of war, the little bit of insanity that kept us sane. Still, it was gratifying to hear the laughter, to know that my words had a hand in making people forget what they wanted to forget, even if just for an hour.

The next morning, Liv and I loaded cameras and notepads, gas masks, and lipsticks into our musette bags, and climbed into the back of a jeep that took us to a cemetery near the coast—a jeep not able, inexplicably, to take us to the front. At Omaha Beach, "Jerome Neff, with Graves Registration," introduced himself while men with spades in hand poked about wherever sticks protruded from the white sand, each stick topped with a canvas bag attached like a hobo's burden. A few feet from where our jeep had dropped us, two soldiers pulled a body wrapped in what had been the dead boy's half of a pup tent from the sand, unwrapped the boy, and put him in a clean white shroud.

"We don't get too many newspaper girls here," Jerome said with a smile that seemed out of place in the setting, but I supposed if I spent my days digging up the dead and reburying them, I might grow immune to it, too.

During the first days of the invasion, he explained, they'd buried fallen men shoulder to shoulder in mass graves in the sand so that each new wave of soldiers coming ashore wouldn't see them. They put each dead man's belongings on a stake where he was buried, along with one of his dog tags—that was what the bags were. It was a month to the day after the invasion had begun, and the whole beach was awash in the detritus of war: the remains of half-tracks and jeeps and tanks on the sand, ocean-soaked rucksacks and bedrolls, a typewriter with its roller intact but a wiry tangle where its keys ought to be. The wreckage of the American Mulberry—six hundred thousand tons of concrete towed across the Channel from Britain for a landing port—lay ugly and useless, destroyed by a gale before it could be anchored to the Channel seabed. Antiaircraft balloons dotted the Channel, though, protecting arriving ships, and one high bluff housed a hospital tent, a barbed wire enclosure for prisoners, and long stretches of wooden crosses marking new graves. Every-where, men and equipment rolled inland as others reburied the dead, the Graves Registration staff pausing in their work to answer my questions or to smile for Liv's camera, or simply to watch Liv and me the way the boys back home watched the prettier girls.

We were soaked and weary, ready to return to the field hospital without complaint, when it became clear there'd been a snafu—situation normal: all fucked up. Our return jeep wouldn't be available until morning. Jerome found us bedrolls and a tent (we didn't ask where they'd come from, among all the dead) and took us to dinner in the officers' mess. We were treated to mystery beef, peas, and fresh bread from a nearby village (bread I held to my face to breathe in the smell), along with a good bit of cemetery humor ("This place is so popular—people are dying to get in here"), and assurances they were digging a new latrine just for us. "We're not good at much here," one of our dinner companions said, "but we surely do know how to dig."

As we settled into our bedrolls under a starless sky later that night, a line from a Baudelaire poem emerged from some part of my mind unvisited since twelfth-grade French class. *"Je suis un cimetière abhorré de la lune." I am a cemetery by the moon unblessed.* I hadn't thought to ask for a flashlight, and it was too dark to see my own writing, but I pulled out my notepad. I wrote just a few lines on each page so I wouldn't scribble one line atop another, a full piece taking shape in my mind—the contrast between the commotion of the men and supplies coming ashore to head for war and the stillness of the dead left behind. If the words slipped away, the emotion would go with them, whatever part of my subconscious I might have exposed tucking itself back out of sight and leaving behind nothing but sludge.

I wished I had my typewriter. I could type blind perfectly well.

"What could you write about this place that anyone would print?" Liv asked. "There's no hope here, nothing to suggest victory is just a hedgerow away."

She stood and wandered out into the graveyard as my words ebbed, and with them my pride that I could call to mind the Baudelaire quote, that the poet was French, that two lines from the poem would have been the perfect opening and closing for a piece about this moonless cemetery and the memories buried here.

"'*J'ai plus de souvenirs que si j'avais mille ans,*'" I said to myself, the first line of the poem with which I'd meant to end my piece. *I have more memories than if I'd lived a thousand years.*

In the distance, truck engines whined and gears ground. I took a long drink from my canteen and I followed Liv out into the wooden crosses spooling toward the darkness, toward the cliff and the white sand and the men and tanks and trucks and the dark Channel, the ships.

"Thomas," she said as she sat in front of one of the crosses. "I saw this grave earlier. Thomas James, although if he's any relation to me I don't know it."

Thomas. I closed my eyes the way I was meant to close them when I was necking with Tommy Stahlman in his Chrysler Highlander, down by the Harpeth River, although I always peeked; I always needed to see Tommy falling in love with me. Tommy, whom I'd known since we fished together in Richland Creek the summer Mama, left with no one to care for me after Grandma died, began taking me with her to work, slipping me books from Mr. Stahlman's library and sending me off with an admonition to stay clear of the Belle Meade children.

I said to Liv, "I was in love with a boy back home named Thomas."

"And he's here now?"

"Lordy, I sure hope he's not *here!*"

There was nothing funny about this *cimetière abhorré de la lune*, but we both laughed. It sounded eerie, our laughter among the graves.

Liv said, "That's who you write to? Those long letters you write at the picnic table. That's who the letters you don't share are from?"

I reached out and touched the dog tag nailed to the cross, thinking of the D-Day letter Tommy had written to me because who else could he write to—I knew him better than anyone. Thirty-mile-an-hour winds and the troops vomiting into the sand from the fire buckets or using their helmets or puking their guts out over the rails. They were relieved to pile onto the landing crafts despite

German fire and bodies falling everywhere. That's what Tommy had written: "I thought I'd rather die quickly, Jane—a bullet to my chest." And German machine gunners firing and boys begging for help in the bloody water and Tommy's boat passing right by them. They were not a hospital ship, he kept telling his men, all the while praying to the god he never did believe in.

Liv asked, "Will you marry your Thomas after the war, Jane?"

He'll be marrying one of the Miss Ingrams— that's what Mama had told me when I came home far later than a nice girl ought to one night to find her sitting in her rocking chair on the front porch. I'd been so angry at her—not at Tommy, who was necking with me even after he was engaged to one of the Miss Ingrams, but at Mama, who spent her days washing the Wedgwood china he ate from and her evenings washing our own plain white dishes while I was out trying to ruin my reputation with a boy who never did mean to marry me.

I fingered the raised name on the dog tag of this Tommy who wasn't my Tommy, who wasn't anyone's Tommy anymore. "I don't know," I said.

Liv and I returned the next morning over roads pounded dry overnight, the traffic kicking up a caustic dust, to find our field hospital settling into a new field closer to the front. A medic chased two cows through the long grass to uncover trip wires or mines left by the Germans, and gear was strewn everywhere. Not so much as a tent set up in the shade of a moss-covered tree yet, though, and the place stank to high heaven, a dead animal smell.

"In no time, they'll have the unit back up again. They just have to clear the area first," I told Liv.

Clear the area, as if the nurses were moving rocks and twigs, maybe the occasional rusty plow blade. But the dead animal smell was no run-over ground squirrel. No dead cow like those we heard were everywhere at the front. Liv slid a cut-film holder into her Speed Graphic and focused on a nurse waving over a stretcher crew, then on the crew laying the stretcher in the grass and gently lifting a dead soldier, an involuntary hero who'd made it across the Channel only to end up here with the dice he carried for luck still in his pocket, his Saint Christopher's medal at his chest. Where his legs ought to have been was a stringy mass of muscle and skin and a sharp shard of thighbone the dirty red-black of dried blood.

Liv adjusted the bellows but didn't take the shot.

"If that boy were my brother," she said, "I wouldn't want anyone to photograph him like that. I wouldn't want anyone to photograph his face."

The stretcher crew carried off the dead boy, and the nurse returned to walking the field, looking methodically, mechanically, for the dead.

Other nurses and medics dragged a large canvas out over a cleared section of the field, the tent's red cross in the white circle taking shape, albeit deflated and creased. I left Liv to photograph it while I helped Marie set up our smaller tent, then fetched water for a sponge bath and examined the prior day's mail: letters from Mama and Tommy, and one with the return address simply "The White House, Washington." I carefully peeled open that envelope as if it might not really be meant for me, to find a typewritten slip no longer than a bread-and-butter note:

July 2, 1944
Dear Miss Tyler,
Your compassionate portrayal of the nurse helping save the wounded boy in "Operating Room by Flashlight" will surely help convince American women how dearly the auxiliary military services need them. Thank you for writing it.
Very Sincerely Yours,
Eleanor Roosevelt

I tucked the note back into its envelope, wanting someone to assure me it was real and at the same time trying to understand how Mrs. Roosevelt could have been left with the impression that Joey was back home eating peach ice cream. I read Tommy's letter (a short thing, mostly about how the watermelons at home would be ripe), thinking perhaps the censors had cut the last paragraph of my "Operating Room" piece, or even just the last line. And when Liv and Marie went out to the latrine that night (Marie saying she hated moving forward because the shelling was always worse, but at least we had newly dug latrines), I puzzled over the note one last time before burying it in my rucksack without mentioning it to anyone. I only asked Liv and Marie, as we lay in our cots that night, whether there was ever a scrap of truth left when the censors finished.

"Never mind that the fellas' stories are wired off while ours go by carrier pigeons, with the darn birds stopping to party in Brighton and Crawley on the way so our news is old and moldy before anyone reads it," I said. I felt like a fraud, some-one claiming to understand the meaning of this war when all I saw was its wreckage, when even the wreckage I reported was edited into something else. "At least you don't have a problem, Liv," I said. "The Signal Corps staff might ruin your film in the darkroom, and the censors might crop a shot or blur a face or censor a photo out of existence, but no one is going to cut pieces out of your shots, paste together what's left, and put your name to it."

Five days and five more "regrets" by the CO later—with just a few days left in Marie's and my three-week accreditations and not much more than a week in Liv's—a jeep became available to take us to a nearby landing strip: planes taxiing to a stop, loading litters of wounded boys through their wide double doors, and taking off again for England. Twelve minutes, that was how long it took each plane, not much longer than it took the pilot to smoke a cigarette and all the notice we'd been given about the jeep. When we returned to the field hospital—mercifully the same evening—we resolved to keep our rucksacks always at the ready: a change of fatigues and socks and underthings; a canteen, a mess kit, and a few K ration breakfast boxes; a tin tube of cold cream, a towel and soap, lipstick and powder; poncho; folding spade and gas mask; notepads and pens. Liv forsook her spade in favor of film and flashbulbs, and her gown and gloves. And as we organized ourselves, Liv began talking about Helen Kirkpatrick's *Herald Tribune* piece that had first exposed the German rearmament of the Rhineland.

"In March of '36," she said, her awe communicating an ambition even she wouldn't voice, that she longed to break a major story like that. Kirkpatrick had left Switzerland for Freiburg, Germany, on rumors of activity along the riverfront, and found German soldiers in the streets and Nazi flags flying everywhere in open violation of the Treaty of Versailles.

Marie said, "Can you imagine that woman leaving

a perfectly good marriage by cabling her husband from Europe simply 'NOT RETURNING'?" She giggled the way she did, at that rumor which was the truth of how Helen Kirkpatrick had ended her marriage.

Liv said, "Helen was the sole newspaper representative coordinating the invasion press coverage, and still they won't let us beyond the hospital camps."

Marie said, "For pity's sake, Liv, you can't mean to go on and on again about getting to the front."

By the time the CO found us a third jeep, Liv was scheduled to return to London in three days. Marie and I each had been granted three more weeks at the field hospital, but her request for more time in France had been denied. "It wasn't my call, Mrs. Harper. You'll have to take it up with your Public Relations Division friends," the CO had insisted, "or perhaps with the First Lady." Liv, too, had received a note from Mrs. Roosevelt by then, one dated after mine, which referenced Joey's death—a fact that Mrs. Roosevelt must have come to understand some-how in the days between the two notes. And still I didn't share my note. It was hard to explain why I'd kept it secret, and I wasn't sure how Liv would feel to know of the mis-impression her photo-graphs had left.

As we stood with our readied rucksacks, waiting for our jeep—this one to take us to a recently liberated village to meet with a woman sharp-shooter who'd trained the French resistance in weaponry—Liv suggested that if we could get our driver out even briefly, we could hijack the jeep to the front.

I pulled out a notepad and pen and pretended to begin writing a letter. "Dear Mama," I said, "I know you'll think I don't have the sense God gave a goose, but I went AWOL to cover the fighting rather than to run away from it, and now I'm locked up in England, waiting to be put on the next ship home."

"We wouldn't come back, not before Paris," Liv said. "I could say I think one of the tires is flat, and one of you can agree."

Marie said, "You're such a card, Liv."

I laughed uneasily, imagining my mother kneeling at mass the way I'd knelt during the mess tent mass that morning, and knowing her prayers would be for me.

The sharpshooter—Jeanne Bohec—told us of gunfire at dawn and urgently coding telegrams to London and carrying messages by bicycle, letters that weren't letters at all. When Germans stopped her, she told them that she was going to visit her grandmother, that she carried a map because she didn't know the area well. She told us, too, of a last-minute sermon held under a parachute, the look of her camp as it was destroyed by the Germans, the frustration of being able to do nothing to fight back, having been refused a weapon because of her gender even though she'd taught the boys to shoot.

As we headed back to the field hospital that evening, Liv said the little town reminded her of the first photo her mother had ever shown her, a Margaret Bourke-White aerial shot that ran in the debut issue of *Life*. The town in the photo wasn't really similar to the French town disappearing in the distance—houses and fences all the same dull brown-gray—but there was the same sameness about it, the same house after house not much different from the next.

"My mother told me Bourke-White was a chubby girl who dressed abominably," Liv said. "She was called Peg, and she wore cotton stockings and no makeup, and she once took a snake to school. 'And she's divorced'—you could sure hear Mother's disapproval on that. But still, she was awed by those photographs." Liv looked to the pockmarked road ahead. "'Imagine that, Livvie.' That's what my mother said to me as she admired that photograph, and she looked right into me the way she did, and I had no idea what I was supposed to imagine."

I touched her arm lightly, sure it was the fact of a woman photojournalist that Liv's mother had meant for her to imagine, wishing that my mother, like Liv's, could imagine a life for me that was different than her own.

Liv said, "Photos of the parachute sermon itself, the gunfire, the bicycle ride—those are the photos I ought to be taking. Not photographs of a woman in a safely liberated French town recalling them."

In less than seventy-two hours, Liv was to return to London and perhaps even to the United States, where the head of Immigration and Naturalization, a Mrs. Shipley, would likely pull her passport and give her a devil of a time before giving it back. Mrs. Shipley held that women had no business being in war zones. She and the CO, we liked to joke, must be from the same austere Vermont whistle-stop.

"Doesn't it feel like one of the tires is going flat?" Liv said loudly enough that no one could fail to hear her even over the rush of wind in the jeep.

Our driver glanced in the rearview mirror, then reached up and adjusted it. "It's not the tires, Mrs. Harper, it's the road," he said.

Marie and I said nothing at all.

The jeep-ambulances bringing back the wounded the next morning came with rumors that Saint-Lô was finally being taken. Gerhardt's Twenty-ninth Infantry had made its way through the German line and taken the high ground a half mile from the city. The road was open. We heard the news from an ambulance driver we'd befriended, a conscientious objector from Colorado Springs named Hank Bend who had the round face and round spectacles of a Bill Mauldin cartoon soldier-innocent. "Gerhardt has a division in the field, one here in the hospital, and one in the cemetery already," he told us. "God help him today." And when Hank returned later with another ambulance load, he brought more news: *Boston Globe* and BBC correspondent Iris Carpenter and Liv's fellow AP correspondent Ruth Cowan were at Saint-Lô.

"They can't be!" Liv protested. "They're assigned to a hospital like we are, the Fifth General outside Carentan."

Hank shrugged and said the story he heard was they got tired of the lizards and the mosquitos, tired of yellow dust all over everything they owned, so they caught a ride on an ambulance to the front. "Story I heard," he said, "is when they were found thumbing a ride back to file their stories and asked what the hell they were doing— they were war correspondents, weren't they? didn't they have jeeps?—Miss Cowan said yes, they were, but they were 'just women,' they didn't rate being taken care of like the men."

"Don't rate being taken care of like the men," Liv repeated later that evening as I struggled to apply bleach to my roots—a thing I'd never have thought to do back home, where people tallied that kind of thing against a girl. The idea to bleach my hair (which, unbleached, was the dingy color of autumn weeds plastered flat after a rain) had come to me as I'd stood before the Saks fitting room's three-way mirror, a professional tailor pinning the skirt of my Intrepid Girl Reporter uniform. Some prettier and more accomplished me had peered back, someone who might carry off shorter, blonder hair set in a permanent wave. I'd only been headed for London then; I hadn't imagined I'd be sharing a tent in a field in Normandy with no privacy to update my look discreetly and nothing more than a helmet in which to rinse the bleach from my hair.

"For pity's sake, can anyone really *self*-apply that stuff?" Marie said. "Here, let me."

She took the bottle and set to work, the tent air sharpening with the bleach scent as we talked about the problems with trying to look anything like feminine here: the boots that shortened our legs; the slacks that hid them; our skin so quickly toughened from living in the foul weather, from washing with harsh soap.

"I've stopped getting my period," Marie said.

"Me, too," Liv said, swatting at a mosquito on her too-thin arm and missing.

"Well, a small blessing that," I said. A result of the travel, the work, the stress, but a convenient one.

Liv, who lay on her cot in her long underwear, launched into a funny little riff about how I might react if German bombers interrupted the bleach routine, then another imagining herself as a blonde. "Can blondes wear red?" she asked. And she started talking about her gown, then, which she'd never unpacked. "It's the only red thing I've ever worn," she said, although that wasn't quite true; she'd never worn it, not the dress and not the gloves either.

I said, "You brought your dancing slippers, too, I hope, Liv. You can't be dancing in a red gown and combat boots. They'll revoke your dance card!"

"I suppose I'll have to dance barefoot," Liv said, and she tossed a dirty sock at me.

I said, "You'd best find a dancing partner who's light on his feet!"

Marie rinsed the bleach from her hands in the water in my helmet, and I wiped the bottle with my towel, tucked it back into my rucksack, and settled in to wait for the bleach to work its magic on me. And we sang more softly than ever as we lay in our cots later that night, torn between the too-hot bedrolls and the too-hungry mosquitos. "We Mustn't Say Goodbye." "She'll Always Remember." "We'll Meet Again."

When I woke not long before dawn the next morning, Liv's rucksack was gone, and her bedroll and cameras. I threw on my slacks and stuffed my typewriter into my musette bag, grabbed my pack and ran, dragging my sprawling bedroll behind me. Liv was already setting off, but Hank

Bend, in the driver's seat, said, "I think that's Miss Tyler," and they stopped and backed up.

"Livvie, they won't give you time to repack your nightie before they take your passport and send you home," I whispered.

"You can have the front seat if you want it, Jane," she answered. "But we'll get Hank in trouble if we dawdle here."

She had already promised Hank this would be a one-way ride, that she would find her own way back rather than take space needed for the wounded.

"Lordy, I should have seen you for trouble the day I met you, Liv," I said as I threw my rucksack and my sprawling bedroll into the jeep and climbed in, doubling Hank Bend's crime. "You surely don't believe in the easy way, do you?" I said, wondering how long we could last outside the field hospital before the military police found us, or how we'd get our work censored and sent home, or what we'd eat beyond the breakfast rations in our packs.

As Hank shifted into gear and we set off, Liv said to him, "I always did think passports were overrated, didn't you, Hank? They don't get you anywhere you want to be."

And I supposed she was right. I supposed we could cross our bridges when the river ran too high to wade across, when the water ran too fast to swim.

SAINT-LÔ, FRANCE
◆
TUESDAY, JULY 18, 1944

I learned to appreciate a nice, deep, muddy ditch which I could roll into during shelling . . . to take a satisfactory bath in my helmet without upsetting it . . . to live like a gypsy, out of my bed roll, and to sleep almost anywhere.
—Photojournalist Margaret Bourke-White

The narrow dirt road was rutted and shell-pocked, and hectic with GIs in Volkswagen command cars and BMW motorcycles left behind by the Germans, with spotted cows in the fields mooing to be milked, with abandoned dogs. Hank chatted nervously, filling the empty ambulance with apologies for the jarring ride and look-at-thats and explanations for so many things that didn't need explaining: fuchsia bushes bright against old stone walls German gunners might be hiding behind, an improbably white rabbit tail disappearing into the rubble of what had been a cottage, and everywhere the remains of tanks and airplanes and gliders in the fields or pushed off to the sides of the roads. "Our tanks burn when hit, which the German tanks don't," Hank explained, "and only one man can get out at a time."

As we approached Saint-Lô, Hank fell silent, no longer even honking at fellow ambulance drivers or leaning out to call greetings to the soldiers securing the area, standing every few hundred yards on the road. I welcomed the quiet at first, before I began to doubt myself or to doubt what we were doing, disobeying orders, coming to the front. The silence of the jeep, though, was nothing compared to the silence of Saint-Lô.

A single part of a cathedral spire stood awash in a wreckage of collapsed stone. We saw it as we topped a distant hill. All the rest of the city was strewn across the landscape in great sprawls of broken building timbers, vast rubble piles of stone, heroic trunks of trees spilled like tooth-picks, all dulled to the sooty gray of ash. Allied bombs—not German ones—had leveled the city. Tons of American-made explosives dropped by American boys from American-made B-17s and B-24s.

Hank pulled to a stop when the jeep could no longer plow through the rubble. "We sure liberated the hell out of this town, didn't we?" he said, a choke in his voice even though he'd approached this city ruin before. I made the sign of the cross over my chest.

Hank and I climbed from the jeep-ambulance,

but Liv only stood on the passenger seat and raised her Speed Graphic toward the ruin of the cathedral. There a dozen or so soldiers gathered around a jeep-ambulance that had come from another direction. Two of them were removing an olive drab blanket from a body laid out on a wooden door while two others carefully unfolded an American flag. They laid the flag reverentially over their commander, Major Thomas D. Howie of the 116th Infantry. He'd led the attack on Saint-Lô under orders to take the town if he had to spend the whole battalion to do so. Spend the whole battalion, as if hundreds of men's lives were no more than pocket change.

Liv photographed the soldiers, their helmets removed out of respect as they lifted the flag-draped body up onto the pile of cathedral rubble. She flipped the cut-film holder and took the second shot before climbing from the jeep. She wasn't the only one to capture their stricken faces; a knot of photographers and reporters had followed the men all the way from Hill 122, staying the night in the shadow of the jeep-ambulance. No one broke the silence. No one questioned this display of emotion from men known for their hardness to the realities of war.

Liv switched to her Leica as I looked to the others, feeling a want to have someone to share this silent emotion with, not that Hank Bend and Liv Harper were no one, but for this moment I needed a whole congregation around me, the comfort of all those understanding glances and silent prayers. A photographer who'd had his camera pointed in our direction lowered it and put it into a changing bag to swap out the film, his square shoulders and his eyes and his stubbled chin ordinary, really, with only his generous ears and his hair—prematurely gray—at all remarkable. British, by the uniform. A small parenthesis of lines lingered at the edges of his mouth, a note of recognition. He finished changing his film and tucked his spent roll into his musette bag, and he took a drink from the canteen on his utility belt. Without a word to anyone else, he split off from the group and headed toward us, his lanky frame in his military garb moving easily.

He addressed Liv as he reached us, saying, "He took a shell fragment in the lung yesterday, before dawn. He was looking out over his troops, making sure everyone had their heads down."

His eyes were the green-brown of moss, the skin below bruised with exhaustion. His Adam's apple bobbed in the stubble of his neck. I wondered who he was, and how he knew Liv.

"He taught English literature," he said, "before the war."

"English literature," Liv repeated dully.

He said to me, as if it might be an easier question of me than of Liv, "You ladies do have your CO's permission to be here?"

Liv focused her Leica on the flag-draped body, the red and white of the stripes, the stars against the blue. I stared down at the notepad that, by some instinct, had found its way into my hands.

"Livvie, oh, Livvie, you are daft." His voice lingering on the last perfectly hit *t*.

Liv adjusted the lens and took photograph after photograph in rapid succession while I scribbled my words. She spent the whole roll, as if she had film to waste.

"How will you manage to get your film out?" he asked softly, the solid set of his lips suggesting he wasn't challenging or reprimanding; he was just being practical.

Liv lowered her camera, finally, and said, simply, "Fletcher."

I looked to Hank—poor Hank, doubting now that he should have brought us here. I wanted to reassure him, but something in his eyes behind his round glasses reminded me so much of the wounded soldiers waiting patiently outside the hospital tent that I thought better of saying anything.

Liv put her Leica, a fresh roll of film, and a lightproof canister in her changing bag and, with her hands in the armholes to work inside the bag, removed the exposed film and enclosed it in the canister, taped the canister closed, and loaded the new roll.

Fletcher took the spent film from her and placed

it in a condom. "To keep it dry," he explained as he tied it closed, like tying a balloon. He hesitated for a moment—the awkwardness of having to hand her the film-filled condom? But then he did so without seeming to think the least of it.

"You might have a go at it in Kodachrome, Livvie," he said. "The shot wants color." The suggestion offered gently. That had been his hesitation: he was uncomfortable suggesting how Liv ought to shoot her photographs.

Liv had only one roll of Kodachrome, but she put the canister in the changing bag with the camera. "If we'd followed the rules, Fletcher," she said quietly as she swapped in the color film, "I'd have no pictures to worry about getting out, and Jane would have no stories."

Fletcher smiled a little sadly in my direction, his slightly crooked teeth white against his sun-worn and unshaven skin.

I said, "We haven't a fool's clue how we'll get our work out."

At the pile of rubble that had been the church of Saint Croix, soldiers and civilians alike began to put flowers on the flag-draped corpse. Liv resumed taking photographs with the Kodachrome, cap-turing the flag and the flowers against the rubble gray.

Fletcher sighed. "I do have an idea. For today, anyway."

Then to me, again with the charming little bit of smile, just enough to convey warmth while remaining respectful of the circumstances, "I'm Fletcher Roebuck, by the way. I'm afraid Livvie here has lost her proper manners. Her husband, Charles, and I are chums."

He shook my hand, his fingernails dark with dirt.

"Fletcher," I repeated, lingering on the comfortable flick of his name.

OUTSIDE SAINT-LÔ
◆
TUESDAY, JULY 18, 1944

[Lee Miller, under house arrest for her actions at Saint-Malo] was rubbing eau de cologne all over herself because she'd been bitten by fleas. I told her calamine would be better, and gave her some of mine.

—Journalist Catherine Coyne

Fletcher's jeep—a thing with no doors and a hairline crack in its windshield—had a propensity to find and share every bump and hole in the road. Liv sat in the passenger seat, her lens trained on the military trucks moving troops and supplies, the roadside littered with gum wrappers and cigarette butts, the summer-green landscape ahead carved with unexpected strips of black. I braced myself with one hand and held my Corona in my lap with the other as we banked into a turn, our rucksacks shifting sideways, pressing the two side buckles on my boot into my leg. I righted my typewriter again, and as I tried to make something of the flag and the flowers and the door stretcher and the soldiers we'd left behind, the dust everywhere, I envied Liv and Fletcher their cameras, their ability to capture a moment as they observed it and then leave it behind.

Fletcher relaxed his grip on the steering wheel, leaving a single index finger there. "Your military will have someone looking for you two in no time, Liv," he said. "They probably already do."

Liv had met Fletcher just twice before that morning, although Charles and Fletcher had known each other for years. The first time she'd met him, at the *New York Daily Press* office just after she and Charles had become engaged, Fletcher had asked Liv to bring him tea—with lemon, he'd said; his blunder, his presumption, mistaking her for an office girl—and she'd set him right, she'd answered, "You must be Fletcher Roebuck, then," in a tone meant to leave no doubt she'd heard enough about him to disapprove and didn't mind if he knew she did. Still, she'd been the embarrassed one.

They'd met a second time when Liv and Charles had bumped into Fletcher at the Palm Court in London, the day before she was to cross the Channel. Fletcher invited them to stay the night at his family's country home, Trefoil Hall—which Charles had visited when he and Fletcher had returned from Poland years before. It wasn't far from the port where Liv was to disembark. Fletcher hadn't meant to go with them to

Chichester, he'd meant to stay the night in London, but Charles somehow persuaded him to drive them down.

As the high turrets flanking the arched central entry to Trefoil came into view, the vaulting windows and stone gargoyles, Charles said to Liv, "Didn't I tell you it was a castle? Tell her the story about your grandfather, Fletch."

"My great-great-great-great-grand*uncle*," Fletcher said.

Charles waved off the correction with a flip of his hand and a dismissive "Uncle, grandfather. He won the place in a card game."

"A game of *vingt-et-un* did have a bit to do with it," Fletcher conceded. "The ace of clubs my distant uncle flipped up didn't win him the property, but it did gain him the fortune to build it. Yet it makes rather a better story to imagine the house itself at stake, doesn't it?"

"The house is shaped like an ace of clubs," Charles explained to Liv. "A third turret over-looking the sea in the back matches these front two."

"The neighbors think it in abominable taste," Fletcher said. "Which indeed it is."

Inside Trefoil Hall, a white-haired butler met them in a vaulted-ceilinged receiving hall frescoed with a crowd looking down from a balcony and romanticized heads of horses and swirls that weren't really anything at all, a painting that somehow made the cavernous space seem less so. "Larkins," Fletcher said, greeting the old man with genuine enthusiasm as the improbable sound of giggles spilled from above. Up a wide sweep of steps, the stairway paused at a landing before splitting into two narrower stairways, right and left, down which a dozen little girls—seven- and eight- and nine-year-old schoolgirls—came tumbling, peering through the banister.

Fletcher bounded up the stairs and scooped two of the girls into his arms, laughing and saying, "My sweet cherubs!" in a tone that suggested he knew how ridiculous he was.

Liv started up the stairs after him, but Charles remained with his feet planted in the entry hall, his hand reaching to the vulnerable balding spot Liv could see from the higher elevation of the stairs.

"Now listen," Fletcher said to the girls, "you must give a grand hello to Mr. Charles Harper. He runs a whole newspaper in New York."

"That's in the United States," one of the girls said. "It's the biggest city in the world."

All the girls peered down at Charles, who peered back at them like a child who wants to play ball but is awkward with bat and glove. Liv longed to coach him, to say, *It's just like with grown-ups, Charles, you touch them on the arm and say something charming.*

Fletcher said, "I suppose that makes him rather

an important chap, doesn't it? And he has the extraordinary fortune to have married quite well, as you can see. This is his wife, Olivia James Harper. She's a talented photojournalist, can you believe that?"

Another girl, one with the same wispy, off-blond hair most of them shared, tilted her head up at Liv. "But she's a girl!"

Fletcher peered exaggeratedly at Liv. "Emily, by golly, you're right. That she is."

They all giggled.

"Well, you'll have to take my word for it. She may be a girl, but she's on her way to Paris to photograph the liberation. I expect she plans to be the first to take pictures there. I imagine she intends to march in before the troops will have done!"

Charles, below, crossed his arms, creasing his jacket. "It isn't a race, Fletcher."

"To Paris? Don't be a berk, Charles." Fletcher bent down on one knee so that he was at the girls' level and said to them, "Of course it's a race. One every journalist and photographer in Europe is eager to win, all in good fun. And do you know on whom I would place my wager, girls?" He nodded at Liv. "I'd like to point out, too, that I'm a pretty fair gambler."

" 'Cept Cecily always wins at dice," the girl he'd called Emily said.

"Well, yes, but then Cecily is awfully lucky."

Charles frowned. "You've taught them to shoot craps?"

Fletcher looked down at him, a mock scolding look. "Please, Charles. *Dice.*" Again, he addressed the girls conspiratorially. "Liv is going to be the first into Paris all right, and you can bet she'll be famous then."

The girls crowded around Liv, everyone speaking at once: "You want to see my shrapnel collection? I got some of them when they were still warm." "I got gum wrappers, thirty-six of them." "I have cigarette packages. Pippa has a hundred." "A hundred and *eight.*"

Liv stooped to their level and said hello to a sad-eyed, curly-haired brunette in white cotton pajamas who hadn't said a word in all the chaos. "What's your name?" she asked.

"Ella doesn't speak," Emily said. "She used to talk, but then her mum stopped coming and now she doesn't say nothing."

Liv leaned back against the banister, trying not to look startled. "Doesn't . . ." She took the girl's hand, which was birdlike, fragile, wanting to scoop her up and take her to a safer world, one where daughters married in their mother's white silk dresses and fathers, rather than twin brothers, gave them away.

Dinner at Trefoil Hall that evening was served in a vast dining hall flanked at each end by cavernous fireplaces, their mantels of gray-white stone carved with lions and leaves and frippery, and with crests carved of onyx and some other stone Liv didn't recognize, something a deep, rich red. It had been all she could do to get out of the bath she'd had before dinner, but now she and Charles and Fletcher sat alone at one end of a table meant to seat thirty, Larkins serving crisply roasted duck with rosemary new potatoes and carrots and peas Serle had prepared from the estate's victory garden. The wine was a wonderful Bordeaux that had been aging in the cellar since long before the start of the war, Fletcher assured them, but still Liv felt the guilt of drinking it, the sense that it was somehow inappropriate to enjoy this wine in the relative safety of England when Hitler might be drinking the same wine while his soldiers trampled the vineyard where it was made.

Fletcher suggested someone ought to do a story about what girls like those living at Trefoil were enduring. They saw their mothers only on Sundays, when special coaches brought them out. Liv felt the tug of that, the sympathy for these evacuee girls pulling against her need to get to the front.

"That girl Ella," she said to Fletcher. "Her mother . . . ?"

"The other mums are kind to her," he said. "She has an aunt who comes when she can as well, and her sister, until a few weeks ago, but now her sister is in France with a nursing unit. Her mother was killed in the Bethnal Green tube shelter last year. Someone stumbled as they entered the shelter, and the crowd pushed on, and in the end more than a hundred people were trampled to death, I'm afraid."

"One hundred and seventy-three," Charles said.

"But that's impossible," Liv said. "We'd have heard about something like that."

"It was kept from the newspapers," Fletcher said. "The location. The magnitude of the disaster."

Charles nodded. "March eighth."

Liv stared for a surprised moment at the carve of lines around her husband's eyes, at the grooves between his nose and mouth. He knew the exact date, the exact number of the dead. He knew what was printed, and he knew what was too awful to print.

"And Ella's father?" she asked.

Fletcher said, "Somewhere in France."

Liv looked down at her meal, no appetite left as she listened to Charles and Fletcher recount the time they'd spent in Poland the way men who never shared much with anyone liked to retread their common ground. Charles said to Liv, "I'm not sure Fletcher and I would have stayed if Julien Bryan hadn't showed up with his Leica in one hand and his Bell & Howell movie camera in the other just as everyone else was leaving. But Fletcher here couldn't bear to let an American take the show away from him."

Fletcher took a studied sip of his Bordeaux and said he was glad to see the American censorship rules loosening. "So now you show your dead but you airbrush the poor sods' faces so their mums won't recognize them?"

From the first full-page, full-bleed shot that had run in the American papers—George Strock's three dead Americans on the sand at Buna Beach—there were no faces on the American dead. They were shown facedown, like two of the three in Strock's shot, or with faces hidden or turned away from the camera or cropped out or blackened in or obscured by shadows. Liv hadn't thought about it in the negative; she'd thought, *My God, how can these photos be so moving? They don't even show the faces.*

Fletcher said, "Even the dead you half show are the few dead, casualties from an otherwise successful outing in the park."

Charles said, "But, Fletcher, imagine if your own mother—"

"My mum would have you print the faces," Fletcher said.

Charles ran a hand through his hair, through the gray creeping in at the temples, the tidy, almost military cut.

"March third," Fletcher said. "Bethnal Green—that was March third."

"Yes, wasn't that what I said?" Charles answered.

Fletcher fingered the stem of his wineglass.

"Showing women the faces of their dead sons and brothers and husbands would no more help win this war than would sending those women directly to France," Charles continued. He looked to Liv, his eyes behind the glasses white against the deep tan of his long, intelligent face. "Honestly, Olivia, I can't imagine why you should be the one made to go to Normandy just to photograph soldiers with bandages on their heads."

Liv lifted a plate of butter—real butter—feeling the silver at her fingertips as cool and soothing as a shutter release. "I'm not being made to go, Charles," she said quietly, trying to understand this new resistance in him.

Fletcher said, "You'd be in Normandy yourself, Charles, if you hadn't let yourself get strapped to an editor's desk. You'd be—"

The dull realization of something passed in his expression. He reached for the decanter of wine, refilled his glass and Charles's. Liv's was still full, but he tipped the heavy decanter over the more fragile crystal of her glass, emptying into it the last little drop.

Liv looked from Fletcher to Charles to the rich bloodred of the wine, the deep brown of the duck, the tender orange and green of the tiny carrots and perfectly round peas. She reached for her wine, the stem cool in her fingertips. She inhaled the wine's musty cranberry and took a single, hesitant sip.

Fletcher speared a bite of duck. "You would have gone back if you could have done, Charles," he said. "If your father hadn't taken ill. If you weren't needed in New York."

Charles cut a substantial bite of meat but let it rest there on his plate. "Yes, of course I would," he said, the slight squint of his eyes catching Liv off guard, reminding her of his expression as he'd asked her to marry him, as if for the briefest moment he'd imagined she might say no. She looked away to the fireplace, the smoke-darkened stone, but not before she heard the truth in Charles's voice: Charles would never return to war.

"Fletcher could be in France, too, but he's not either," Liv said, feeling even as she spoke that she was betraying Fletcher somehow, embarrassed by her need to betray him for the sake of Charles's pride, and perhaps her own.

In bed that night at Trefoil, when Charles traced a finger over Liv's breast, she pressed her tongue lightly to her bottom teeth, the tension in her shoulders ebbing with the slight motion, sinking into the small of her back, her hips. His hand moved down to linger at her thigh before brushing upward, over her hip bone, her belly. "Shall we try for a Charles Jr.?" he said as he pulled the tie of her nightgown, releasing the fabric to expose her bare skin, releasing the longing. It wasn't a fall-back position, he'd said months before; having a baby wouldn't make up for her being stuck taking photos of women knitting caps for the soldiers rather than photos of the soldiers wearing the caps in Africa or Italy or France. But now he said, "Come home with me, Liv, and we'll have one of each. A Renny and a Charles."

She touched the curl of hair on his chest, dark still, but with gray sprinkled here and there— editor in chief gray, and who wouldn't take that position, especially with his father too ill to do the job himself? He smiled down at her the way he was always smiling—at women having tea in fancy hotels, at sources he thought could give him a scoop, at the young New Hampshire gal he'd wanted to charm into working for him two years before, a young photographer who hadn't even begun to think of herself as such, who hadn't needed to be charmed.

The next morning, when they awoke nestled together under the smooth, clean sheets, Charles reached for his glasses and put them on. He leaned back against the pillows, put his arms around her, and said, "Come home, Liv. It's time to come home."

She curled into the warmth of him. "If we weren't married, Charles," she said gently, "if I were still working for you, you'd *make* me go to France."

He didn't respond for such a long moment that she turned her face up to him. Before she could recover from the shock of it, the realization that he was crying, he said, "You'll get yourself killed, for God's sake."

She entwined her fingers in his sturdier hand and stared at the window, the blackout shade down but beyond it the Channel and the ship that would take her to France, if only she kept her nerve.

"I'd lose my AP credential, Charles; I'd never work again," she said in the gentle voice, willing away the ache in her chest, thinking she wouldn't curl up with Charles every night while she was in France, but he would have the entire pool of AP photos to choose from and he would choose hers to run in the *Daily Press*, and that would be enough.

Fletcher, with one hand on the steering wheel, extended a pack of cigarettes to me. I took one and ducked down toward my typewriter to light it with my Zippo. Liv declined the pack. Fletcher took one between his lips and returned the cigarettes to the netting liner of his helmet, where he'd learned to keep them after too many attempts to light soggy fags with soggy matches. Around us, new roads were being bulldozed through banks of rocky field scrap and thick, impenetrable hedges. Cacophonous collections of road signs directed in French, German, and English: code names like "Madonna Charlie" and "Vermont Red" for the invasion beaches, towns like Luc-sur-Mer, and arrows nailed over signs reading *"Umgehung"* (*Bypass,* Fletcher told us), the kilometer markings all painted over with miles. White tape along the roadsides indicated where mines hadn't yet been cleared beyond the banks, and boards painted with skulls and crossbones barred the way into fields that were unlikely riots of daisies, poppies, gorse, and Queen Anne's lace. Military police directed traffic at the busiest of corners, aided by children wearing pinafores and the MPs' military caps. The children's mothers waved from the side of the road at the endless caravans, trucks full of soldiers and supplies headed away from the Channel, and the wounded returning. The MPs weren't looking for us, at least not yet.

I turned to my typewriter and banged out a sentence: *The war is thick in the long shadows, not just in the shattered buildings and the broken road, but in the French faces as well.*

"What are you two doing at the front?" Fletcher asked, still with the cigarette between his lips. "Neither of you has to be here, and besides, Liv, I heard you—"

He frowned abruptly and lit his cigarette, holding the steering wheel steady with his knee while he cupped the fag.

"I'm what?" Liv asked.

He cleared his throat. "You're expecting—"

The jeep clipped the edge of the road, throwing

Liv and me against its side as Fletcher gripped the wheel, straightening back onto the road and cursing himself.

"I'm expecting what?" Liv asked as I righted my typewriter and smoothed the creased paper.

Fletcher glanced at her. "I thought you were expecting."

Liv said, "Expecting what, Charles?"

"Fletcher," I said.

"What?" Fletcher said.

"She just called you Charles," I said. "Liv, you called Fletcher Charles."

"Fletcher," she said irritably. "What are you taking about, *Fletcher?* Expecting *what?*"

Beyond the cracked glass of the jeep's window, land that might once have been a vineyard was a stretch of blackened earth.

Fletcher flicked the cigarette, though there was no ash buildup to dispose of. *"Expecting,"* he said. *"With child."*

Liv and I both laughed.

"Having a *baby?*" Liv said. "Who started *that* rumor?"

"I don't . . ." Fletcher tugged at his ear with the hand that held his cigarette as I remembered Mama's words the night of Tommy's engagement party: *A rumor makes a reputation, whether it ought to or not.*

Fletcher said, "I don't remember where I heard it."

"Can you honestly imagine, Fletcher, that I'd be here—going AWOL!—if I were carrying a child? Can you imagine Charles would allow it?"

The car engine hummed lower as Fletcher disengaged the clutch and threw the gearshift forward.

"The only thing I'm expecting at the moment," Liv said, "is to arrive in Paris before anyone else does."

"No one is going to Paris," Fletcher said. "Eisenhower intends to circumvent the city."

Liv leveled a look at him. "And you believe that?" Then to me, "No wonder he's a photo-journalist."

"I'm not. I'm a military photographer," Fletcher said.

Liv said to me, "Of course he is. He's far too gullible even to be a photojournalist."

"No one is going to Paris," Fletcher repeated.

But Paris was what we'd broken the rules for. We'd gone AWOL so we'd have a chance to document the Tricolor raised high over the city, Parisians celebrating in the streets as Allied troops marched across the Seine, down the Champs-Élysées, through the Arc de Triomphe.

"Really, Livvie," Fletcher said, "you ought to let me take you back to your field hospital."

Liv, looking through the cracked windshield, said, "My brother is over here somewhere."

Fletcher downshifted again, easing the jeep to a

96

stop at the side of the road, looking at Liv as if he'd somehow followed whatever chain of thought it was that had brought her to say that, to say Geoff was here somewhere. "Isn't that all the more reason to stay safe yourself, Liv?" he asked. "What would your parents do if—"

"I might have that cigarette, after all," Liv said.

I watched Fletcher watch Liv, his dark eyes and dark brows softened by the premature gray of his hair. He extracted the Chesterfields from his helmet liner and shook one loose from the pack. Liv coughed as he lit it for her, unused to the burn of tobacco in her lungs. She stared at the glowing ember, the graceful swirl of smoke. Her awkward grip on the cigarette made me self-conscious of my own sturdy fingers, the dirt under my nails. She switched it to her left hand, then back to her right. She turned in the seat so she could see Fletcher and me both. I wondered if what she'd said about her brother was true, even. Was Geoffrey in France?

"Why do you wear two wedding rings?" Fletcher asked her.

She looked to me as if I might answer for her. "One was my mother's," she said. A thin gold band of fading crosses and hearts.

"I'm sorry," he said.

"It was a long time ago."

Fletcher cupped a hand under the gray ash teetering at the end of Liv's cigarette, knocked it into his palm, and dumped it outside the car. "You don't smoke?"

"I'm learning," she said.

He tossed his own cigarette and lit another, and inhaled deeply. "My brother, Edward, died at Dieppe," he said quietly, exhaling smoke with each word. "Twenty-two months ago." Then to Liv, "Charles is wrong about not showing the faces. It's the faces that make the deaths real. It's the faces that make people give up that last of whatever it is they're reluctant to give, to win this war."

Liv took another drag of her cigarette, and coughed again. She didn't agree with him, but she couldn't possibly disagree with him now, when he was talking about his dead brother.

"Tell us about your brother, Fletcher," I gently suggested.

Fletcher's moss-brown eyes expressed the words he held back, that Liv was wrong to listen to Charles.

"Edward was three years older than I," he said. "We shared a bedroom all our lives, and we loved the same things: cricket and maths and trifle. And Jane Austen novels as well—not that we would ever have admitted that to anyone but each other."

"The ideal brother," Liv said.

Fletcher smiled slightly. "There was that time Edward boxed my ears for something I said about a girl."

"What did you say?" Liv asked.

"Oh, that," Fletcher said. "Tell us about your brother, Liv."

"Geoff," she said. "He's twelve minutes older than I am. He used to call me Lousy Livvie and put lizards in my bed."

Fletcher and I both laughed.

"Dad called us Mutt and Jeff, like in the comic strip," she said.

I sat watching and listening from the backseat, trying to imagine what it would be like to have a brother who would help keep me in line, to have a father who had affectionate nicknames for my brother and me. To know who my father was.

"I was Mutt even though I was the short one, the Jeff," Liv said. "Even though Geoff, at ten, already towered over me. 'Not *Mutt,* Francis,' Mother used to scold him. 'You'll leave her thinking she's a dog, for goodness' sake.'" Liv laughed, then, and she told us about her mother forever showing her photographs in magazines even before she bought Liv a camera. "I remember when she showed me that photograph Dorothea Lange is so famous for, the migrant mother," she said. "'This is how you make people care, Livvie,' she told me. 'This is how things change.'"

"Of course, that would be the migrant mother's *face* that moved people to understand what the poor in America were enduring," Fletcher said.

"But the migrant mother isn't dead," Liv

answered. "No loved one would be made to see her death in a photograph. And Lange was careful with faces. The children's faces in that photo are turned away. That's what makes it so compelling, the fact that the children's faces *aren't* shown. Would the mother's face be so compelling without the protection her weary shoulders afford those children?"

Fletcher quietly smoked his cigarette. He didn't agree with her any more than she agreed with him, but I saw what she was saying, I saw that if you took the children from that photo you had only a woman, not a mother. It was the motherness of the woman that was so moving, the fact that she would bare her own emotion to the camera if the shot might help others understand her family's plight, but she would protect her children from prying eyes. I supposed my own mother was like that, trying to protect me.

"Geoff and I love the same things, too," Liv said more lightly. "Bicycling, and cherry pie, and 'maths.' "

" 'The ideal brother,' " Fletcher said.

"Though there was that time he bloodied my nose for something I said to a boy," Liv said, echoing him, and Fletcher and I both laughed.

"What did you say?" I asked.

She touched the small bump at the bridge of her nose, the shame of who she had been as a girl in the gesture: a skinny, awkward tomboy whose only friends were her brother's friends. "A new boy at school," she said.

Someone as odd-looking and awkward as she had been, too fat where she had been too skinny. When had she come into her beauty?

"I called him a cow," she said.

He'd taken the last seat at the lunch table, excluding her.

Fletcher tossed his cigarette onto the ground outside the jeep, then took Liv's and tossed it, too. "You were nicer than I was," he said, "and my brother merely boxed my ears."

"A retarded cow." She sighed. "God, the hurt in that boy's chubby face, and the mortified look in Geoff's, his embarrassment at my cruelty to this poor kid who . . ." This poor kid who would have been her, if not for her brother. Who *was* her that next year, when Geoff was sent to an exclusive boys' school where he was captain of the football team, class president, first in his class, while she, at the girls' high school, cleaned erasers at lunchtime to avoid having to eat by herself. Their mother had already been sick then, although they hadn't known how sick, hadn't known she was dying.

"An 'ugly, retarded cow,'" she said. "He got up from the lunchroom table, like I'd meant him to, and I took his seat. God, what a brutal kid I was."

THE U.S. FIRST ARMY PRESS CAMP AT CHÂTEAU DE VOUILLY, NORMANDY

◆

TUESDAY, JULY 18, 1944

If SHAEF hears about Carpenter being in this show, they'll discredit her so fast it'll make her head spin.
—Journalist Iris Carpenter's driver, shortly after being shot in the hand as Carpenter covered the taking of Metz, Germany

Fletcher pulled to a stop just before he reached the correspondents' tents in the field outside the Château de Vouilly press camp—the whole estate now covered up with men in military green returning to file their stories about the taking of Saint-Lô. He ought to have parked somewhere farther away and walked in, he realized, but it was too late now. Beside him, Liv took a cigarette— her fourth—and lit it fairly expertly in the jeep.

One day, or two at most, he thought. He couldn't be escorting two AWOL women journalists around northern France any longer than that. He meant to go it alone; he did better work that way. He might not even go to Paris; he wasn't in

103

France to photograph cheering crowds and champagne toasts, and he certainly didn't need the distraction of Charles bloody Harper's beautiful wife, no matter how talented she was.

"Do you know how Charles first described you to me, Liv?" he asked. "He said you think and photograph like a man, but you don't smoke and you don't curse."

Liv looked at him from underneath her combat helmet. "Charles said that?"

"When he first hired you."

She took a drag from her cigarette, blew a thin line of smoke through her nose. "Damn," she said.

Fletcher laughed and said, "We were all skeptical. We couldn't imagine a lady could take pictures—" *Could take pictures like you do,* he'd almost said.

He patted his shirt pocket, his letters to Elizabeth Houck-Smythe, thinking that if he were caught traveling with two AWOL journalists he would be taken in with them, slowed down at a minimum, or perhaps sent back to London. Not that that wasn't tempting. The Allies were stuck in the hedgerows all over Normandy, being mowed down by German guns every time they tried to go over the top, or even when they sat in the low roads, seeking relief in the shade. As you sat reloading your film, a shell could blow your head off.

"I can send your photos as my own back to the

AP offices, Liv, I think I can arrange that," he said. "I can find someone to pass your stories along, too, Jane. Just tell me where you want them to go and I'll figure something out."

Two days, he thought. Certainly not more than three.

"If you have any shots you want sent on the press wireless, Liv, I can have perhaps as many as four transmitted," he said, trying to keep the reluctance from his voice. If his CO discovered he was tying up resources for lady journalists . . . "Those shots will get to the US in seven minutes," he said. "I'll arrange for the rest to go by plane. If they don't get tied up by the censors, they'll be there for tomorrow's evening papers."

The uncertain look in Liv's eyes left him uneasy.

"You should probably wait in the jeep," he said. He patted his pocket again. "Do you have any letters to mail?"

Liv turned to the windshield, looking out ahead. "You'd send my photos as yours?"

Fletcher eyed the front driver-side tire, again losing air. "I can't send them as yours. They'd be confiscated. And maybe I can't send them to AP. If the military police are already looking for you they'll be watching to see where the AP photos are coming from, which ones can't be accounted for. But I could have them sent to Charles. He might be a bit befuddled at first—why am I sending him photographs?—but when he sees them he'll know they're yours, Liv. Hell, he fell for you the moment he saw that first photo of yours as surely as—"

As surely as I did, he'd been about to say. Was that true? Before he'd met Liv, in Charles's office that first time when he'd asked her to fetch him tea, he'd seen her photographs. Charles had shown him her photographs. He'd seen the way she captured so much of a person, and he'd wondered if he could stand to be seen so clearly. But Liv was Charles's girl, and he always fell for Charles's girls, there was that. Just like he always fell for Edward's girls, as if love were a com-petition he needed to win.

"Charles knows your work, Liv," he said, thinking anyone who knew anything about Liv's photos would recognize them. Most artists used light and angle to capture the contours of a face because faces shot straight on tended to show flat, to lack expression. Liv, though, shot faces straight on as if no one had taught her better, and yet somehow, when you looked at her subjects— these images of people you'd never met—you saw something of *yourself* you hadn't known before, something you didn't always want to know.

"Charles will understand," he said, thinking if only she would photograph the faces of the dead, no one who saw them would be able to turn away from the cost of the war. But she wouldn't.

She'd been schooled by Charles and she was unable to deny him, or even to disagree with him.

"He'll know the photos are your work," he said, "and he'll get them to AP for you."

"There's nothing earth-shattering here," Liv said. "Nothing that won't keep."

Fletcher stared at her, trying to drag some understanding from beneath his confusion. The flag-draped corpse in the rubble of the cathedral was magazine-cover material.

"But Liv, the Major Howie photos," he said. "Surely you realize—"

"It's not like I got our boys shooting Germans."

"You've gone AWOL, Liv. You've risked your accreditation to cover the war. And now you don't mean to send your photographs out?"

"The war was over in Saint-Lô by the time we got there."

Fletcher extracted another cigarette, cupped his hands against the wind and lit it, and exhaled.

"Jane?" he said.

A jeep slowed as it passed, but continued on.

Fletcher handed the cigarette pack to Liv, saying, "You're not credentialed to the front, neither of you are. They won't send your work if they know it's yours because you aren't credentialed, and they won't credential you because you aren't men."

Liv and I would never get accredited to the front; we knew that. Not in any event and certainly not

107

now, not after we'd left the field hospital in flagrant violation of our CO's direct orders. I watched through the cracked windshield as Fletcher disappeared into the château, thinking we were going to be found out before the day was over, turned over to the authorities, arrested and sent back to a nurses' camp in London where they knew now to watch girls like us lest we escape over the fence like Martha Gellhorn had.

Liv said, "Why is it a bad thing, Jane, to want to get to Paris?"

"A bad thing?"

"'Make your career.' Marie repeated what I said with such distaste. But photos like Capa's D-Day shots, you can't see them and not want to—"

A jeep pulled up behind us, the driver puzzling over Liv and me as he headed on foot toward the pale stone and pale shutters and slate roof that reminded me of the Stahlman mansion. No columns here, no overhangs to keep the rain off visitors at the front door, if not servants at the back, but there was the same polite quietness here. Even with the commotion of the press hurrying about, the soldiers billeted here to keep communication with London out of German hands, there was a calm here.

Liv said, "The darkroom staff set the dryer too high and melted the emulsion in ninety-five of Capa's negatives. They ruined all but eleven photographs he might have died getting."

I was trying to make sense of what she was suggesting—that it was better to keep her work in her pocket than to risk a snafu in the darkroom?—when she said, "He has two mistresses. Two that Charles *knows* of."

"Capa?" I said.

"Fletcher," Liv said. "One of them is his own dead brother's fiancée."

I stared at the château's arched doorway, trying to reconcile what she was saying with Fletcher's lanky limbs and perfectly hit *t*'s, Fletcher who as a boy had shared a love of cricket and maths and Jane Austen novels with his now-dead brother. The specificity of the charge weighed in favor of it being true, though, or there being some truth in it. His own dead brother's fiancée.

Liv took out another cigarette and offered me one. As we sat smoking, I wondered if I would have gone parking with Tommy Stahlman if I'd known about the Ingram girl. I wondered how I would hear from Tommy to know that he was still alive now, and how I would get word to Mama that I was okay. I remembered the first cigarette I'd ever smoked, the green Lucky Strike package in Tommy's hands, in his car at the banks of the Harpeth River. I hadn't wanted him to know I didn't smoke, that no boy had ever before offered me a cigarette. I'd only ever smoked with Tommy until I became a journalist, the day my boss at the *Banner* called me in to tell me another of his boys was headed off to war and did I want to try a piece for the books page? "The books page?" "You do read," he'd said, and he'd offered me a cigarette—a Lucky Strike, too, the green package by then swapped for a white one with a red circle on it and the slogan "Lucky Strike Green Has Gone To War" because green dye was needed for the military. My boss had said, "You were just comparing the *Mrs. Miniver* movie to the novel for the other gals. You've been fixin' my grammar on the sly for years, too, putting things in better words than I ever would. The books page or the society page, that's what Mr. Stahlman told me to offer you. And you seem more a books girl than a society gal to me."

To Liv, I said, "But you said your husband and Fletcher are friends," thinking maybe her unwillingness to let go of her photos had nothing to do with mistrusting Fletcher Roebuck; maybe it was her husband's reaction to the fact she was traveling with Fletcher that Liv worried about.

Liv said, "You best be careful, Jane. Fletcher Roebuck is partial to pretty, long-legged blondes."

Without Fletcher, though, Liv and I had no way to get our work to the United States short of sweet-talking wireless operators into giving us lines out the way we'd heard Martha Gellhorn was doing, filing stories whenever she could. And neither Liv nor I was Martha Gellhorn, who'd been covering war for nearly two decades and was now doing so for *Collier's*, no less. Without Fletcher claiming our work as his, anything we managed to get out would be identified as ours and confiscated to be used against us—destroyed, or as good as destroyed.

Fletcher, Liv, and I found our way to a bombed-out farm not far behind the front northwest of Saint-Lô that night. The barn, though in shambles—a new door had been tacked on not long ago, as if that alone could hold the thing up—still stood in a barnyard that had, alongside slit trenches dug well into the earth, surprisingly tidy if unweeded rows of pole beans and feathery carrot tops, and great sprawling vines of yellow squash. The farmhouse itself was a roofless collection of tumbling-down walls, and dead cows lay rotting in the field, but we ate vegetables from the garden along with our dinner rations, and we laid out our bedrolls in the barn's hayloft, Fletcher at one end and Liv and me at the other. I lay awake listening to Liv breathing in steady rhythm, Fletcher rolling over in the hay across the barn, talking in his sleep. Something about Edward. I listened more intently, trying to make out his words, but he grew quiet again, and I dug more deeply under the warm hay, left listening now to the night sounds: the low moo of the farm's single surviving spot-eyed cow; the birdlike chirp of frogs down by the pond; the scampering feet of barn rats, which only occasionally scurried across me, never near my head, as I willed myself to remember they were just harmless little creatures seeking the relative warmth of a barn I certainly was not ceding to them.

I heard Fletcher moving, making his way to the ladder and down it. When he didn't return in the time it might have taken him to relieve himself, I slipped down the ladder to find him sitting just outside the barn door, an emergency kit opened before him and the small scissors from it in hand. Mixed with the country smells was a hint of chocolate.

I sat next to him and leaned back against the rough wood of the barn. "Can't sleep?"

"I am in sorry need of a trim," he said.

"And outside in the dark in the middle of a war zone with no mirror is just the time to be cutting your hair? I do see how that would keep you awake at night, though, being a little unkempt."

I took the scissors from him and told him to scoot forward so I could get behind him. "I can't promise much, but I'm pretty sure I can do this better than you can."

I'd cut Mama's hair for years, although I didn't offer up that fact.

I knelt behind him and slid the fingers of my left hand through his hair, which was dirty-rough with the living outside, the coarse gray strands obstinate against the dull blade.

"It's Tuesday night," he said—a comment I gathered was meant to explain why he couldn't sleep.

Snip. Snip.

"How do you keep track?" I asked.

"The girls back at Trefoil will have had a splendid weekend with their mums," he said, the emphasis on "end" rather than "week." "But they'll be sad now, with their mums gone back to London."

While I cut his hair, he told me about the evacuee schoolgirls Liv had met, who'd arrived at his family's country house with their cheap little suitcases gripped in one hand, their gas masks in the other. Little girls whose mothers came on special weekend coaches to see their children but returned on Sunday nights to jobs at military barracks and airfields and munitions factories while their husbands fought in Africa, or Italy, or France. The way he spoke of them—particularly of a little girl named Ella who hadn't spoken since her mother died—left me wondering if the longing in his voice was for home or for fatherhood. His parents, like the girls' mothers, lived in London, but the butler and housekeeper who cared for the Roebuck country home cared for the girls as well.

I imagined Mrs. Serle as a woman like Mama—

who had lived on the servants' floor at the Stahlmans' until she'd become pregnant with me. I suppose it said something about my mother, or perhaps about the Stahlmans, that they kept her on at all then, although of course they couldn't have an unwed mother and her child living in their home. Mama had moved back in with my grandmother and taken the long trolley ride to Belle Meade every day. "Mrs. Tyler," the Stahlmans started calling Mama then, the dignity of the married title not for Mama's sake but rather to preserve the fiction that their help were all decent and respectable.

Fletcher said, "Serle says the girls spend their Mondays throwing toys out of the pram, and Tuesdays picking them up."

"The girls are babies?" I said.

"It's an expression."

I said, "Like my mama. The summer I was nine, I was getting so thin I had to stand up twice to cast a shadow." I didn't say that was the summer after Grandma died, the summer Tommy and his friends peered through the garden shed window to spy on Old Cooper and found me sitting amidst the fertilizer and shovels and rakes, reading a book and eating a cheese sandwich because cheese would keep all morning in the damp heat. I didn't describe their taunting, or my happiness the first time Tommy came to the shed alone, the first time we snuck out to play in the stream. I

114

said, "I grew so fast that year that Mama said I'd be able to hunt geese with a rake by summer's end."

Fletcher tilted his head back a little, laughing warmly.

I said, "I take no responsibility for this hair, Fletcher Roebuck, if you're going to be flopping your head all over the place."

And I thought of how well my height had served me. I'd been sixteen when I graduated from high school and started typing for the *Banner*, but no one seemed to realize how young I was. It was 1938 and jobs were impossible to find, but Mama had worked for the Stahlmans, who owned the paper, since she was sixteen herself.

I said, "That was the summer I got my first dictionary."

Old Cooper had found a discarded one somewhere and brought it to the garden shed for me.

"The summer I started schooling Mama on vocabulary," I said lightly.

Every night on the trolley home, she asked me to teach her a new word. "Tell me a word I don't know, Janie," she would say, and I would offer up words like "copious" and "writhe" and "gambit," and she would repeat each one. When I replay those trolley rides in memory, I hear the bone-tiredness in Mama's voice, the worry, but as a child I heard only her curiosity. She would ask me to tell her what each word meant and

115

how it was used in whatever I'd read, and about the book itself. Others on the trolley would join the conversation, maids like Mama heading home after the long days I spent reading in the garden shed or the tree, or sneaking out to play with Tommy. Sometimes, if I ran out of talking before we reached our stop, Mama and I would sing together, the way we sometimes did at the Stahlmans' sink. She never let me stay for more than one song when she was washing dishes; she always sent me off to read. But if I offered up a good word on the trolley, one she'd never heard before, she would sing with me all the rest of the way home.

Fletcher asked about my father, and I started to say that my father was no longer with us or something similarly vague, to leave the implication that I had a father but he'd passed away. In the stillness of Fletcher's head under my hands, though, I felt him waiting for my answer. And some worry kept him, too, awake at night, and maybe it was the war, but it seemed to me to have something to do with a more personal shame like mine, like never having known your father. I imagined saying it: *Whoever my father was, my mother was never his wife.* But I just kept trimming Fletcher's hair with the scissors, not wanting to lie to him and yet not wanting him to think of me that way.

Shelling began to sound in the distance, far

enough away to be background war to us. Fletcher pulled a half-eaten chocolate bar from his pocket and peeled back the wrapper.

"Hershey's finest?" he offered.

"I do like chocolate," I said, trimming carefully around his generous ears to avoid snipping his skin, although the scissors weren't sharp enough to be much danger. "Even ration chocolate." It was fortified with an overabundance of flour to prevent melting. "But I don't much care for hair-covered chocolate."

"How can you tell with this chocolate?" he asked, and he laughed as he broke off a piece and set it on my tongue.

SAINT-LÔ–PÉRIERS ROAD
◆
FRIDAY, JULY 21, 1944

> I don't want any women attached to my
> unit. Send them back!
> —Associated Press North African
> bureau chief Wes Gallagher, according
> to AP journalist Ruth Cowan

All we needed was a break in the incessant rain.
We'd been at the front for days, and we were wet
through and through despite our rain ponchos, so
chilled that we couldn't imagine it was really July,
that back home people were drinking iced tea
and fanning themselves on front porches, eating
sliced watermelon and corn freshly cut from the
cob, and peach ice cream. We weren't alone—
everyone at the front was wet and miserable.
Everyone anywhere near it was. Wet from the
rain and being out in it every minute, cold from
being wet and from the chill coastal air.

"One clear day, one clear morning," Liv said,
"and the breakthrough will come."

Breakthrough. The word was everywhere. The
troops and supplies were amassed on the beachhead, ready for the push to take back France.

Getting tired of being ready. General Bradley himself—the commanding officer of the American troops in Normandy—had shown up at the Vouilly Château the day before, slipping quietly into the barn opposite the old bakery, coming to the press rather than calling the press to headquarters so as not to alert the Germans to Operation Cobra, which he was there to explain. The weather needed to clear enough for air support to go in first, though—the US Eighth and Ninth and the British Royal Air Forces: B-17 and B-24 heavy bombers, B-26 Marauders, and the fighters, the P-38s, P-47s, and P-51s. The largest air strike ever ordered—that was what we were waiting for at the Saint-Lô–Périers road.

Now Eisenhower was here, too. He'd flown in from London in a heavy storm, only to have General Bradley tell him the attack he'd come to witness had been called off due to weather and admonish him for risking the flight.

Fletcher did a great imitation of Eisenhower flicking his cigarette into the mud, and in a rotten imitation of the general's voice said, " 'Perhaps the only perk to being Supreme Commander is that I can't be grounded, even by you, sir.' "

"This damned weather is going to be the death of me," Eisenhower was said to have remarked.

"The death of us," Fletcher said. "He means the death of all of us here at the front. The death of the Allied effort."

Waiting. It takes a bigger toll than you might imagine when every second offers the specter of the military police taking you into custody, or of a battle beginning that would be the end for so many and might be the end for you. I'd done what I was supposed to do while I waited. I'd written a piece on the waiting:

All of war is waiting for something. Waiting in a mess tent line for bad food. Waiting for orders, or for daylight or darkness, for the weather to clear enough for planes to fly. All of war is waiting except when you're in it and you wish all you had to do was wait.

We waited, and Fletcher taught Liv and me to shoot.

The first time Fletcher put the revolver that had been his brother's in my hands, it made me more nervous than I would have imagined.

"Lordy, Fletcher," I said, "correspondents aren't supposed to carry weapons!"

"Of course they aren't, Jane," he agreed. "It's against international law. But you and Liv are AWOL. What's one violation more?"

"And you, Fletcher?" Liv said.

"I'm not a correspondent. I'm a military photographer, one of the few benefits of which is that I am allowed a weapon."

He turned me toward a tree and wrapped his arms around me, guiding me in the aiming of the thing. I hit the trunk that first shot, with his hands warm on mine, the stubble of his beard brushing the edge of my brow and his chest against my back so that I was sure he could feel the thud of my heart. My gaze was not on the tree I was to aim for but rather on my arms lined up with his, my hands in his palms, my breasts pressed together in the posture. When Fletcher let go and told me to fire on my own, the bullet hit nowhere near the target.

"For someone who so obviously loves the feel of a gun in your hand, it's sad that you're such a bloody lousy shot," Fletcher said.

As he dipped his head to reload the gun, Liv mouthed, "A playboy," and made a face that left me wanting to laugh, and feeling slightly ridiculous, too.

When Fletcher looked up, she said, "I think Jane needs a man in her sights rather than a tree"—her voice as serious as if by "a man" she meant a German soldier. She cut me a sly look only when Fletcher again tended to the gun.

Liv hadn't done much better when her turn with the pistol came, but then Fletcher hadn't put his arms around her to show her how to shoot.

That was the first of our daily shooting lessons, after which Fletcher left the gun with us and set off in the jeep for the press camp at the Vouilly

Château. He went to the ten a.m. press briefings most mornings, and sometimes to the late-afternoon ones as well. He went to deliver his film to a contact who sent it on to military intelligence so it could be used to plan the attack. Or that's where he said he was going, anyway, often giving us shooting lessons first and always leaving us the Webley, always asking Liv and me if we were sure we didn't want him to send out our work. He could have slept nights at the press camp, in a dry tent in the château's pasture, waking to pressed clothes and a hot breakfast, food not scooped from ration tins but rather served on china that was washed afterward by staff while he attended the press briefings in the château's living room. But sleeping at the press camps would have meant leaving Liv and me.

I saw him headed away from the press camp, though, when he said that was where he was going, and in the hours before dawn, too. The Germans were just a few thousand yards away here, so he used his telephoto lens to peer over at them, capturing what the terrain on the German side was like, what equipment they had, and how they were dug in. I didn't know whether Fletcher would go beyond the front into German territory, but I tried to watch him go whenever he left us, in case he didn't come back. I had no idea what I would do if he didn't return, but I knew that if it were Liv and I, he would come after us, and it seemed I ought to at least know where someone might begin to look for him if it ever came to that.

We gathered with a number of other journalists and military men in the bombed-out farmyard each morning, already used to the stench of dead cows. Ernie Pyle was there. Fletcher introduced us to the Scripps-Howard columnist, who took off his helmet and smiled shyly, his eyes about the saddest I'd ever seen. I took his hand, not quite a handshake—so few men could comfortably greet a professional gal. His palm was sweaty-nervous in mine.

"Looks like a lousy day for a bombing, doesn't it?" he said.

I remembered a column of his I'd read, one from Africa: Pyle had shared a ditch with an American soldier during a German strafing run, and when the plane was gone he'd tapped the soldier on the shoulder and said that had been close, hadn't it? The soldier hadn't answered him, though—the boy was dead.

Pyle said to Liv and me, "There's a snowdrop making his way around this splendid French countryside looking for you." He ran a hand through his hair—red and thinning, and gray at the temples. "But I suppose you know that?"

I scanned the barnyard almost involuntarily. Military men were everywhere, but none were wearing the snowdrop-white helmet, gloves, and belt that distinguished the US Army military police from anyone else in a class A uniform.

Liv said, "A snowdrop," repeating Pyle's words without appearing to care as much as I knew she did.

"Average height and build, with a ridiculous little mustache and a nose tilted just so." Pyle tipped his nose up comically. "As if to sniff for prey. Piggy, almost colorless eyes, too—although you don't want to get close enough to him to see that."

"Wouldn't I?" Liv said with a lift of one dark brow. Then, "I hope you've worn your track spikes, Mr. Pyle. Miss Tyler and I plan to sprint the whole distance to Paris once we've broken through the German line here, and we'd hate to leave you behind."

Pyle and everyone listening laughed—of course they did. Liv had that way about her that left men wanting to feel charmed by her. She could read aloud nothing more than the orders calling off the strike each day, and if she meant to make them laugh, they would laugh. She could read the arrest-on-sight order with our names on it and men would laugh.

The same thing about her that drew their laughter caused them to allow her to win at the poker games we played to pass the time while we waited, although they let me win, too. We played for sticks of gum and for cigarettes, which we bet singly or in the three- or four- or nine-packs that came in the ration accessories: Lucky Strikes ("Lucky Strike Means Fine Tobacco"), Chesterfields ("Milder—Cooler—Better Taste"), Camel ("Turkish & Domestic Blend"), and Chelsea (packaged inexplicably slogan-free). Even after the others started going down badly and began to play in earnest, we kept winning. Liv had to be reminded that three of a kind beat two pair, and she claimed "trips and a pair" once, not realizing that was a full house, but she won more than anyone. She was up four sticks of gum and thirty-six cigarettes, including two fancy French ones we all agreed could count as a ration three-pack each, when the men took to calling her Pitiless Livvie. The French cigarettes were thin and black, and Liv and I felt rather glamorous as we smoked them together, flaunting our success. I'd have thought that would be just the kind of thing to turn the others against Liv—her lighting those two fancy cigarettes and handing one to me even before the game was over, so that their owner had no chance to win them back. But it only made the men love Pitiless Livvie all the more.

We harvested the few green beans and carrots and squash left in the farm's garden for dinner after the others had returned to the press camp that night. I said a quick, silent prayer the way Mama and I did at home ("Bless us, O Lord, and these Thy gifts . . .") and I made a tiny, surreptitious sign of the cross over my heart before brushing most of the dirt off the vegetables and eating them with an M tin of meat and beans. We slept, and when I woke in the darkness, I knew Fletcher had left us. His bedroll was there, though, and his gear was in the jeep still parked below.

Liv woke as I returned to the hayloft. "Can't sleep?" she asked. Then, "Where's Fletcher?"

She and I opened the doors in the gable and sat with our feet dangling over the edge, high above the ground. Somewhere in the distance, a cow mooed into the moonless night. I wondered how long it would be before Fletcher had enough light to get whatever shots he was trying to get, and when he might return.

"Charles came to London to see me off even though we'd said our good-byes in New York," Liv said. "That's why we spent the night at Fletcher's country home, why I know Fletcher. I'd still be back in New Hampshire, developing my film in a sink at night, if not for Charles."

She reached up and pulled a piece of hay from my hair, rolled it between her fingers.

"'You must be Olivia James. I guess you're pretty good with a lens.' Those were his first words to me."

Her brother had enlisted by then, and she'd been living alone in the home they'd grown up in.

Charles had seen a photograph she'd taken of a friend of her father's, and he'd arranged a train ticket to New York for an interview. When she'd presented her photos, Charles had studied the top one for a long moment before removing his glasses and cleaning them, replacing them for a second, closer look. She hadn't known at the time what the gesture meant, but she'd learned soon enough that if she found some excuse to stop by his office with her shots, she could sink into the succor of Charles, in that small gesture of cleaning his glasses, delivering praise no words could replace.

We peered over the edge to our dangling feet and the rough wood of the barn, the dark ground below, and we wondered together where, exactly, Fletcher was. I wondered to myself if he would come back alive—a fear I wouldn't vocalize lest the speaking of it could somehow bring it to be.

"I was terrified the morning I shipped out. Were you, Jane?" Liv said as if she could hear the fear in my silence. "Looking through the barbed wired fence to soldiers picking wildflowers from a scrappy field and presenting them to girls in WAC uniforms."

Smelling the brine and rotting fish guts and diesel exhaust, I remembered. Listening to the nervous laughter and too-loud voices, the clanging of the shipyard, the lap of the sea.

"The ship nearest me was boarding when I arrived," she continued. "Women's Army Corps nurses climbing the long, narrow wooden planks, or already on the deck, leaning on the ship's railing, looking down at the safe, dry land. At the end of the line, a young American soldier handed a motley collection of wildflowers to one of the nurses, who filled her seasickness bag with water and put the daisies into it, to keep them fresh. He had a long, narrow face and a white smile, that soldier did, and he was tall, too, like Charles is, except that where Charles moves with an easy grace, this boy was all skinny arms and legs, all oversized hands and feet."

She dropped the piece of hay from my hair over the edge, and it fluttered away into darkness.

"Perhaps Charles was like that as well, though," she said, "before he grew into himself."

We both listened for a moment to a sound that might have been Fletcher returning, but was only the breeze rattling the barn door.

" 'Talk American to me'—that's what that boy was saying to that nurse," Liv said. "It's not something a camera can capture, though, the ache of a voice."

She started talking about a photo she'd taken at the troop marshaling area then, raising it the way she raised her camera, to ward off emotion. A hundred women crowding the railing in one neat

129

horizontal line of skirt hems, military "pink"—a warm gray, actually—a regulation sixteen inches from the deck. "All those baggy-stockinged legs upside down on the ground glass," she said. "Women no different than the women I'd spent the whole war photographing—women supporting the war effort when what I want is to photograph the war itself. Like those women I shot for 'The Homefront.'" A dozen Long Island grandmothers who'd met daily for bridge before the war now sitting in the same parlors knitting for the troops. Women working the swing shift in a munitions plant outside Newark. A typists' pool at the Pentagon.

"That was some of my best work, that spread," she said, "although it could have used a better title. Not my department, though, titles. Charles is forever reminding me of that."

I listened to her untempered pride—that, too, a shield. I supposed it was why she hadn't been popular as a child, because insecurity masked as arrogance rarely played well in a girl. Bragging on herself, people back home would have said. A bossy girl who bragged on herself. But maybe not. Liv was a rich girl, and rich girls were held to a different standard.

"I turned back to the gate after I boarded the Channel-crossing ship," Liv said, "so sure that Charles would have changed his mind and come to see me off. But the eyes I met were those of the boy who wanted to talk American with that sweet young WAC, who was no longer anywhere in sight."

I took Liv's hand in mine, the distant cow the lone sound as I tried to make sense of her words. Her husband had come all the way from New York to England to see her off to this war, but then hadn't? I remembered boarding the Channel crossing ship myself, swallowing against the dryness in my throat, the breakfast toast dry in my stomach, too, as I'd climbed the ramp to a ship that was more cruise ship than military craft, where I had a private cabin complete with a waiter bringing lemon squash to the door, where dinner was served on china and I ate guiltily, aware that the extravagant routine was meant for the boys the ship usually took across the Channel, who might end up with dog tags nailed to wooden crosses here in France.

"When I wrote Charles about the crossing," Liv said, "I told him there was a Renny on the boat."

A Renny and a Charles Jr. Marie and I wanted children, too, but Liv alone had imagined names.

"Charles was the one who first told me I had to get to Paris," she said. "Charles said the war would be won with the liberation of Paris and having the first photos out would make my career."

I said, "Maybe when it came right down to you

actually coming here, your husband was afraid for you, Liv."

"He wrote me later that he wished he'd come to see me off," she said. "I ought to have written him back that there was no Renny on the boat, no Renny anywhere."

In the distance, the cloudy darkness lightened, a suggestion of moon that darkened again, that might have been an illusion all along.

"The girls before me, they were beautiful and charming—rich New York girls Charles grew up with, mostly," Liv said. "Girls who couldn't imagine Charles's newspaper would mean more to him than they would. Or not exactly more, but . . . Do you suppose all men are like that, Jane?"

"I don't know."

"Charles thinks he wants me to come home, but he wouldn't love me if I were the type of girl who would come home after she'd gotten to the war, or even the type of photographer who sent back photos that weren't the best. He can't see how plain I'd be to him without my camera."

SAINT-LÔ–PÉRIERS ROAD
◆
MONDAY, JULY 24, 1944

At last I've seen with my own eyes the front I've been writing about.
—Journalist Sonia Tomara from "Italian Front at a Standstill" in the April 13, 1944, *New York Herald Tribune*

The morning of the twenty-fourth of July dawned, if not clear, then at least not as thickly overcast as the days before. The word went out that the planes were taking off through the cloud cover, and everyone gathered again in the farm-yard. Ernie Pyle, who'd slept in a bombed-out farmhouse the night before, looked so weary that I wondered if what people were saying was true: that he was considering going home, that he lay awake nights for fear of dying, that he'd written his editor that he didn't know how he could keep covering the war, nor how he could abandon the troops.

Pyle said to Liv that morning, "I hate to think the gal who shot 'Operating Room by Flashlight' might be prevented from doing more work like that. 'Operating Room by Electric Torchlight,' it was captioned in the London papers. No credit line, but people know."

Pyle paused, considering, as I registered his words: Liv's photos had run without attribution, as AP photos often did. Mrs. Roosevelt would have had to go to some trouble to find out who'd taken the shots; she wouldn't have known from the photographs themselves to write to Liv any more than she would have known that the piece of mine she read was a different thing altogether from the one I wrote, that Joey hadn't lived. She might have come across my piece only in searching for Liv, through my byline that ran in the *Banner* with Liv's photographs.

Pyle said, "You're a smart girl, Liv, not to file your photos. The minute you do, this Major Adam Jones fellow knows exactly where you are."

Liv and Pyle talked and talked then, as if they were alone rather than standing in a farmyard in Normandy with a gaggle of journalists and military types. They talked and the others talked, and Fletcher and I stood silent. He stood watching Liv and Pyle.

Before I realized what was happening, Fletcher headed toward the highest of the remaining stone walls, making an assault on it in hopes of gaining some visibility in this land of flat fields and high hedgerows. Or trying to impress everyone. Trying to impress Liv, who was so taken with Ernie Pyle. Fletcher got only a few feet up before stones tumbled away under him and he was forced to leap back and off. He landed on his seat in the mud.

Pyle gave him a hand up.

The military types discussed moving closer to the Saint-Lô–Périers road that was to be the bombing line. It was marked with long strips of colored cloth laid on the ground, beyond which the planes would be headed. If you stayed behind the cloth line you might be okay. But in the end everyone agreed that we were close enough, that moving closer would be an unreasonable risk to take.

It didn't matter. Just as the first of the B-17s dropped their loads, the strike was called back, the day left to the same dull waiting.

After Liv had gone up to the hayloft that night, Fletcher and I sat side by side against the barn, looking up at the starless sky and sharing a chocolate bar from the rations we'd eaten for dinner. "Sunday," I said. "My mother had a special milk pitcher we used only at Sunday supper." *The color of Liv's eyes in the morning,* I thought but didn't say, and I imagined Mama back home where it was so much earlier, kneeling at church without me beside her, without even knowing if I was alive or where I was.

"It's Monday, actually," Fletcher said.

"Is it really?"

135

Fletcher asked, "What will you do when the war is over, Jane?"

I held the chocolate on my tongue for a long time, trying to sort out an answer that would be true enough.

"I can't imagine going back to Nashville," I said finally, "but I can't imagine not going back. Mama doesn't have anyone else."

"No chap back there awaiting your return?"

"If I had a chap I expect I'd be the one awaiting," I said. "What about you?"

"No chap awaiting back at home for me either," he said.

"Just the schoolgirls whose mothers will have been to visit them yesterday?" Sounding easier than I felt, wanting him to say he had no girl. Two mistresses that Charles knew of—that was what Liv had said. Girls like I supposed I was to Tommy. Like my mother must have been to my father, at best.

"Elizabeth Houck-Smythe," Fletcher said finally. Just the one name.

He offered up no more detail than I'd offered about my missing father, and I wondered why he didn't. I imagined, too, how sweet he must be with the little girls at his country house, and maybe that was part of it: the one house in London and another in Chichester, houses big enough to host whole school classes of evacuee girls. Not just a neighborhood or a city or a state away from the wrong side of Nashville, but a country on the other side of the world. I'd liked England the time I'd spent there before I shipped off to France. Folks were charmed by the hint of Southern accent I couldn't manage to shed, and it rained in the same long slow drizzles we got at home and the countryside was just as lush, and yet no one there judged me by who my parents were or were not.

I said, "I suppose Elizabeth Houck-Smythe . . ." But then Mama's voice came to me as surely as if she were sitting beside me: *If you aren't the prettiest, you just pretend you are.* When had she stopped telling me that? Sometime before the night of Tommy's engagement party, two hundred guests under the stars on the back lawn and they'd needed extra help, and Mrs. Stahlman had particularly requested me. *That cute little daughter of yours, you bring her along to help serve, Mrs. Tyler.* But it was Mama herself who had handed me the plates for the bride- and groom-to-be, admonishing me to hold my head up and serve them proper. A rumor makes a reputation, whether it ought to or not. Tommy had sat silently as I served his plate that evening and the next week I'd been offered the books page at his daddy's paper, where I'd been a typist for years.

"I suppose Elizabeth Houck-Smythe can burn water," I said to Fletcher, although, like the Miss

Ingrams back home and like Liv, Miss Houck-Smythe didn't likely need to cook anything.

Fletcher said, "Of course that's why I've come to France, for the fine dining," and he offered me another bite of the floury chocolate.

He extracted from his pocket a photograph of a woman who, in the dim light, looked a bit like me, her light hair in a wave like mine. But pretty, very pretty. He tucked the photograph back into his pocket, then took another bite of chocolate, and chewed it, and swallowed. "Elizabeth was my brother's girl first," he said, "before Edward died."

Then he was telling me about the last time he'd visited his brother's grave. Two hours, that was how much notice he'd been given before he was shipped out—more than two hours in the foul weather and he might not be able to take off, his CO had said, and Fletcher had stuffed down the hope that the English weather offered. Two hours left no time for dinner with his parents or drinks with his mates, no showing up drunk at Elizabeth's, no midnight drive down to Trefoil to watch the evacuee girls sleeping safely in their makeshift beds. Two hours left time enough only to drive to Saint John's, the Anglican church he'd grown up in. The chapel was empty at least; he was thankful for that.

He stuffed a one-hundred-pound note into the tin contribution box beside the candles and lit them one at a time. He left the last candle in the front row unlit, and he leaned over the warmth of them, the brightness, not so much praying as letting the past trickle through him: the lavender-water smell of his mother; the warmth of his father's smooth, strong hands over his own on a cricket bat; the prick of a thorn in the rose garden as he'd stolen his first kiss. If Fletcher's time was up, he didn't want the reliving done only in a quick flash as he was dying. He'd had more than his share of good times, he knew that, he appreciated that.

He took the single unlit candle from its small glass cup and left the church through a side door. He passed sunken tombs tilting at odd angles and grave markers overgrown with creeping vines before climbing the broad steps to the upper cemetery, the hillside. On clear days the sea was visible from up there, but the sun that day was lost behind a thick covering of gray that was not yet a storm. The air was as still and heavy as that in the walled part of the cemetery below, but it wasn't musty, or dank, or decaying.

"Edward," he whispered as he'd done so often late at night from the bed beside his brother's.

He sat in the damp grass just in front of the simple stone marker. "I'm off to France, Edward," he said, pressing a palm flat to the headstone, the carved "Dieppe, France, August 19, 1942."

"You'll have to watch over Father and Mum, Edward," he said. "And Elizabeth as well."

He smoothed the clean white wick of the votive between his finger and thumb, put the candle on the headstone, and used his Zippo to light the wick. A tiny flame struggled against the shade, the dampness, before rising into the grayness, flickering in the soft exhale of his breath.

To me, he said, "I'm sorry. I oughtn't be mawkish."

"Mawkish." A word I might have presented proudly to Mama on the trolley home.

"It's barmy, I do know that. This idea that a final visit to Edward's grave might save me from his fate."

He offered me another bite of chocolate. I held his hand steady as I put my mouth to the bar, my fingers lingering on his.

"I have to stay," he said, "I can manage this when I'm here. It's the . . . I'm not sure I would be able to make myself come back."

"You'll stay then," I said.

He set his hand on mine. "Elizabeth loves chocolate," he said, leaving me to wonder why boys always counted me as a girl who would listen while they professed to love someone else.

"When she was pregnant she couldn't get enough," he said.

I shifted uneasily against the barn, confused. Fletcher was married?

"It was Edward's baby," he said. "She miscarried.

140

She said it was better that way, with Edward dead before either of us could marry her and make it right."

"I'm so sorry," I said.

He said, "She would have been a good mum, Elizabeth would have been. Edward would have been so much better a father than I."

Maybe it was a gift we bequeath to the dead, this idea that they would have been so good at all the things at which we fear we'll fail.

He said, "Do you suppose I would love Elizabeth if she loved me?"

From somewhere beyond the barn, a hoot owl sounded a lonely call into the distant sounds of the guns.

"Elizabeth doesn't make love to me," Fletcher said. "She makes love to the memory of Edward." He folded the chocolate in its wrapper and tucked it in his pocket. "We both do," he said, something he'd both known and not known when he was with Elizabeth.

He took a sip from his canteen. He offered me a sip, and I took it. We sat for a long while, looking out into a night sky devoid of stars.

"I was in love with a boy from back home," I said finally. "But he's a rich boy, and rich Nashville boys don't marry their maids' daughters except in the movies, not if their parents have anything to say about it."

In the quiet moment that followed, I wondered if

my Saks Fifth Avenue uniform and my new hair and my new career fooled anyone.

"We rich chaps have no sense," Fletcher said. "And our parents even less."

Liv woke with a start later that night, from a nightmare she tried to rid herself of by waking me and explaining it. She'd dreamed a hollow-eyed woman was sweeping glass from a sidewalk, sweeping recklessly, the shards scattering onto a Persian rug that was clearly inside somewhere.

"An indoor sidewalk, now that *would* be a nightmare," I said, trying to make her laugh.

"I dreamed a baby smiling up at me from the rug crawled right into the spray of glass, and the woman just kept sweeping, sweeping. Then my father in his surgical mask was tending the baby, and the baby died, and it was all over the newspapers but they'd gotten it wrong, they said Daddy had killed the baby when he'd been trying to save her. Then Charles was reading the newspaper, the story about my father. He took off his glasses and his eyes were so frighteningly pale, Jane. Then we were making love, Charles and I were, and I was trying to stop him, I was telling him I had to go to Paris."

In the silence, only the cow and the frogs. The rats, mercifully, had been stilled by Liv's voice.

"Was your father somehow involved in a child's death?" I asked, pulling the truth from the shadow of the dream somehow, or one bit of the truth.

"It's what the newspapers said," she answered quietly. "After Mom died. They said Daddy oughtn't to have been delivering babies. They said his grief had made him unfit to work and he knew that, he knew he ought to have called in another doctor. They said the baby died when any other doctor would have saved her. And then Daddy killed himself."

"I'm so sorry," I said.

The newspapers had gotten it all wrong, she whispered. About her mother. About the baby her father had tried to save the morning of her mother's funeral. About everything that happened afterward.

I thought of Mrs. Roosevelt's note tucked into my rucksack, all those people who read "Operating Room by Flashlight" or saw Liv's photographs imagining Joey eating his peach ice cream.

"Geoff slept on the floor beside my bed after that," Liv said, "until the battle over Daddy's estate began and we were sent to live with different relatives. We finished school and turned eighteen in the same week, and we moved back home, just Geoff and me, and he started at Dartmouth so he could live at home. English literature, even though Daddy had always wanted him to study medicine. Then Pearl Harbor was bombed and Geoffrey signed up, and it was just me."

143

I intertwined my fingers with hers, and we lay there, staring up into the darkness of the barn rafters, the silence of the war taking a few hours off.

"Geoffrey is out there somewhere," she said. "I'd feel it if he were dead."

I squeezed her hand.

She said, "I don't know if I could bear this now if you weren't here, Jane. Thank you for coming after me."

"Well . . ." I said.

"Thank you for not trying to stop me," she said.

"I meant to," I said.

A creature burrowed in the hay several yards away and we both turned toward the sound.

Liv said, "If you meant to stop me that morning, Jane, why did you bring your rucksack and your typewriter?"

She started singing then, the way we used to sing in the tent at the field hospital, with Marie. Softly. Barely over a whisper. And I sang with her. "The White Cliffs of Dover." "Always. "As Time Goes By."

"Liv?" I said as we settled into silence again, heading toward sleep.

"What is it, Jane?"

"Thank you, Liv."

"What do you have to thank me for, except dragging you out into this dreadful war?"

"Yes," I said. "Thank you for everything, Liv."

SAINT-LÔ–PÉRIERS ROAD
◆
TUESDAY, JULY 25, 1944

Glad to learn that some of my photos are at
least doing a little bit of good.
—Photojournalist John Stephen Wever,
upon hearing that his shot of a
wounded man receiving blood plasma in
an alley in Sicily caused record numbers
of donors to stream into Red Cross
blood banks across the United States

Fletcher awoke in a sweat, his heart pounding. He
sat up abruptly, relieved to see only the shadow of
the barn walls around him, the closely studded
timbers and the yellow clay dried in between
them in thick, unsmoothed clumps. He exhaled:
just a dream. Liv was on the other side of the
barn—or at least she wasn't beside him, naked in
his arms. And Charles was not there either;
Charles was back in New York finishing the
important job of moving words around on a page,
or perhaps sitting down to a late dinner with his
supposed mistress, a newspaper magnate's niece.
Hell, where did rumors like that come from?
Hell, where did *dreams* like that come from?

Though a part of him thought the dream had been lovely, really. Much better than the other. Better to be found by a jealous husband than by a lousy bastard German.

A part of him wanted to climb back into the dream.

He longed for the cigar Charles had been smoking in the dream. Did anyone make cigars anymore?

The rumor about Charles's mistress—*that* he'd heard again at the press camp two days earlier, along with the dawn reports from the front and the news of the progress of the war. It was the kind of gossip people fixed on because it amused them even though there was certainly a logical explanation: the girl was visiting her uncle in New York, perharps, and her uncle brought her along to dinner with Charles, and Charles and the niece were seen alone in the moment the uncle had left the table to use the loo.

Fletcher brushed the hay from his sleeves, pulled off his helmet and got a cigarette from the pack in the liner, then, thought better of lighting anything in the barn. The hay was warm and he hated to climb from it back into the constant chill, but he did want the cigarette. He grabbed his camera out of habit and headed down the ladder.

It was early, the dawn not even close to breaking over the barnyard, the air thick with the night damp. He stood outside, thinking of the cow that had made all that noise, imagining how delicious fresh warm milk would taste. But when he closed his jacket up to his neck and set out to investigate, he found that the creature was a single, lonely bull.

He thought he should return to the barn and its warm hay, perhaps to write Elizabeth another light letter that would make the war seem an easy thing, that would make his homecoming seem sure but would say nothing about what they would do when he returned. He knew he ought to write her, and he knew he shouldn't write her, just as he knew he both loved her and didn't love her at all.

He would have loved the child. He was sure of that. He would have loved Elizabeth's child even more because the baby would have been Edward's.

He smoked, leaning back against the wooden counterbalance gate, the cigarette tip glowing red until it nearly burned his finger. It was foolish to smoke out in the open in the near darkness this close to the front, but it was foolish, too, to carry around two AWOL American women. It was foolish even just to sleep in a barn, especially one recently abandoned by the Krauts. The bastards slept in the barns and they knew you would, too, and so they often left the haylofts mined as they retreated. Just as you poked your foot in deeper to get a little warmer, you could be looking at a leg without a foot, if you were left with eyes to look. And even if the barn wasn't mined, airmen and artillery both liked to blow up barns just for fun.

Sometimes you needed a good night's sleep in a barn, though. Sometimes you needed the freedom of being able to have a cigarette wherever and whenever you wanted even more than you needed to stay alive.

He crushed the butt into the muck and moved cautiously, climbing through a few hedgerows toward what was now the front and had been for days: camouflaged tanks hidden in the brush, most equipped with the new "rhino" hedgerow-cutter steel prongs thanks to one soldier with a good idea; artillery at the ready to move forward after the bombing; and men—everywhere there were men, all dug in. GIs slept in foxholes around the tops of which were the necessities for keeping themselves alive: rations and water, bandages in their musette bags, ammunition clips, hand grenades. Some slept on the earth above their foxholes, drier but more dangerous ground. They stretched south almost to the Saint-Lô–Périers road—the front until the troops had fallen back a few days before, reluctantly giving up a thousand hard-fought yards to allow the air force some margin for error.

Looking over the scene, Fletcher sighed in appreciation of the night spent in the warm hay.

He listened carefully, heard soft voices, followed them to a gun pit he'd visited the first night, a circular pit a meter deep and three wide, rimmed with sandbags. He always looked for the gun crews in the predawn because they were awake and had an ear to their telephone connection to the battery at all times, ever ready for orders to fire. They tended to know what was what.

This crew had had a quiet night from the looks of it: only a dozen empty 90mm casings were stacked behind the pit to be collected and returned for refilling. Fletcher called out softly to let them know it was him, and waited for one of the gunners to peek over the back edge of the pit.

"It's Baron von Flash, the mighty Brit!" the gunner said into the pit. Fletcher liked these chaps for the nicknames alone—and not just the one they'd given him. While most of the gunner teams named their guns things like Tomahawk or Thor, this crew had named theirs W-w-w-w-wobbly, the stutter perfectly describing the way the gun jittered as it was aimed.

Two soldiers manned the gun's bucket seats and a third the phone line, but one of the others snored and another ate a ration. Fletcher offered them cigarettes, and they turned to the chap on the telephone, who shrugged. The weather made flying as difficult for the Germans as for the Allies.

Two Midwestern twangs and one smooth Virginia drawl accepted fags and pulled the camouflage net over the top of the pit before lighting up. With the pit closed up like that, the smells grew stronger: bodies that hadn't showered in weeks, morning breath, the egg-meat mixture of the K rations, damp blankets, the mud itself, the brush, the smoke.

Fletcher lit his cigarette and inhaled deeply.

One of the GIs coughed, a deep, racking cough. Fletcher wondered if the poor chap ought not head to the battalion aid station; surely he could use hot food and clean hospital sheets. But if he was sick enough, his buddies would make him go back to the aid station. For the most part, though, the men toughed it out at the front. They could no more abandon their mates than Fletcher could abandon Liv.

The thought startled him. As soon as the break-through was under way, he told himself, he would set off on his own again. He worked better on his own.

He touched his pocket, where he kept the photograph of Elizabeth Houck-Smythe.

"Any word yet?" he asked the soldiers. "Is today the day?"

The Virginian said he sure hoped so. They were tired of waiting, antsy from the waiting.

Fletcher chatted up the chap on the phone, who would know the most. Nothing about the morning bombing had yet come over the field phone or the radio.

"All right, then," Fletcher said, and he climbed from the pit and continued on past the colored-flag markers, creeping over to the German side.

SAINT-LÔ–PÉRIERS ROAD
◆
TUESDAY, JULY 25, 1944

I'm sure that back in England that
night other men—bomber crews—almost
wept . . . But I want to say this to them.
The chaos and bitterness there in the
orchards and between the hedgerows that
afternoon have passed . . . Anybody makes
mistakes . . . The smoke and confusion of
battle bewilder us all on the ground as well
as in the air.

—Journalist Ernie Pyle

The sky was larger, lighter, and I was awake,
eating the compressed corn flakes from a K
ration, when Fletcher returned to the barn. In
minutes, we'd have the company of other
journalists hopeful that today would be the day.
Maybe even the sound of engines overhead.

We climbed back into the hayloft and called
quietly to Liv, found her sleeping, openmouthed,
bits of straw webbing through her hair.

"Liv," Fletcher said, popping open a tin of
breakfast rations near her ear to wake her.

Liv's complexion was an odd mushroomy shade

I imagined only a strong pot of coffee could overcome.

"We've a lovely bit of breakfast for you this morning," Fletcher said.

She pushed the can away.

I said, "What? This is America's finest. Egg and . . . what kind of meat is this anyway, Fletch? All mushed together in a tiny tin."

Liv closed her eyes again. She had never been much for breakfast even back at the field hospital.

Fletcher sniffed at the awful muck. "You told me yesterday that you loved this, Livvie."

Liv sat up, and she asked for a biscuit, and Fletcher handed her one of the cracker-like little pucks along with the rest of the breakfast ration box. She took a bite of biscuit, then examined the fruit bar and handed it and the Nescafé and sugar tablets back to him. She pocketed the chewing gum for the next poker game.

Fletcher dug into the disgusting egg-and-meat mixture.

"Sadly, there's nothing left in the garden," I said.

Fletcher pocketed the water purification tablets and downed the rest of the ration. He tucked the second ration back into his rucksack.

Liv took the toilet paper from the ration and headed behind the barn.

Ernie Pyle didn't come that morning. He'd gone farther forward and slept in a foxhole at the front.

We watched with everyone else, though, as the first planes passed overhead, as they dropped the smoke to mark the bomb line, the smoke floating to a field not far ahead. Fletcher stood stoop-shouldered between Liv and me, his beard coming in a steely gray despite his attempts to shave it back. Already we could hear the dive-bombers coming, the P-47s. The world filled with the hurricane swirl of them—the sharp crack of the bombs landing and the screams of the diving wings and the slick rip of the machine guns—and everywhere we looked, there they were, circling and diving and rising back up.

A deeper rumble arose from behind us, louder and louder.

"The heavies," Fletcher shouted over the noise.

Flying Fortresses, that's what they were called, and that's what they looked like, flying close together, twelve at a time in groups of three dozen until there were hundreds of them, everywhere you looked.

I leaned back, a thrill of anticipation welling in me as I looked straight up, my helmet falling to the ground behind me. I shivered for the enemy on the other side of the colored cloth that marked the bomb line.

Fletcher stooped beside me while Liv set her camera for infinity, estimated the exposure, and pointed upward, took a shot: the underbelly of all that destruction.

Fletcher stood and set my helmet back on my head, and buckled it tight. He set his hands on the sides of it as if trying to shield my ears from the roar of the planes. In that moment, I thought he might kiss me. I imagined his lips on mine, his tongue pressing, his breath slightly rank from living outdoors, his beard rough, and I imagined cutting his gray hair for him again, having only that moment and glad for it.

The big bombs started falling then, the dust and debris rising up from the earth in front of us, like the world's end. As the sky grew slowly darker, I breathed in the sharp smell of burning.

Fletcher said something right into my ear, but I couldn't hear him. I leaned close, wanting the words, whatever he might say, but there was nothing but the sound of the planes and the rumbling through my feet, my unsteady legs, the sudden sick feeling in the pit of my stomach. Each gulp of sooty air seemed a gift.

And all the time, Liv kept the Leica raised.

Fletcher began taking photos, too, the die-cast body bumping his cheek as he swung to take photograph after photograph: of the dive-bombers, the bigger planes, the distant spewing earth, the smoke rising higher and higher in the sky. Though we couldn't have been any closer, these shots would be nothing; this could not really be committed to film, not from this distance, not probably in any event. And yet I felt almost as if the bombs were moving closer to us rather than farther forward. The bombing line was tight up against the Allied soldiers, just a hundred feet south of the Saint-Lô–Périers road, but we were well enough behind it to be safe. It was the sound: bomb after bomb exploding until no loud noise would ever startle us again.

I felt more alive than I ever had.

The ack-ack of German guns joined the fray. And Fletcher was behind Liv then. Right behind her. Shouting words she couldn't possibly hear over the noise. I was sure, suddenly, that he would kiss her, that the way he'd looked at me was some kind of dress rehearsal, and I felt so ridiculous to be worrying about who was kissing whom or not even kissing but only wanting to as all that death rained down, to be so relieved when Fletcher pointed to a plane— one of the Piper Cubs, the little planes flying low, spotting the German guns and radioing back their positions.

Fletcher shouted again, shaking his head.

Liv lowered her camera to broaden her field of view, and I, too, saw what Fletcher did, what he already had his camera fixed on: a plane burning bright against the smoke.

Another burst into flames, and another, slashing the sky. Still the planes came forward, forward.

A parachute opened white into the smoke, another here, another there, and a gasp broke through the clamor, a sound escaping improbably from my own chest as a single parachute hung up on a wing, a man suspended underneath it, struggling to free himself.

The yellow-orange flames crept toward him. Leapt at the white of the parachute. Caught it in a burst.

The flyer disappeared, leaving only the flames, the smoke.

A tiny black figure fell from the flames.

Fletcher swung his camera, but the airman was already gone.

The sick expression in Liv's eyes as she lowered her camera: yes, she'd gotten the shot.

This is it, I told myself. *The breakthrough. Good Lord, at what cost?*

Fletcher raised his camera again as the ground exploded in great heaves, the spewing earth filling more and more of our world, so close that Fletcher kept wiping his lens with a cloth and Liv couldn't keep her camera steady; she kept lurching back from the shots.

Another plane burst into flames, seemingly right overhead. I could feel the explosions now in the trembling of my fingertips as I tried to get words onto my notepad.

What the hell were they doing? The bombs *were* getting closer.

Maybe the smoke being carried back toward us by the breeze confused the planes about the location of the bombing line. Maybe something had gone wrong in the equipment in the lead plane, which determined where every bomber in the formation dropped its load so that 288 bombs fell in one great blast. Whatever had happened, the bombs were falling short of their target.

I said, "We're bombing our own men."

A bomb exploded right there, just beyond the barn, and Fletcher was pulling Liv and me both down into a trench, the cameras tumbling, too, so that the hard metal of one pressed into my stomach in the soaking brush at the bottom of the trench.

Fletcher lay over me, his belt buckle digging into my back, my heart pounding, pounding, pounding. The loamy smell of the mud. Liv's cheek on the rough straw beside me. Fletcher's hand on Liv's, deathly white.

"Correct course, you lousy bastards," Fletcher said, his voice close in my ear.

I closed my eyes to the dank smell of the tomb and the suffocating press of Fletcher's weight, to the possibility of a bomb dropping on us, exploding, with only the thin wall of earth around us and nothing but smoky sky above. *Breathe, Fletcher, breathe!* I thought, wanting the warmth of his breath on my earlobe, the certainty that we were alive, like Mama's breath as she set my book aside and lifted me from the chair in the garden shed, where I sometimes fell asleep.

Something exploded just above us. The ground shook, threatening to crumble, to collapse.

Fletcher breathed out, a rush of hot moisture, almost a groan. His weight sank more heavily into me. For once, I was thankful for the dampness, for the muffling effect of the sodden earth, the heavy mud that allowed the blasts to sink in, that kept the shrapnel from flying quite so far.

There was nothing to do then but listen, and feel, and pray.

Listen to the approaching planes, the scream of bombs falling, the thunder as they struck.

Feel the shaking of the earth, the dirt spraying across the top of the trench, the vibrating air.

Pray for myself and for Fletcher and Liv and for everyone else, pray that somehow this mistake would be realized before it was too late. And try to forget the blackened figure falling to earth.

Finally, Fletcher lifted his weight slightly, saying, "Bloody hell."

With his lips at my ear, the words hurt.

He rolled over onto the muddy straw beside me, and Liv and I rolled over, too.

I looked up through the steep walls of earth to the smoky sky. Planes continued overhead, but they were passing again, holding their bombs until they were farther forward and dropping them where they were meant to be dropped.

I climbed from the trench finally, my joints corroded from the tension, my muscles locked.

Around us, others were climbing from foxholes, looking at one another in dazed disbelief.

Fletcher touched my arm, looked into my eyes. "Jane, are you okay?"

He pulled me close, his other arm pulling Liv to us. I closed my eyes to all the people, to the blank stares and the muttered obscenities, the heavy exhaustion, the disbelief.

"We'll return to the press camp," Fletcher said, his breath soft in my hair, his lips warm on my scalp. He turned to Liv then, and kissed the top of her head, too.

I looked away from him, from the longing in his eyes as his lips lingered in the dusty dark of Liv's hair. A longing for the war to be over, I told myself as I looked to the other journalists, some watching us with curiosity but most still flummoxed by the fact that they were alive.

I called out to them, "This place is nothing like it looked in the brochure!"

Those within hearing distance laughed, those who'd been in this war long enough to laugh when the laughing was good.

I turned to Liv, remembering the Robert Capa quote she so loved. "Was that close enough for you, Liv?"

She tucked away what had to be her own fear without missing a beat and said, "Pffft . . . *That?*"

I wiped the dust from my lips with my muddy hands. It was everywhere around us, the gray soot:

on the roof of the barn, on the water in the trough, on our helmets and uniforms and gear. Soot the gray of the newsprint that would *not* report this mistake the next morning because men like Charles would think the news of 111 GIs killed and 490 wounded by their own bombs was less important than the perception that this war was being won. Men who would hold tightly to that belief even when they learned that one of their own was a victim, that AP photographer Bede Irvin was killed as he was trying to retrieve his camera during the short bombing at the Saint-Lô–Périers road.

"We have to turn back," Fletcher said.

We looked not backward, though, but to the horizon, to what was left of our troops digging out from the debris, taking stock, preparing to move ahead. Liv climbed back into the trench to retrieve her camera. She handed me my ruined notepad and Fletcher his camera, too, and they pulled their spent film and stuffed it into condoms, and reloaded. Fletcher lowered the cracked windshield of the jeep so it lay flat on the hood lest the glint of it attract sniper fire, and we climbed in, and we moved slowly toward what once were lines of colored cloth and beyond them, to leafless trees and dead cows not yet reeking, to empty bunkers abandoned by Germans in a moonscape of bomb craters that were sharp-edged, not yet worn smooth by the back-and-forth crush of tanks.

BEYOND THE SAINT-LÔ–PÉRIERS ROAD
◆
TUESDAY, JULY 25, 1944

The nearer the front, the easier things are—in a base section where everything is carboned in triplicate and thrown away before reading, there are shower baths, sheets and no fleas, but the cigarette ration doesn't arrive nor the mail, there is no milk for the coffee, and no paper for the toilets which really flush. At the front there are heaps of cigarettes for everyone to help himself, matches, paper and fleas, hitch-hiking transports without signing chits, guys who hear you're out of film and bring you theirs, coffee enough because by the time you've found the method of making smokeless fire to heat the water you've saved up enough Nescafé packets from the K ration to have plenty for seconds and thirds.

—Photojournalist Lee Miller,
from her original manuscript of
"The Siege of St. Malo," written for
the October 1944 issue of *Vogue*

As the sky reddened the evening after the breakthrough, we caught up to a crew operating one of the ack-acks, the 90mm antiaircraft guns charged with keeping the German airplanes away from our troops. The soldier on the phone to the command post as we arrived at their newly dug pit nodded to Fletcher and said, "Flash," but frowned at Liv and me. He wasn't happy to have women in his gun pit, and with a word into that receiver, the MPs would know exactly where we were.

"Nighttime is the busy time for these chaps," Fletcher told Liv and me. He said Liv ought to get what photos she could in the last of the evening light because she couldn't use flash at night here, but most of the action these boys saw came after dark, with the German planes.

"Eleven twenty," one of the boys in the gun's bucket seats said without pausing in his visual search of the horizon. "Set your watch."

"Where are your manners, Flash?" the other bucket seat boy asked in a Virginia drawl.

"Sorry." Fletcher set a hand on the side of the big gun and said, "Liv and Jane, may I introduce you to W-w-w-wobbly, the finest gun in Normandy."

The crew laughed.

"*Five W*'s, not four—since I see you're writing that down, Miss Tyler," said a GI loading cubby-holes dug into the walls of the pit with shells.

"Jane," I said.

"Jane," he repeated. "Five W's because we have five W's in our crew. William—that's me, Bill Singleton, S-i-n-g-l-e-t-o-n, but I'm a William. And Willy and Wade." He pointed to two others on the gun team. "Walter on communications." The fellow on the phone. "And Warren is cooking up some chow. Do tell us you're staying for dinner? Just rations warmed over a stick fire, but the meal is included in the price of a ticket for tonight's show. You've bought your tickets, right?"

Fletcher said to the soldier with the Virginia accent, "Virginia, Liv and Jane are here to make you famous, so you might run a comb through that hair."

Liv photographed Virginia smiling right at her from his bucket seat, the big gun behind him. But we wouldn't make him famous. We weren't sending our work out so we wouldn't get caught, and these boys would be old news by the time Paris was freed.

"Our ninety-millimeters are the big daddies," Virginia said proudly. "They can shoot thirty thousand feet up and fourteen miles. We can do twenty-five rounds in a minute, too. And we don't like to miss."

"Eyes on the sky, Virginia," frowning Walter on communications reminded him.

The night was spent like so much of the war: waiting. I asked the boys where they'd come

165

ashore (Omaha Beach) and when (D-Day plus three) and what they'd been doing since then, and I made notes in the waning light. There hadn't been much to do with the guns their first days in France, they said, so they'd acted as infantry, which was brutal. Now they targeted not only German planes but also ground fortifications, troop concentrations, and armored vehicles.

At 11:20 the pit went silent as, in the distance, a plane thrummed. Perhaps just one. Perhaps not.

I turned to Walter. It was dark now, impossible to read his expression.

"Stand by," he said finally. "Three rounds."

The big gun buzzed to life, the long barrel jerking up, down, left, right, like a barn rat sniffing the air—the aiming controlled at the other end of the electric cable. My mind jerked just as wildly, from Fletcher's assurance that the gun pits could survive anything but a direct hit, to my mother at home without me, to an unbearable thirst and the need to listen and take up my pen. I focused on the shadow men, the energy palpable in their hushed voices.

The gun settled.

"On target! Three rounds! Fire!"

I braced myself against the force of the gun, the blast, the muzzle flame illuminating the crew for a moment, beautiful and vulnerable. They shot and reloaded, shot and reloaded, shot again, the smoke thick around us.

"A flamer!" someone said, a hushed exclamation, as if the sound of the gun weren't enough to alert the entire German army to our position. The crew looked over the rim of the pit, and I looked with them to see a fiery airplane plummeting.

Virginia said, "We don't often know whether we've made our targets like that until someone tells us."

"That is fucking satisfying," one of the *W*'s said. Then to Liv and me, "Excuse me. Excuse my language."

I thought, *That* is *fucking satisfying*.

I opened my canteen and took a long drink, hoping none of the shells had landed beside a German field hospital, knocking out the lights in their operating room.

We followed the tanks down the coast in the days after the breakthrough, rolling over roads and crossing open fields, always on the offensive. We drove with our windshield down and our helmets on, watching for military police and avoiding communications officers who might alert them to us as we followed Patton's Third Army on the slow creep through French towns—Coutances on July 28, then Bréhal and Granville and Sartilly. We found relatively safe positions from which to watch minesweepers clear streets, tanks roll over cobblestones, infantry creep from house to house to find, as often as not, that the Germans had fled from the fighter planes and the bombers that cleared our way.

By night we slept in foxholes under skies reddened by the flames from bridges the Germans burned in their retreat. Fletcher didn't sleep much at all as near as I could tell. He and I would talk and eat chocolate together late at night while Liv slept. He sometimes went out on night patrols with the soldiers or crept forward alone in the early mornings, always to the places he insisted it made no sense for Liv and me to go. We didn't object. We appreciated the way Fletcher positioned us to observe the war well enough without putting us in more danger than was necessary. And he always left the Webley with us.

We continued our shooting lessons, with progressively more distant targets. "You'll not want to be asking a German soldier to move up a bit so you can hit him," Fletcher said, putting his arms around me to steady my aim, which was perhaps intentionally poorer than it might have been had I not known that a poor shot would bring his touch. We played poker with the soldiers. We smoked the cigarettes they let us win, and refilled our lighters from a leaking jeep tank, not ours. We won "liberated" bottles of wine and cognac, which we opened and passed until they were empty. And when soldiers asked us to "talk American" to them, we did so, trying not to think of the cemetery back at Omaha Beach and the wooden crosses we passed at the roadsides, crosses with American helmets set atop them. The ones with flowers, we were told, tended to be the mine-sweepers, boys killed making the way safe for everyone else.

We gave up bathing more or less altogether. We needed the available water for our canteens, we told ourselves, but in truth no one bathed at the front. Mobility was far more important than cleanliness, and it was hard to remain mobile with your pants down. So we lowered our pants only to do our business, which we did quickly. A latrine would have been a luxury.

When Liv and Fletcher ran low on film, Fletcher found a photography shop in one of the newly liberated towns, its door hanging loose from its hinges and the owner hiding in a basement or somewhere else altogether. Fletcher took what he and Liv needed and left behind a hundred-pound note, more than enough to cover the supplies. No one with the Allied forces was to spend money in France; that was one of the regulations about which our CO back at the field hospital had been "crystal clear." If Allied soldiers started throwing money about in France, the civilians wouldn't be able to afford anything. But Fletcher couldn't do his job without film, and he couldn't bear to take the film without leaving some payment, and he had nothing but hundred-pound notes.

When the Third Army split, we followed the column heading west toward the port of Brest on the Brittany peninsula over Liv's protests that we were going away from Paris rather than toward it.

"Your American papers will want photographs of American soldiers, Liv—without the faces of the dead, of course," Fletcher said. "If we go east to find Montgomery's troops, your photographs will be of British chaps."

When she refused to be swayed by his logic, Fletcher said, simply, "I'm a military photographer, Liv. I have my orders."

"And your orders are to follow Americans so Jane and I can get caught and sent home heading away from Paris rather than toward it?"

Fletcher said, "I'm sure I can find you another ride, Liv, although I can't say that you'll be completely happy about where they will take you."

"We can find our own ride," Liv said.

But we stayed with Fletcher, who decided not much later to turn back in the direction of Paris after all.

We'd been able to get gasoline and rations from the Allied supply trucks when we were traveling with the troops, but finding gas on our way back toward the press camp, now at Canisy, was a challenge. The sun was high and hard in the sky, and the gas gauge read dead empty when we stopped in a small town: a square, a church on the corner, a butcher shop, a *boulangerie*. The town had no water, no light, no gas, and little food, but it was liberated and the café owner was happy to bring us what little she had.

"*Vous n'avez pas a me payer. Je vous l'offre,*" the woman said. She wouldn't allow us to pay.

She served us a loaf of crispy bread, a few apples, and three glasses of eau-de-vie at a tiny outside table from which we watched a raucous crowd collect in the square. Old women and young. Children. Old men.

"What's happening?" Liv asked.

A young woman emerged from a building across the square—"*Commissariat de Police,*" a sign over the door read—pushed by a fat, balding old man. The skin of her upper arm blanched under the grip of the man's fingers as the crowd surged toward her, shouting "*Salope! Putain!*"

Liv raised her camera and focused on the agitated face of an older woman who stood apart from the crowd, weeping as she watched the girl. Liv didn't take the shot, though; this wasn't the war, and she didn't have film to waste.

The café owner pulled off her apron and laid it across the back of a chair at another table.

"Is the girl German?" Liv asked.

"*Est elle une femme allemande?*" I asked the café owner.

"*Elle est une collaboratrice horizontale,*" she answered, and she pushed toward the square, disappearing into the crowd.

Fletcher stood and followed her, and Liv and I followed Fletcher, slipping in his wake through the circle of townspeople. In the center of the crowd, the balding old man gripped the girl by the long dark hair curling down her back. He forced her into a chair set out on the flagstone. Sitting there, she looked more womanly, thicker.

Fletcher crossed his arms over his chest and stood watching.

Another old man, as round and balding as the first, stood by the chair, waving something at the girl-woman. The old man who'd brought her out pushed her head down between her knees with a single rough thrust of his hand.

"What are they doing?" Liv asked.

But for his immobility, Fletcher might have been one of the mob.

The sun glinted off the thing in the man's hands—a large pair of shears.

"Fletcher." I echoed Liv.

Liv focused her camera as the scissors sliced through the girl's hair in a single, metallic *shhhhht*. Long dark curls tumbled to the ground. The crowd's voices rose higher, their arms thrusting in angry triumph, "*Danse avec ton soldat maintenant! Couche avec ton soldat!*"

"*Help her!*" Liv said, moving through the

172

crowd before Fletcher caught her shoulder and pushed past her.

Two men caught Fletcher's upper arms and held him back, scolding him in French. Liv tried to raise her camera, but one of the men took it from her, saying, *"Pas de photographe."* The girl in the chair sat eerily still, her gaze to the ground as the barber sliced off her hair. He set aside the shears and began with the razor, the crowd egging him on. He shaved off the last remaining stubble to leave only a patch above her left ear in the shape of a swastika.

The men draped a sign around her neck—*"J'ai couché avec un sale Boche"*; *I slept with a dirty Hun*—and forced her to stand, and the crowd booed one last time. Fletcher was beside the girl then, and although the crowd continued to jeer, the anger had ebbed.

Someone handed Liv back her camera, and she took a shot of the girl's naked scalp—a startling white against the bent-armed cross of hair and the red where metal had nicked skin. "Swastika," from the Sanskrit *"svastika,"* meaning a talisman. I'd written a column on it back in Nashville. The German word meant, literally, "it is good."

Fletcher lifted the girl and carried her off, bending his head low and murmuring some small, soothing words as the older woman who had been weeping hurried after them.

Liv and I ducked into the nearest building, an

empty schoolhouse, and sank into little chairs in the first room we came into. The seats were hard, the smell of eraser dust stifling. The room had been used as some type of command post: There were lists written in German on the chalkboard. Maps and elevations taped to the walls marked the locations of troops, planned lines of attack, points of the earth seeded with mines. I went outside again, but that was worse: the bright sunlight, the dark curls blowing across the square.

I found Liv again in another of the schoolrooms, one with German tourist posters decorating the walls and German and French words chalked in blackboard language lessons: *"Vater—Père, Mutter—Mère, Bruder—Frère, Schwester—Soeur."* Liv stood with her camera focused on the word *"Bruder."*

Fletcher called to us from outside: his voice, and then silence. The door to the schoolhouse creaked open, the smell of the warm summer air flushing into the chalky, dusty room. Liv took the photograph of the chalkboard—*"Vater Mutter Bruder Schwester"*—then turned the camera on him. He held a gas canister with German words like those on the chalkboard marked on it, along with a swastika.

"We have petrol," he said in a dull voice. "The last of it in this town. I suggest we move along before someone sees we have it."

"Is she all right?" My voice low and soft.

"She's . . . She'll be fine."

I said, "Those people, they . . . they were *thrilled* by it."

Fletcher set the canister down heavily on a desk and rubbed his hand where he'd held it. "They had nothing, and she had petrol. She ate beef and candies when they were starving. She never wanted for soap or warm water."

"You don't know that," I said. "You think that because you want to think it, you want her to be that person. You have no idea who she is."

He rubbed the edge of the gray stubble on his neck. "She was a source of information for the Germans, Jane. She fingered fellow townspeople working with the resistance, people she grew up with."

"You don't know any of that," I said. "Those people, they just wanted to be cruel, and she was someone they could be cruel to. And she—"

"Have a look at what the Germans do to French girls who help hide resistance fighters," Fletcher interrupted. "Or—"

"But she was pregnant, Fletcher!" My hand going to my own waist.

Outside, the sound of someone passing, laughing. I wondered where the boy was, if he would survive the war, if he would grow old with a wife and children back in Germany, untouched by the disgrace that would be this girl's and her child's, too.

"She was pregnant," Liv repeated—a fact, it was clear from her voice, that she hadn't realized.

We slept in an open field that night, Liv and I with our bodies under the jeep but our heads out so we could see the stars, so many stars in the clear sky. Our helmets on, though, and Fletcher discretely several yards away, under a tree.

"Liv?" I said.

"What it is, Jane?"

"Do you suppose that girl loved the boy who got her pregnant?"

She turned her head in her helmet toward me. I kept my gaze on the sky.

She said, "I don't know."

"Why do people judge like that, just because a girl falls for a boy they don't think she should love?"

"Why do people judge anyone for anything?" Liv answered.

"I could have been that girl."

"I know, Jane. We all could."

"I'm not smart at knowing who to love," I said.

"No one is," Liv said. "That's the problem with love."

Planes sounded faintly, and a church bell tolled from the direction of the town.

I said, "But the mistakes ruin us."

Liv said, "Yes. Even when they aren't mistakes."

OUTSIDE CANISY, FRANCE
◆
THURSDAY, AUGUST 10, 1944

The men don't want us here.
—AP correspondent Ruth Cowan
in a wire to Eleanor Roosevelt
that never made it out of Africa

I awoke in the passenger seat to a change—some difference in the environment that made me sit bolt upright. The silence. No grinding of truck gears, no spinning of tires stuck in the mud, no low rumble of tanks, no gunfire. That and the slowing of the jeep. I felt the motion high in my stomach as Fletcher turned the wheel and braked, stopping the jeep alongside the road.

Liv reached into her pack for the last unopened B tin—a biscuit, a "confection," Nescafé, and sugar—and extracted the biscuit. She offered me a bite of the dry, floury puck, and I took it. I preferred compressed corn flakes, but we were out of breakfast rations and down to a very few provisions. We'd opened our last package of halazone a few days earlier, and the chlorination tables lost their effectiveness after they'd been opened for a day or two. We'd had no option, though. We couldn't accept the soldiers' supplies and leave them without good water.

I pulled my jacket tighter, thinking that might explain why I was queasy even riding in the front.

Fletcher opened a can of meat-and-vegetable stew and sniffed it—as if it might smell any better than it always did. "We're outside Canisy," he said. "It won't be a half mile to the First Army press camp."

We were hoping to catch up with the First Army, which was said to be meeting German resistance in Mortain, or to join the British Second, where Liv and I might be safer. American papers didn't want photographs and stories about British boys, American papers wanted pictures and stories about American boys, but we wanted to get to Paris and we weren't sending off our work anyway, for fear that it would lead the MPs to us.

Liv set the ration tin back in the pack with the last of the biscuitless rations and all the letters we'd written since Saint-Lô, letters we couldn't mail if we didn't want to be found out and sent home, but still we'd written them. Fletcher tucked his own letters in his pocket, took out his revolver, checked to make sure it was loaded, and handed it to Liv.

"I should be an hour or perhaps two," he said. "Any special requests? The delicious chopped ham and eggs? Hershey's chocolate? We have cigarettes and a bit of tinned meat but not much else, and our film is about at an end as well."

Liv took another nibble of the biscuit, then stuffed the rest in her pocket and focused on the revolver. The metal, she'd told me, was as cool as the metal of her Leica, and similarly empowering.

"Correspondents aren't supposed to carry weapons," I said, an old habit by now.

We all climbed from the jeep, and Liv took aim at one of several cigarette butts littering the road twenty yards up, not waiting for Fletcher to pick out a target. The gun popped and the butt flew into the air, blown by the force of the bullet striking the macadam in front of it.

Fletcher smiled at the new scar on the road. "You're still aiming a bit low, Livvie, but if I were a German in your path, I wouldn't hang about to give you a second go at me."

Liv handed me the gun, and I aimed at the butt, now just in front of a coil of telephone wire dangling from a pole. I took the shot, and a second, a third.

Fletcher put his hand on mine on the gun, saying, "That poor, wretched butt is quite dead enough, isn't it, Jane?"

He took the gun from me and set the safety, then handed it back to Liv. The butt remained on the ground just beyond where it had been. Like Liv, I was still aiming low.

"Why don't you take the jeep, Fletcher," Liv said.

"So, you've got—what?" he said to her. "A month's worth of exposed film?"

"Take the jeep, Fletcher," she said.

"French film isn't like French wine," he said. "It won't improve with age."

"Take the jeep," she repeated. "It's not like Jane and I are going anywhere."

"I can send it as yours, Liv. I can manage that. Don't worry, I don't intend to pinch your—"

"I know."

"Beastly hell, Liv! You won't shoot the faces, that's your own decision even if it is mistaken, but why the devil won't you send the shots you *do* take?"

A transport truck loaded with Americans sped past, splashing mud behind it. It was not raining at the moment but likely would be again soon. We watched the truck disappear around the bend, the soldiers staring out the back at us. I wondered where they were going, whether they'd get there, if they'd be lucky enough to come back alive.

Fletcher sighed. "Stay with the jeep," he said, "and do mind the woods."

Always, there were Jerries in the woods. An Allied unit would clear an area, pushing through it or surrounding it, forcing out the few soldiers left behind by the fleeing German army, but within hours the woods would be thick with them again.

"Take the jeep, Fletcher," Liv insisted.

180

Fletcher slung an empty rucksack for carrying back supplies over his shoulder and added a smaller musette bag, also empty. "Mind the woods," he repeated, directing the words to me now as if Liv couldn't be trusted. Then to Liv, "Reload the Webley and remember what I said about hard surfaces. The bullet will skip and fly about and you'll end up plugging some poor sod you haven't meant to shoot, and Jane here is too attractive alive to be shot dead."

Too attractive.

Liv tightened the strap of her helmet as Fletcher set off down the road. "A playboy, but a charming one," she said, leaving me holding my pathetic little heart upright, as I had when I'd served dinner plates back home on the Stahlmans' lawn.

Liv and I sat on the hood of the jeep, the metal cool through the seat of our fatigues and the French countryside sprawled out around us: rolling hills that allowed for some measure of vista, hedgerows giving way to fences of granite slabs. A jeep sped by, then a transport truck, each slowing to see if we needed help. Ten or fifteen minutes later, an American soldier approached on a BMW motorcycle left behind by the Germans. No snowdrop helmet, I noted as he stopped to walk the bulky bike through a shell-pocked portion of the road. He, too, asked if we needed help. It was an odd sight, I supposed, the two of us in American fatigues, helmets, and combat boots, sitting atop a jeep in the middle of a war zone.

A second jeep hurried by a few minutes later, then stopped abruptly a few yards ahead and backed up. My throat tightened, but the two were newsmen, NBC radioman John MacVane and AP correspondent Hal Boyle. We'd gotten to know them while following Patton's army, and they liked to give us a hard time about our AWOL status, our careful avoidance of the press camps.

"The party won't be the same without you," John said.

"No ladies' latrines there," I answered.

They were already late for the briefing, they said.

As they hurried on their way, Liv raised the pistol and took aim at a tree overhanging the road, the bullet rattling the leaves over their heads.

"Damn, Liv," I said.

"What do you say we get out of the path here so all these boys will stop gawking?"

"I don't mind the gawking," I said, only half in jest. But we'd made ourselves unobtrusive enough at the front to avoid attention, or we'd gotten lucky, or the MP charged with finding us was too cowardly to come after us as we followed the front. Farther away from the danger, though— back here near the press camp—who knew who might say what to whom about seeing us?

I climbed from the hood and took the driver's

seat, Liv beside me, and drove a few yards across the scrub. I tucked the jeep under some low-hanging oak branches at the edge of the woods so it wasn't easily visible from the road.

"I have half a mind to set out into the woods, the way Geoff and I did as kids," Liv said.

"You drove, or your brother did?" I asked.

She took aim at the road, but didn't shoot. "Our friend Oscar Miller, too, sometimes," she said. "Never during hunting season, though."

A few minutes later, a jeep came from the other direction, not in a hurry. We sank lower in our seats as it approached: a driver in a snowdrop helmet. I hoped we were tucked back well enough. I was glad Lucky Strike had given up their green dye for our sake.

The MP seemed to be going so slowly, but he passed without seeing Liv and me.

As we watched his jeep disappear down the road, I whispered, "I sure hope he wasn't looking for us. It would be such a shame for him to have missed us when he was so close."

Liv whispered, too, although the MP was too distant by then to hear us. "Well, he came up the road from the press camp, so it does seem unlikely he was looking for anyone from the press."

"Certainly not women correspondents," I said. "No ladies' latrines and all that."

She closed her eyes. She looked in sad need of a rest, and I supposed I did, too, despite all the attention we'd drawn. In a war zone you didn't have to be gorgeous. Being female was enough.

At the sound of rustling leaves in the woods, I whispered, "Just a bird."

"A squirrel or a rabbit," Liv agreed.

"A wild boar, maybe," I said. "Aren't there supposed to be wild boar in the French woods?"

Liv set the Webley in her lap and closed her eyes and slept, or pretended to.

I closed my eyes, wondering if the MP was our Major Adam Jones, thinking how lucky we were that he hadn't passed by just minutes earlier. Wondering if he'd been at the press camp when Fletcher had arrived, and who he'd talked to there, whether he'd learned anything about us.

I must have dozed off, as I was jolted awake by an explosion. Liv sank lower in the seat, turning at the same time to aim the pistol over the pile of gear and the spare tire, toward the road.

An Allied jeep skittered to a stop at the road's edge, headed away from the press camp, like the MP had been. Two men, cursing loudly, piled out of the jeep and stood scowling at their blown front tire.

"We are fucking gonna be the last ones to Paris at this rate," one of them said in a thick Alabama accent. "The champagne bottles will be empt and the dames all shacked up with soldier boys."

Liv recognized the pointy nose and chin, the scrawny cheeks and red-rimmed eyes as those of a journalist to whom Charles had once introduced her, whose name she couldn't recall.

The rat-faced man's companion grabbed the jack, and the two began to repair the wheel.

Gossip. The favorite pastime at the press camps, Fletcher had told us. We could only hear the rat face, but that was what these two were doing now as they fixed their tire. We listened a little more carefully. Well, why not? It wasn't as if we ever got much gossip from Fletcher.

Lee Carson had vanished from a "facilities tour" in Normandy, the rat face was saying. It comforted me to know the experienced International News Service reporter—whom people said could get anything she wanted just by flexing a pretty ankle—had to resort to going AWOL to get to the front, too. The rat face and his friend talked Lee Carson to death, then started in on Iris Carpenter's husband taking up with someone else—Iris Carpenter, whom I would have thought to be beyond gossip's reach. She was one of the most gracious women I'd ever met, impeccably British and proper and yet so warm, and she'd given up her post at the *Daily Express* to care for her children before the war. She couldn't be accused of having ambition. She'd come back to work for the BBC only when the British government summoned her.

I wanted to give the obnoxious American a piece of my mind. He couldn't hold a burned-out candle to Iris Carpenter. He was putting her down the way men were forever putting down women more talented than themselves. His reproach had nothing to do with anything other than making his little rat face turd of a self feel manlier.

The rat face's companion stood again and tossed the jack and the pump back into the jeep, and the two climbed in.

The briefing must be over if these two were leaving; Fletcher would be gathering supplies. He'd be back soon.

"I heard Bourke-White has hooked up with some counterintelligence fella down there," the rat face said. "Some Major Poopart. Must be the lady's ass that guy is after, not her tits." His Southern accent dragging through the words in double syllables—*ay-ess, tee-its*—leaving me ashamed to be Southern.

"Tits-wise, she's got nothin'. My grandmama's got better tits than her. *I* got better tits than her."

"*Papurt*—Major Jerry *Papurt*," Liv whispered, raising the gun and sighting the rat face's pointy nose, right between his dull eyes.

The motion—the emotion—must have frightened her. She held the revolver away from her, as if her aiming were the gun's doing and not her own, and as the two fired up their jeep, she bolted from ours into the woods, lurching forward from the waist just in time to choke up the biscuit into the underbrush. By the time I reached her she was sitting with her back up against a tree, wiping her mouth with her hand, and the rat face and his companion were puttering off.

"God, I might have shot that little jerk," she said.

I said, "Oh, but he *did* need shooting."

I reached for my canteen to offer her a sip but Fletcher had taken the canteens to the press camp to rinse out the sediment and fill them from the château's clean water supply. It was a rare treat, water that wasn't cloudy, like so many simple things we'd always taken for granted at home.

The fact of not having water made me thirsty.

"Three ration-can meals a day, that's what the brochure promised, but you didn't read the fine print, did you?" I said. " 'P-38 included with every C rat so you can leave your can opener at home, and one free package of halazone tablets . . . but drink the water at your own risk.' " The last bit offered in my best fine-print voice.

Liv closed her eyes and rested against the rough bark of the tree trunk. I did the same, the damp ground soaking the seat of my slacks.

A minute later or ten or thirty—I didn't know how long—I gasped as my eyes flew open to see Liv already aiming the revolver.

Fletcher, I thought.

I said, "Don't shoot, Liv!"

A German soldier drew back, reaching for his rifle.

Liv pulled the trigger, the blast of the gun absorbed by the forest as the bullet buried in the ground just in front of him.

He dropped his rifle and raised his hands over his head, all knobby wrists and dirty hands and thin blue eyes sunken and scared under a military cap that wouldn't protect him even from the nonexistent sun.

The revolver shook in Liv's hand, the four inches of metal ahead of the trigger jittering.

The soldier cowered, pleading in German, the Adam's apple of his thin neck bobbing above the neatly buttoned military jacket.

"No!" Liv said, moving to her feet now, the guttural sound of his voice tugging at her trigger finger.

He looked from Liv's face to the revolver and back, his wide-set eyes unblinking over smooth cheeks filthy with the dirt of living outside. He started speaking again, hesitantly, quietly. Mixed in with the unintelligible rest, I heard, *"Gunther."*

"No," Liv said. "No. I don't care what your name is. You're not human. You . . . You put guns to their heads and laugh. You cut their belts and buttons off so they have to walk humiliated, holding their pants up. You . . . God, you . . . You shoot them when they're surrendering, when they're unarmed and kneeling on the ground."

Though she didn't know, really, what the Germans did to their prisoners. Charles had been talking about what Allied soldiers did to the Germans when he told her that—facts he'd heard from journalist friends but which no responsible editor would print. Allied boys shooting terrified, exhausted German boys who'd already laid down their guns.

The German began to murmur again. He'd wet himself, the dark stain spreading down the leg of his pants.

Liv held the revolver in one hand—shaking a little less wildly—while she wiped her eyes and nose with the back of her other hand. I heaved a big breath, but the air didn't fill my lungs.

"His gun," she said to me.

I approached him, trembling like hell, turning sideways toward him as if that might be safer. Liv, with the gun fixed on his face, motioned for him to step back, and I kicked the Mauser away from his feet. It was surprisingly heavy, and I had to kick it several times to get it out of his reach, backing it awkwardly through the undergrowth on the forest floor. When the gun was far enough from him, I stooped to pick it up, grabbing it by the wood stock.

Liv trained the revolver on the German's chest now, the second coat button.

The boy's washed-blue eyes watched our every move.

The Mauser weighed on my muscles, the creep of exhaustion emerging in my arm and in my shoulder as I backed away from the boy.

If this German was here, others likely were as well.

The boy blinked pale eyelashes as straight as mine, as straight as Tommy Stahlman's. He was as tall as Tommy, too, but gawky-thin, a young man not yet grown into his size. His uniform was well kept but for the stain where he'd wet himself. He was not missing a button.

"Geoff was on an intelligence mission," Liv said quietly, not to me but to the German. "He was on an intelligence mission and he was reporting in like he was supposed to and then he wasn't, he went missing. That's what the telegram said."

The German looked from his Mauser in my hands to the Webley pointed at him.

"He was on leave in London when I was there and I didn't even know it," Liv said. "I didn't even see him. Then he was sent on an intelligence mission somewhere, I thought he'd be here in Normandy but by the time I got here he was already missing from wherever he was supposed to be. No one knows if he was captured or if he's hiding in the woods or if . . ." She tightened her grip on the pistol, tears spilling down her cheeks.

The soldier leaned away from her and raised his arms higher. Again, the softly spoken, guttural words.

"Geoff could have escaped," Liv said, suddenly insistent. "He wouldn't give up. He would escape."

The German, his face still a deathly white, remained silent.

With the gun pointed at him, Liv reached into her uniform blouse pocket and drew out a letter, which she unfolded awkwardly with her free hand, exposing the easy, looping handwriting, the "Dear Mutt." A photograph of her brother wrapped inside fell to the ground, landed almost in the putrid bit of biscuit she'd not been able to keep down. Without taking her eyes off the German, she picked up the photo, brushed the mud from it, and handed it toward him.

"Liv," I said, alarmed that she would approach him.

"My brother," she said to him, stopping well out of his reach.

The German looked from the photograph to her, still with his hands raised. He risked a glance at his rifle in my hands.

Liv held the photograph up for the German to see. She lowered the revolver slightly. "Do you understand? My twin brother."

The German looked at the picture, a flick of pale eyes and then a longer, steadier glance.

"Geoff," she said.

Mutt and Jeff.

The German lowered his arms slightly as if to move toward her and take the photo. Liv aimed the gun squarely at his chest, and he again raised his arms. He wore no wedding ring.

"Surely someone is helping him," she said. "Surely some mother or sister or someone has found my brother and she knows all we can do is help each other."

After a moment, the German spoke, soft words that sounded like agreement that some German mother somewhere was helping Geoff.

Liv's skin stood white against the cold metal, against the khaki of her sleeve. "It's only the soldiers who kill, isn't it?" she said. "The mothers, even the German mothers . . ."

The boy kept his hands in the air, still with the stain on his pants. "*Ja?*" he said.

With the gun trained on him, Liv awkwardly folded the snapshot back into the letter.

I set the barrel end of the soldier's rifle to the ground, held it like a cane. "Yes," I said. "*Ja. Not the *mutters*."

I reached into my pocket, moving slowly so as not to alarm either of them. I didn't have much—just a chocolate bar and a pack of cigarettes—but I tossed them to the ground in front of the boy.

Liv, with the gun still pointed at him, said, "Look for my brother." She began to cry again. "Find him. Tell him I'm here."

The boy looked at her, his Adam's apple bobbing in his too-thin neck.

She nodded toward the candy bar, the cigarettes. "Take them."

He hesitated, looking to me, and I nodded. He lowered his arms slowly, keeping them in a surrender position but his palms at the height of his shoulders now.

Liv lowered the pistol, still gripped tightly in her thin, pale fingers, to aim it at the muddy ground. She nodded again to the chocolate and the cigarettes, her tears trickling over her jaw. With her free arm, she used her sleeve to wipe her nose, the little bump from that childhood fight.

The German squatted carefully, his eyes fixed on her. He picked up the chocolate and the cigarettes with his right hand while keeping his left raised, returning both to the surrender position as he stood.

"Go," Liv said. "Go."

The German took a step back, watching us, and then another. He said a few words softly, *"Sie werden nicht schiessen?"* A question, I knew, from the inflection, from his pale expression.

"Go," I said. *"Allez."* Wishing I had any idea how to say the word in German.

He took another step back, then lowered his hands and turned and ran. His boots struck hard on the muddy ground. He splashed through a puddle and veered through the trees, the gray of his uniform blending with the tree trunks, the brush, the leaves, then disappearing altogether into the thick green of the woods.

OUTSIDE CANISY, FRANCE
◆
THURSDAY, AUGUST 10, 1944

Who got to a town or across a river first was a silly game the newspeople played. I'd never realized how intense the competition was for datelines.

—Journalist Andy Rooney

Fletcher caught a ride from the press camp back to the jeep with two *Stars and Stripes* journalists, including a young American named Rooney he'd gotten to know a little at the briefings. When they got to the side of the road where Fletcher had left us, he was startled to find nothing there—no jeep, no Liv, no me. "Liv!" he called out, ignoring Rooney's joke that it wasn't like him to lose a dame. "Jane!"

He spotted us in the jeep under the tree and rushed over, calling our names again.

"Whatever is it, Fletcher?" Liv answered with a calm I certainly didn't feel.

What I felt was utter exhaustion. The face-to-face encounter in the woods was somehow more frightening than the bombs or the night in the gun pit or the days following the tanks and clearing the towns, even though it had been us holding the gun on the German boy and him in danger. Or maybe because of that, because we might have killed him. I felt exhausted and, at the same time, as if I might hold the gun on the frightened German boy myself and be glad for doing it.

"Beastly hell," Fletcher said. "I was sure you two had stumbled into the hands of the Germans."

"Oh, yes, of course, Fletcher," Liv said. "We just made friends with one in the woods." Making a joke of a truth she couldn't tell him lest it provoke him to take us directly to Major Adam Jones himself. *Don't tell anyone,* Liv had whispered after the German was gone. *Not even Fletcher. I couldn't bear for anyone else to know.* Leaving me wondering if she meant about shooting at the German or about her twin brother being missing in action all the time I'd known her. *"Missing" or "missing, presumed dead"?* I'd wanted to ask, but I'd been afraid to suggest a death that hadn't been mentioned.

I made myself smile, and I said, "We were pretty damned close there, Liv. You did get his photograph, didn't you?"

Liv said, "I'm afraid we weren't quite *that* close."

Fletcher took the Webley from Liv and cocked it open, spilling out the empty shells. "You didn't even reload," he admonished us as he reloaded. "What if you actually had run into trouble?"

He took out a cigarette and offered it to Liv, then to me when she declined. I declined, too; I couldn't stop my hands from shaking, and I didn't want Fletcher to notice.

Fletcher extended the cigarette pack to the *Stars and Stripes* journalists, who were just catching up, offering, "Have the last of Mrs. Harper's poker winnings?" He lit his own and said, "We've got another damned flat."

He set about jacking up the jeep for the third time that week, a task made no easier for the jeep being off the road, near the woods. He removed the tire from its rim, took out the inner tube, and pumped air in it to find the hole as the Americans told Liv and me what they had learned at the briefing: We'd taken Guam and Tinian in the Pacific, and a thousand German prisoners at Rennes. Canadian and British forces had opened a new offensive south of Caen, thrusting four miles into the German blockade of the roads to Paris.

Rooney said, "Listen to this, the latest ploy in the race to get the first dateline. Have you heard this, Mrs. Harper? You head for a city that maybe hasn't quite been taken but is about to be. You go as far as, say, a road sign on the outskirts of town, something that shows that, technically, you're in the boundaries. Then you scurry on back to the correspondents' tables at the press camp to write your story as the news comes in, with the dateline the city."

"You can't do that," Liv said, the repair kit in her hand, its metal cap already removed. "No one would try to do that."

"The patch?" Fletcher said.

Liv looked down at the kit, then back up at him. "No hot patches left," she said, handing him the cap. "Only cold."

"You underestimate the human desire to be first, Liv," Fletcher said, and he began sanding the inner tube with the rough side of the cap.

"No one reputable would," Liv said.

But the culprits included correspondents from the Associated Press, INS, Reuters, and UP.

"I don't want to malign anyone," Rooney said, "but Hank Gorrell—you know him, right? Harry Harris and Bert Brandt have taken to calling him X-ray Eyes."

Liv cut a piece from the red sheet of cold patch and shoved the rest back into the cylinder. I watched her, still thinking of the German boy in the woods, Liv with the empty pistol pointed at him. Thinking about what Liv had said to him, wondering how she could have tucked away the telegram about her brother being missing in action and made polite conversation that first morning at the field hospital, with a nurse tending a wounded German boy.

Fletcher dabbed the glue on the inner tube,

slapped the patch over it, and looked up at me as if he might know I was keeping something from him.

"So the good news for you photographers," Rooney's companion said to Liv, "is that a photograph of a road sign at the outskirts of Paris doesn't sell as well as the story written from it might."

At that, Rooney suggested they hit the road before everyone got to Paris ahead of them. Fletcher retrieved the jerry cans of gasoline and his rucksack from their jeep up on the road, and they puttered off.

Fletcher returned his attention to the tire, inflating it. "I understand Martha Gellhorn has joined the Poles in Italy and no one is troubling her," he said.

I looked out across the landscape—the sharp-edged bomb craters, the dangling telephone wire—wanting to object, to insist that we follow Patton's troops straight to Paris. We could get to Paris and I could write my story and Liv could take her photos, and we would go home.

"Some of the lads of the Thirtieth Division are holding Hill 317 against all odds," Fletcher said. He shoved the tire back on and tightened a lug nut, then another. "They *are* surrounded by Germans, though, and I can't fathom how we could get to the hill to photograph them. The word is the Seventy-ninth Infantry have taken Le Mans and—"

"They'll get to the road signs for Paris and say they're already there!" Liv said.

Fletcher's hands slipped on the lug wrench and the thing thumped onto the ground, smashing his finger. "Hell," he said, shaking his hand to try to ease the throbbing.

"Listen to me, Liv," he said. "What have I been telling you? No one is going straight for Paris. Rooney was yanking your chain." He picked up the wrench, fitted it back onto the lug nut. "The plan is to encircle the Germans west of Paris, with the Americans coming from the south and the Canadians and the Poles from Caen, to the north. We can connect with the Poles or the Canadians."

"Eisenhower isn't going straight for Paris?" Liv said. "Why not?"

Fletcher gave the wrench one last frustrated yank, then stood and stowed the jack and climbed into the driver's seat, still nursing his finger. "Do I look like Eisenhower?"

Liv leaned back a little as if to get the whole view of him. She looked slightly better now, her color returning.

"More like de Gaulle," she said, a mocking little smile creeping into her slightly pink-rimmed eyes. She raised one brow, with a glance at me.

"The sharp nose, maybe?" I said.

Fletcher smiled slightly despite himself. "I'm leaving you two behind if you don't get in the jeep," he said.

Liv took the passenger seat, peering exaggeratedly at him. "The weak chin?"

"I expect it's my ears," Fletcher said.

"De Gaulle's ears are *not* that big," I said, settling into the backseat.

"It's just that hat he wears," Liv agreed.

"I should have left you both back at Saint-Lô," Fletcher said. He rubbed the finger he'd banged with the jack, saying, "I expect Eisenhower wants to avoid the destruction of Paris and the cost of supplying it. The fuel and food needed for a liberated Paris could support eight infantry divisions in the field."

The Allies had spared Paris in their bombing, hitting only the rail yards and other outlying facilities, but would the Germans, if forced to retreat, grant it the respect of surrendering it unscathed?

Fletcher sighed and said, "It happens that I just missed your snowdrop chum, Major Adam Jones. I'm told he is well aware that we're traveling together, and in this neighborhood."

Liv and I glanced at each other. Maybe our luck with the MP, like our luck in poker, would stay with us, or maybe it was just about to run out.

Fletcher had heard two other pieces of news at the press camp, which he reluctantly shared: Three French journalists—Pierre Bourdan, André Rabache, and Pierre Gosset—were captured when their car was halted by machine gun fire at

Rennes. Worse, Bill Stringer was killed doing just what we'd been doing, following the tanks.

Bill Stringer. He was an American, a Reuters photographer.

Fletcher focused on the jeep's choke although it wasn't cold enough to need it, averting his gaze lest we see the truth in his eyes: that if we insisted on following the Americans, he would take us; that he was scared for us all, whichever way we went.

Liv, in the passenger seat, shoved her hands underneath her thighs. My hands, too, were still shaking.

The engine cranked to life, but Fletcher didn't shift into gear.

"I would have taken his picture," Liv said, "but I didn't think I should waste the film."

"You would have taken whose picture?" Fletcher asked.

She tilted her head toward the woods and said, "Our German friend."

Fletcher reached into the back of the jeep and pulled out the musette bag he'd taken with him to the press camp, and set it in his lap.

"Fletcher," I said, "do you think you could kill a German?"

A jeep passed on the road. Fletcher didn't turn to look.

"Fletcher?"

"At Dieppe there was a barbed wire fence," he

said, staring blankly through the windshield, his voice flat, "and we were getting slaughtered, the dead and the wounded falling on the wire, and the bodies . . ." His Adam's apple bobbed once, twice. "The bodies formed a human bridge over the barbed wire. Edward . . . he stood up right into German fire and called his men to follow him over the bodies."

"You were there?" I asked, confused.

"I was in London with my photos of stuffy old men, and a girl in bed beside me that I'd just met that afternoon."

"Oh," I said, startled by his frankness. "I'm sorry." Meaning about his brother.

"It wasn't even . . . We had no hope of holding Dieppe. It was more of a . . . Would the landing crafts work? Could we make an assault on the beach? Six guns. We were after six bloody guns defended by barbed wire and pillboxes and flak towers.

"My brother suffered burns all over his face and chest from a mortar explosion," he said. "He lived for . . . for I don't know how long."

"I'm sorry," I said again, thinking of the German soldier, regretting having let him go free.

"How do you do that? How do you charge into enemy fire over your own mates' dead bodies?"

I thought of Tommy commanding his men past the drowning soldiers on D-Day. "A friend of mine from home," I said, "he says you don't find courage, it finds you."

Fletcher said, "My brother told me that courage is merely another form of cowardice, that you fight because you don't want to humiliate yourself, that on some level you know you'll likely die but you can't fathom it so fighting is easier than running away."

Instinct. Self-preservation. The need to live. That was what had driven Liv to fire at the German boy.

Fletcher said, "I thought it was something my brave and modest brother said to spare me the dishonor of my lack of it."

I pulled my hands from underneath my legs. They'd finally stopped shaking.

"Do you ever think you'll die out here, Fletcher?" Liv asked.

"Don't you?"

She considered this.

"You didn't imagine you would die even when we were caught in the short bombings at the Saint-Lô–Périers road?" Fletcher insisted.

He fingered the musette bag in his hands for such a long time that I feared he was gearing up for another lecture on how Liv should photograph the faces of the dead and Charles should print them.

"That last day in Poland," he said finally, "Charles and me kneeling in the street, a German soldier with his pistol pressed to my temple. I do think about dying, all the time."

"Charles was nearly killed in Poland?" Liv asked.

"I can still feel that small circle of metal. I can hear Charles telling the German that we were journalists, that we could tell his story. I can feel the selfish relief when the German turned the gun from me to Charles. I have no idea why he didn't shoot us. It's so random, who lives and who dies."

Liv said, "Charles never told me he almost died."

Fletcher said, "He wouldn't have wanted you to worry, which you would have done had he returned here to cover the war.

"Well then," he said, "I've brought you a present, Livvie." He upended the contents of the musette bag into her lap: dozens of rolls of 35mm film.

She cupped her hands to catch the flow of film canisters.

"Fletcher, do you think Pyle was right?" I asked.

"About . . . ?"

"About the MP knowing where we are once we've sent my stories and Liv's film?"

"If you send them as your own?" Fletcher asked.

"Yes."

"Likely so," he said.

"And if we send Liv's photos as yours? If we get someone to send my stories as his?"

We might have died back in those woods, Liv clutching her spent film to protect Charles from what he must already know, that she was traveling with Fletcher, and me clutching my stories without even that excuse. Fletcher's brother, Edward, was dead and Liv's brother, Geoff, might be dying in some POW camp, a German guard holding a pistol to his head, and Tommy might be, too. Everywhere soldiers were dying while Liv's photos and my stories remained in our rucksacks.

I pulled out the last piece I'd written and handed it to Fletcher. Liv hesitated, but she gathered her spent film, dozens of sheets and rolls all enclosed in canisters and stored in condoms. And as Fletcher walked back to the press camp to send it all out—Liv's photos as his and my piece under someone else's name if he could find someone, which he thought he could—I unfolded my typewriter and slid in a fresh sheet of paper, and tried to find a way to start a piece about the German boy in the woods.

CHAMBOIS, FRANCE
◆
SATURDAY, AUGUST 19, 1944

Using a camera was almost a relief. It interposed a slight barrier between myself and the horror in front of me.
—Photojournalist Margaret Bourke-White

When the Polish infantry of the Tenth Dragoons finally fought their way into Chambois early in the evening of August 19, we were with them, documenting the taking of the tower and the march of forty German prisoners—their hands on their wool caps, their expressions impassive— toward the relative safety of an Allied POW camp. Before the day's light faded, Patton's Fifteenth Corps came up from the south and joined the Poles, closing the Falaise pocket to isolate fifty thousand German soldiers—a major strategic victory, with Paris not much more than a hundred miles away. Liv took photos and I tried to get down the words of the hurried toast between the two commanders (Polish vodka) as their troops took up defensive positions to hold the city— a story every newspaper and magazine in the United States would want to run.

As we covered what followed, though, we knew that censors and editors like Charles would again and again discard our photos and words. German infantry and artillery soldiers spilled out from the Gouffern Forest and fled down the single road through the low valley as US artillery, posted every ten yards on the hillsides above them, rained a constant fire. Allied tanks and fighter planes pounded incessantly at the valley's narrowed end. German soldiers were shot dead in horse-drawn wagons and in tanks flying white flags that were shredded along with their bearers. They were shot abandoning their vehicles. Shot being dragged by horses. Shot trying to scramble up dirt side roads and over wire fences, or with their hands high over their heads. Their remains were everywhere, skin and innards tinseling the hedgerows. The Allied military police already had more prisoners than they could guard; that was what was said. Horses were caught in the fire and wounded, some still hitched to teams and dragged along by frantic survivors, but the Allied soldiers took pity on the horses, standing by the banks of the Dives River and shooting them to save them from drowning, or from the slow death of a bleeding wound.

On the second morning, Liv moved into the valley to better photograph the fleeing Germans, and because she did, Fletcher and I did as well. We went down toward the confetti of paper and clothing and supplies, medical paraphernalia and food packages. The twisted metal of abandoned vehicles. Blackened trees. Well-creased letters stuck in the mud, and frayed photographs of wives and children, of parents, of sisters and brothers. Sprawling tangles of hooves and necks and manes and bleeding horseflesh, and corpses.

"Photograph their faces," Fletcher urged Liv again and again. "You can't control the censors, but you can photograph the faces, Liv."

Liv focused, though, on the medics with crosses on their uniforms, German and Allied medics working together, risking their lives to save fallen German men. The earth exploded around them and bullets flew past their bent backs as they applied tourniquets, administered morphine shots, and loaded the living onto stretchers.

"Do you think he's here?" Liv asked.

It took me a minute to realize she was searching not for her brother but for the washed-blue eyes we'd seen in those other woods, the straight blond lashes. She was dreading that the next boy she focused on would be the German boy we'd left without even his Mauser, who was somehow to help Geoffrey survive.

We left, finally, climbing into the jeep and turning it around, heading away from the rattle of gunfire until the smoke of the burning tanks could no longer be seen across the landscape, until the firecracker smell of the bombs was faint and the sounds of the war distant, only an undertone to the metallic hum of the jeep engine and the gravelly crunch of the wheels.

As the road turned to follow the Dives River, the faint burble of water flowing, Liv said, "We're never going to get to Paris, are we?"

Fletcher touched his dirty fingertips to his dirty combat helmet on his dirty face. "They'll go around Paris, but does it matter?"

The bumpy road passed under us for perhaps another quarter mile. I pulled out my typewriter to make some sense of the soldiers and the horses and my own emotion, but no words came. I hadn't tried to stop even a single soldier back there. I might have saved a life or two or twenty, two hundred. But I stood silent, stewing in the satisfaction of seeing Germans dying after all the Allied dead we'd seen. Or not satisfaction, but something uglier, some filthy part of me I hadn't known before.

Liv said, "My brother and I used to swim in a stream like this. It was where Geoff and I went after Dad's funeral, that stream. It was the first place I took Charles when I took him back to the town where I was a girl."

"Could we swim?" I asked quietly, wanting to weep and knowing I couldn't, I was a war correspondent, I couldn't weep in front of anyone, and there was so little private space in this war.

Fletcher glanced at me, still with the gray skin, still with the sunken eyes. He wanted to push on as fast as possible, to leave this behind, but I said again, "Please, let's stop and swim." I hadn't had a proper wash in weeks, and I felt the need for it now more than ever. "Just a short bathe in the river."

We passed an abandoned cottage alongside the river. A garden. A barn. As the road cut away from the water, Fletcher pulled off, bumping over the rutted earth toward the clean flow of the stream.

"If we stop, this jeep may never start again," he said.

The river ahead disappeared through a stand of beech trees. The stout, gray trunks spread branches almost to the ground, standing hopeful, their leaves rustling in the breeze.

"Just for a minute," Liv said.

Fletcher pulled alongside the trees, cut the engine, and commanded us to stay in the jeep while he checked the area. He left us the Webley.

He returned a few minutes later and said he would wait until we were in the water.

"We're never going to make it to Paris," Liv said more quietly but more certainly. "None of us are."

The water was deep here, the bottom not visible through the murky green. Liv and I unbuckled our military boots and skinned off our fatigues, stripping down to our brassieres and gray undershirts, gray panties, dog tags. I pulled Mrs. Roosevelt's note from my brassiere and tucked it into a pocket of my abandoned clothes.

"It's from the boy from home?" Liv whispered. "Your Thomas?"

I thought to tell her what Mrs. Roosevelt said about my "Operating Room by Flashlight" piece, to ask how a piece about a boy dying could have been made into one about a boy being saved. I thought to tell her how I'd tucked it away out of pride but now it weighed on me, a reminder to imbue every word I wrote with what needed to be said lest it be misconstrued.

"Tommy is married," I said. "He married a friend of mine when he came back on leave after basic training." Although none of the Ingram girls was my friend. The Ingram girls were Belle Meade children, and I was to stay clear of them not because they were trouble, but because they were the children of prominent Nashville families while I took the trolley out with Mama, who worked for them.

"I didn't know he was seeing her at the same time he was seeing me," I said.

I hadn't known what I hadn't wanted to know; I'd been content to climb from my bedroom window to go parking with Tommy after his Belle Meade friends had all gone home.

"But you still write to him?" Liv asked with a

hint of disapproval, or maybe that was my own guilt creeping in.

You've been my best friend since we were kids, he'd written in his first letter, as if he understood the shame I felt at the girl I was with him, willing to compromise myself for a boy who had never loved me back. Not honestly able to say whether it was him I was in love with, or the big house up on the hill on the rich side of town.

"Tommy and I have been friends since we were nine," I told Liv. "How can I not write him back?"

I dove headfirst into the river, the cold knocking the air from my chest. I swam hard into the current, low to the riverbed, staying under although my lungs ached. I opened my eyes and mouth to the cleansing rush of water. I might cry about everything here. I might let the tears blend with the river water, let the cold keep my eyelids from swelling. No one would know to judge me poorly for being too weak to bear the things I saw here, for having no father, for shaming myself at the Harpeth River, for wanting to go home and yet not wanting to at the same time.

When I surfaced in the shade of an upstream tree, Liv was standing with the cold water circling her bare ankles the way I used to at Richland Creek. Behind her, leaves rustled.

"Oh, I'm desperately sorry," Fletcher stammered, tugging on his ear that way he did when he was nervous, or when he was telling something short of the truth. "I thought you . . ."

Liv dove in, emerging a moment later in the center of the stream. Not two feet away from her, Fletcher emerged, too. He floated on his back, his white legs and arms splayed from his undershirt-clad chest, his boxer-covered hips.

There was nothing between them—Liv was married, and Fletcher had a girl back in England, his brother's girl—but still I felt myself an intruder, still I tucked farther back into the shore as if witnessing something I ought not.

"We shouldn't have stopped," Fletcher said to the sky.

Liv soaked in the green water, the murky surface, the leaves and twigs and weeds and sun.

I sank in as deeply as I could, surrounded by the hanging roots and the shade of a tree clinging to the shore as I listened over the lap of water at my ears. The water billowed my gray undershirt, but did not leave me feeling cleaner.

"If you stop like this, you think about it," Fletcher said to Liv. "If you think about it, it's all too much."

"I needed to be clean," Liv said softly.

Fletcher said, "It doesn't wash off."

Their fingers brushed each other's and intertwined. I supposed perhaps Liv imagined they were Charles's fingers. I supposed Fletcher was reaching for Liv's touch just as he reached for mine sometimes at night, when we shared chocolate bars. And I wanted to be making love then, to Tommy, who was the only boy I'd ever been with; to Fletcher; to the German soldier we'd freed. I wanted to be in a place where the sun always shone and the world was quiet, no gunshots in the distance, no stench of death.

"You go home and you sleep in a real bed," Fletcher said to Liv, "and you eat real meat, drink good hot tea, good brandy. And still, it doesn't go away."

He blinked and a drop of water—was it a tear?—ran down his temple and into the murky green river cocoon. He pulled Liv closer, the soaked fabric of her military-issue panties brushing the cotton of his boxers. I pressed my toes through the mud of the streambed, wanting to make a sound, to say something clever to remind them I was with them in some way that I was not.

"I think you see what we do to each other," Fletcher said, "and I don't think you ever live comfortably again."

BAGNOLES-DE-L'ORNE, FRANCE
◆
WEDNESDAY, AUGUST 23, 1944

In case you don't know, eau de vie is a savage liquid made by boiling barbed wire, soapsuds, watch springs and old tent pegs together. The better brands have a touch of nitroglycerine for flavor . . . I think every American who connects with a glass of eau de vie should get a Purple Heart.
>   —Journalist Ernie Pyle in "Good-Will-Towards-Men Rang through the Air," a June 24, 1944, dispatch from Barneville, Normandy

Liv and I were sitting in the jeep, our boot buckles loosened but our feet sweltering in the leather, our fatigues damp against the seats and my blond wave plastered to my forehead, when Fletcher reappeared, hurrying toward us from the press camp.

"The pistol has been shot, ladies!" he said as he leapt into the driver's seat. "The starting gates are open!"

He gunned the engine and lurched onto the road. Monk Dickson had come over from First Army headquarters to do the press briefing at Bagnoles-de-l'Orne—business as usual, more or less the same talk of what battles were where, more or less the same maps they'd been looking at for weeks. Then Dickson had looked up at the correspondents and smiled mischievously and said, "We may be in Paris tomorrow."

Representatives of the FFI—the French Forces of the Interior—had informed General Bradley that the German commander in Paris, General Dietrich von Choltitz, had received orders to destroy the city if necessary rather than give it up, orders from Hitler himself. Von Choltitz appeared ready to defy Hitler if he could promptly surrender Paris to regular Allied forces. He'd secretly asked for an armistice to allow a peaceful retreat northward. Allied troops could take the city without a fight.

De Gaulle was rumored to have delivered a letter to Eisenhower saying if Eisenhower wouldn't give the order to take Paris, he would. De Gaulle would not risk the possibility of the communists within the city taking charge of the liberation and staking a claim to the future rule of France he saw as his rightful place.

"That's what my husband has always thought," Liv said, "that de Gaulle would liberate Paris, that it would mean the war would be won and anyone who called himself a photojournalist ought to be there."

That had been before, though, when she'd first started working for Charles, when she'd been his protégée but not yet his bride.

"Charles wanted to honeymoon in Paris," she said, "but of course we hadn't been able to, not with the war."

It seemed that since that moment in the Dives River Liv was forever talking about Charles.

The threatening rain clouds had brought no relief from the heat and humidity as we entered Rambouillet, just thirty miles outside Paris. Our jeep was large and conspicuous on the town's narrow cobblestone roads. The shops were all closed and wary, only the occasional flutter of curtains at upper-floor windows. Several journalists loitered outside the high iron gates of the Hôtel du Grand Veneur, a three-story, slate-roofed hotel designated as the press headquarters pending the march into Paris. No troops were anywhere in sight, though. No snowdrop helmets.

Fletcher pulled into a little forested park off the square and stopped under a low tree—scant protection I supposed was meant not against the Germans but against Major Adam Jones, who might be having a cool drink in the hotel bar. If everyone headed for Paris was coming through Rambouillet, we wouldn't be hard to find.

Behind us and about a hundred yards farther on, a wide channel of water beckoned, peaceful and cool. On a church spire up a narrow lane in the opposite direction, an ivory clock face between the bell chamber and the peaked slate roof clicked off minutes, as if meaning to hurry us along before Paris went up in flames. The church's stained-glass windows would cast a forgiving light inside. There would be an old wooden confessional with a private little bench retreat, a priest to slide the confessional door open and murmur low French words inviting me to set down my sins, lest I die here with a mortal stain on my soul.

Liv and I waited and watched through the low branches as Fletcher sussed out the situation, then waved us over. One of the journalists, as we joined them, was saying de Gaulle was back in France for the first time in four years.

"Jolly good of him to show up," Fletcher said.

"He spoke in Rennes to a square overflowing with people despite a pouring rain," the journalist said. "There wasn't room to raise an umbrella."

"The man was stiff as a board, speech-wise—that's what MacVane told me," another said. Then to me, "You know him, Miss Tyler? The NBC radio fellow?"

I had no idea how the journalist knew my name.

I glanced to the church again, the comfort of a confessional giving way to the threat of German snipers. The spire would be where they watched our arrival, if they did. Had the Germans all fled, or were they waiting for better prey than a few journalists before they showed their hand?

The first journalist said, "But the crowd was screaming for de Gaulle, who commanded everyone to sing the 'Marseillaise.'" The emotion of the moment washed up in his sweaty face as he shared the details: de Gaulle's single voice singing the opening phrase of the French anthem to the crowd in the square and the hundreds more who'd climbed onto the roofs of bombed-out buildings to see him; French soldiers standing guard over the scene with their new American carbines slung over their shoulders; the crowd joining the singing, the hope they'd hidden during four years of German captivity finding voice in the forbidden song.

"Some of your lady reporter friends were there," the man continued. "Iris Carpenter and Catherine Coyne. Virginia Irwin. Sonia Tomara."

"And Helen Kirkpatrick?" Liv asked.

We'd heard a rumor that the *Chicago Daily News* London bureau chief had gained Eisenhower's blessing to go wherever she wanted, that she'd gone to see him after the German V-1s started dropping on England and told him that since London wasn't safe she ought to be sent to France.

Fletcher said, "Rennes was liberated *before* the women were allowed in, Liv. Lee Miller is there, too." He paused for emphasis, wiping the sweat from his brow with a sleeve. *"Under house arrest."*

The *Vogue* reporter had gone to Saint-Malo when she heard the fighting was over only to find it wasn't over, bullets were still whizzing through the air.

"No women permitted in combat zones," Fletcher said, "or even in zones they fail to realize are still combat zones."

I startled at the sound of military vehicles rumbling up the cobblestones—a reconnaissance group sent ahead toward Paris by General Leclerc returning from beyond the town, French troops who wouldn't give a blink about Liv and me. They'd lost one soldier, and a second had a bullet in his arm. The road to Paris was not yet clear.

Leclerc's tanks began rolling up the main road and pulling off into the reserve in which we'd left our jeep. Soldiers climbed from their vehicles and removed their helmets to relieve the heat. Several American officers sped into town, and Liv and I ducked into the gated courtyard of the hotel, melting into the doorway.

We might be caught, taken into custody, sent back to the States—here, just outside of Paris.

The Americans didn't stop, though. Arresting us was someone else's job. They sped right out the other way, only to return just as the French had, having found the road to Paris remained in German hands.

One of the French soldiers told us we might find Leclerc at the château. We walked with the other journalists toward several brick chimneys rising above a slate roof as if daring the bombers to try. A small lane off the main road led to guard towers and gates and a turreted limestone castle. A note on the door announced the château was reserved for General de Gaulle.

We found Leclerc in the gardens, poking at a path with his cane, oblivious of the walkways and balustrades and statuary inviting strollers toward the ponds we'd first seen from the park. The general wore his kepi and a pale, tightly knotted tie despite the heat. His stunted mustache was as precisely sculpted as the garden's carefully squared-off trees.

His troops had come too far too fast, he told us. They were not ready to go into battle. And the armistice had been broken. The Germans were going to fight.

Several of the correspondents badgered him for the details of his plan, but he demurred, saying we were only looking for a story. His concern was the liberation of France.

We would have been too conspicuous at the official press headquarters even if we were allowed entrance, so we found a cozier family inn just outside of town, where Liv and I were given a tiny, hot attic room and a private bath with a real porcelain tub, big and deep—unfathomable luxury. A crystal jar on a table beside the tub held bath salts, an indulgence I'd not known even before the war. There were two of us, though, and a single tub, and the nagging memory of signs over hotel bathtubs in London: "The Eighth Army crossed the desert on a pint a day. Three inches only, please." Even the king of England had a low fill line painted on his tub and bathed just once each week.

Liv uncapped the crystal jar and smelled the salts.

"Your three inches and mine would make six," I said, "which with our bodies added might actually fill the tub."

"And would save us from having to knock each other over in the fight to bathe first."

We'd been through so much together that it seemed nothing, really, to add bathing in a real tub to the list of things we'd shared.

I said I needed to do my roots first.

"'For pity's sake, can anyone self-apply that stuff?'" Liv said.

"Remember how Marie used to lay her clothes out so neatly on her cot every morning?" I said, and we laughed as we unbuckled our boots and stripped off our khakis and blouses and under-wear, letting it all fall to the floor.

Liv applied the bleach for me, and I turned the tap—in the middle of one side rather than at the tub's end—until the water was streaming. Liv poured out a handful of the salts, and we sank in with our backs at opposite ends. I lay in the water, remembering a house we'd stopped at to trade for supplies, where they'd had the foresight to fill their bathtub with water—all they would have to drink for weeks, their water and electricity lost in the Allied bombing and the brutal German retreat. I tried to imagine the fancy floors of the Belle Meade mansions back home under German boots, and Mama keeping our own little bathtub full of water, hiding resistance fighters and knowing we would die if they were found. Maybe that wouldn't be more dangerous than what I was doing, running around Normandy in broad daylight, but I couldn't have borne living with the possibility of being discovered and tortured into implicating those I loved.

I soaped Liv's hair, scrubbing out the thick dirt of the road, of sleeping in trenches. Liv lay back in the bathwater to rinse, and she soaped my hair and I rinsed, and she soaped it again to make sure she'd gotten all the bleach out. When we climbed from the tub, finally, I caught Liv's reflection in the small mirror over the sink. Her shoulders seemed bonier and whiter, her collarbones sharper than they seemed in their unreflected reality. Even her face was sharper| and something more, too, something that left her barely recognizable as the person who'd arrived at the field hospital just weeks ago.

We were clean, though, for the first time in weeks, and with a four-poster bed instead of our bedrolls to sleep in, too.

We put on our freshest clothes—damp, but not soaking—and brushed our wet hair and our teeth. We rinsed our extra fatigues and underwear in the bathwater, then hung some in the bathroom and the rest from the long, leaded-glass dormer window, not sure whether to hope for the rain to hold off long enough for our clothes to dry a little or to wish our clothes be drenched if only a good solid rain would bring relief from the heat. We left the blackout shade up for whatever little breeze might cool the room, and we headed down to join Fletcher, who had promised to find us a bottle of wine, or at least a little eau-de-vie.

The small, candlelit dining room overflowed with correspondents who'd pushed tables together to accommodate large groups. In the middle, a bronze woman sat naked on a bronze jug, her graceful shoulders turned to an old man carved in stone as, above them, a cluster of cherubs laughed and sang. The stone walls and stone floor of the room kept it cooler than our top-floor bedroom despite the crowded tables buzzing with talk of history in the making, full-page headlines, and special editions. Fletcher, freshly shaved and with his hair still damp, stood and waved to us, and we set off toward him, stopping as we crossed the room to acknowledge hellos, to laugh off smart remarks about us being "wanted women," and to exchange excited and contradictory speculation: the Germans were reinforcing the ring around Paris; the German commander wanted to surrender to the Americans; Leclerc's French forces alone would enter the city; the French and the American forces would enter together, but the Germans would destroy Paris before they would give it up.

"*We* are going to be the first correspondents into Paris," Liv and I insisted, but of course so did everyone else.

Fletcher, sitting at a table of journalists, pulled out chairs for us, and I sat facing him while Liv took the seat beside him. He introduced us to the others—all British journalists—and sat only after we'd sat, laughed only as we laughed at the banter about how they'd thought we were just a legend, and how we made them look bad by staying forever at the front. One of our old poker pals from the Saint-Lô–Périers road games asked for a rematch and told us where the game would be after dinner if we wanted to play. All the while, Fletcher's gaze shifted uncomfortably around the dining room—looking for MPs, I realized. We were quiet and discreet compared to the Americans at the table behind Liv and Fletcher, but they had no AWOL women sitting with them.

227

I leaned across the table toward Fletcher and said, "Don't worry, they have ladies' latrines here, after all."

Fletcher apologized for the lack of wine as he poured us glasses of eau-de-vie.

"To Paris," he said, and we lifted our glasses.

"To Paris," I said, and I took a careful sip, the brandy taste sharp and warm on my tongue. *To Paris,* I thought, not quite believing still that we hadn't been taken into custody and returned home already, or chosen to turn back ourselves.

Liv asked Fletcher to translate the menu: "beef," "chicken," "duck." Watching him flush with the odd pleasure of her needing him even for this small thing, I wondered at my own proud French.

". . . head shaving. God, who knew a dame would look so ugly?" said an American, a Midwesterner joining the table behind Fletcher. I studied my menu, wondering why American men were so often too loud, why they couldn't have the charming manners of British men.

Fletcher said, "I thought we might never have a decent meal again."

Liv smiled. "We might not after this. Let's order everything."

There was agreement around our table that we should order absolutely everything, but no one ordered the beef. We had too often seen local townspeople coming through fields just after battles, bringing knives with which they carved dead horses into butcher-cut slabs. Fletcher opted for the chicken, as did I. Liv chose the duck.

From the table behind Fletcher, I heard the American again: ". . . crushed to death by one of our own tanks." Fletcher and Liv, too, heard him. I leaned forward and they leaned back to better hear, all of us wanting to know and not wanting to at the same time.

"Tom Treanor, that's who it was," the American said.

Tom Treanor, an *LA Times* journalist Fletcher knew. An *LA Times* journalist Fletcher had known.

I stared at the flame on the little votive burning in the center of the table, knowing I ought to be making conversation but unable to do much more than choke down a bite of chicken.

". . . Grant and Hemingway swinging at each other," we heard from the next table. Bruce Grant of the *Chicago Times* and Ernest Hemingway, who was reporting for *Collier's*. Hemingway and his friends were tying up ten rooms at the Grand Veneur, stacking them high with ammunition while other correspondents were sleeping on straw in the dining room or searching the country-side for beds. "The man says the hotel is his general headquarters," the American said. "Says he's been holding off the Germans for days and it's time he had some help."

I took another sip of the eau-de-vie, trying to

think of something to say but unable to shake the idea of any journalist crushed to death like those soldiers in the mud at Falaise.

The conversation at our table tentatively resumed, no one saying a word about Tom Treanor. The others speculated about which troops would go which way into Paris, and who would be first. We all wanted to be with whichever troop would be first, or claimed we did, although the news of Tom Treanor's death certainly gave me pause.

Liv said little; she was still listening to the conversation at the table behind her: ". . . not over a dame, no. Grant suggested Hemingway stop playing 'chickenshit general' with his 'chickenshit little army,' and MacVane had to step between them to break it up." Hemingway was pissing off Patton and Leclerc both with his ever-present bottle of brandy and his rooms full of weapons and his ruffian companions he wanted to pass off for a private army.

Fletcher raised one eyebrow, and Liv smiled guiltily—over the eavesdropping? Or over letting her duck go to waste when she'd had nothing but tinned food since those garden vegetables at the Saint-Lô–Périers road? She stabbed at a tiny carrot and took a dry bite of crusty bread. She asked Fletcher for a cigarette. He gave her the rest of the pack and a Zippo lighter, and told her to keep them in case we wanted to smoke back in our room.

"At least Hemingway is in the war," the American said. "Better than that coward Charles Harper. He sends his wife over here while he's shacked up with the rich little daughter of—"

Fletcher scooted his chair back sharply as he stood, the screech of the chair legs on the floor cutting off the man's words. Everyone at the table was looking at them now, at Fletcher standing there like an idiot and Liv looking up at him, startled, her cigarette not yet lit. Had Liv even heard the damned American? Although that was just wishful thinking. The flat look in her eyes and her utter upright stillness—yes, she'd heard.

A murmur around the table, stifled amusement. They thought this a lovers' spat of some sort. They hadn't heard the American, then.

Fletcher was standing over Liv, who sat looking from him to the bronze woman and her bronze jug, the old stone man, the cherubs. They were all part of a fountain, I realized, although no water ran.

Fletcher sank back into his chair and unconsciously tugged at his ear. "It's merely—"

A rumor. A dreadful thing.

He wrapped his fingers around his glass of eau-de-vie, and I did the same, feeling the crystal cool in my fingers. Liv met Fletcher's gaze directly, and those of the others around the table. For a moment, I thought maybe she hadn't heard after all.

She leaned into the table and said to Fletcher and me in a low, conspiratorial voice, "They probably believe the rumor that I'm 'expecting,' too."

She tucked her unlit cigarette back into the pack, the pack and lighter into the pocket of her blouse, and lifted her glass of eau-de-vie. "To Paris," she said.

I echoed her words, "To Paris," listening to the tink of glass on glass.

Not much later, Liv excused herself, leaving her dinner largely untouched, saying it was too hot to eat anything and she just wanted to climb into that feather bed upstairs. When I moved to join her, she told me to keep Fletcher company. And even before she disappeared through the doorway, Fletcher leaned across the table, closer to me.

We were with a roomful of journalists in the middle of a war, but there was candlelight and good food and eau-de-vie and the anticipation of Paris, the hope.

"Jane," he said softly, his lips moist, his hair that I'd once cut now combed neatly back. He leaned even closer, the eau-de-vie sweet on his breath.

He said, "Charles Harper is the one who sent the MPs after you."

"Charles?" I repeated, confused.

"Charles arranged for them to track down Liv,"

he insisted. "He wants her home and he doesn't give a toss what Liv wants."

Fletcher leaned back in his chair and took a healthy sip of eau-de-vie. I thought to protest, to ask why Charles would be having an affair and wanting Liv home at the same time. But I thought of Tommy kissing me at the Harpeth River the very night he'd proposed to Miss Ingram, and I raised my own glass to my lips and threw the liquid back. The alcohol was rusty and bitter on my tongue.

Liv was in bed when I returned to the room. I turned off the light she'd left on for me and let up the blackout shade she'd pulled down, and I gathered in the clothes—damp, but no longer dripping. I hung them inside the room's armoire, then sat at the end of the bed and unbuckled my boots in the moonlight, and stripped off my fatigues. My head was thick from too much o the eau-de-vie, from too many cigarettes lit only to be smashed out moments later over too many days and nights of war.

Liv said, "I wanted to strangle that nasal Chicagoan," her voice startling me.

She lay under the covers despite the heat.

"I know," I said.

"I wanted to stuff Fletcher's pity down his damned throat," she said.

I tossed my slacks aside, stood in my blouse

and panties in the dimly moonlit room. "Down Fletcher's throat, or the Chicagoan's?"

She laughed. I was relieved. She might have wanted to stuff my words down my throat, too.

I swatted a mosquito on my bare neck, sweaty again in the hot room. I closed the window. There was no breeze anyway.

Liv said, "I'm being exactly who Charles fell in love with, Jane: a photographer who sleeps in damp clothes in muddy trenches and eats meat from tins."

"I know," I said again.

She pulled the goose-feather coverlet up to her chin. I pushed back the coverlet on my side and climbed in beside her. A real bed with clean sheets.

"It's just a rumor," I said, remembering my mother's words the night of Tommy's engagement party, about emotions that were public and those that were private, about rumors and reputations and ruined lives.

I said, "As early as tomorrow you'll be in Paris, Liv, photographing the freed city."

"It will make our reputations."

"Our reputations," I repeated, looking through the closed window to the trees laced with moonlight, wondering if Mama would be proud of what I was doing or if she would worry whether any man would want a newspaper girl like me after the war.

Liv said, "I try to imagine cheering Parisians celebrating in front of the Arc de Triomphe, with me capturing them on film, but I keep seeing New York. The apartment. Anthony in his white gloves, and his deep 'Mrs. Harper.' The view from our living room over the hushed white of Central Park after a new snow. The sharp line of Charles's chin and his long, slender fingers as he edits. The slightly lost look in his eyes in bed at night, without his glasses."

She climbed from the bed, touching the graceful curve of the bedpost in the muted moonlight and groping for the outline of the armoire beyond it, the cigarette package. She lit a cigarette and stood looking through the window glass despite the blackout. "Charles always sleeps on his back," she said. "Isn't that strange?"

I lit a cigarette, too, and joined her at the window. "It's just a rumor, Liv," I repeated.

Beyond the trees, the moon was slipping into mounting clouds, leaving me peering through the screen of branches just as I forever peered through the confessional screen, trying to see what I wasn't meant to see.

Liv said, "This is what Charles does when he wants something so much he can't bear the thought of not having it. It was the way he dealt with that first, brief attempt to have a child, his disappointment when I didn't become pregnant right away."

She coughed against the smoke in her throat, then, against that truth.

"Charles saw my failure to become pregnant as some fault of his virility," she said. "He would never admit that, though. Not even to himself."

She cranked open the window just as a last bit of moon disappeared. "He wants a Renny and a Charles Jr., too, but he won't allow himself to want anything he isn't sure he can have."

Charles was the one who'd sent the MPs after us. Had Fletcher meant for me to tell Liv he thought that, or to keep it to myself? I wasn't sure I believed it, but I wasn't sure I didn't.

She said, "We'll be in Paris tomorrow or the next day or the next. I'll take my pictures, and I'll go home."

That had been our plan all along, even if neither of us had ever thought of it with such a sharp edge.

"I suppose you should, Liv," I said, not sure what I'd do without her, but sure there was nothing for me back home.

"'You'll get yourself killed, for God's sake.' That's what Charles is afraid of. That's what he can't bear." She leaned out the window. "Of course he can't bear it," she said. "If he were here and I were at home I wouldn't be able to bear it either. And this is what he does. He decides he doesn't want me because he's not sure I'll come back alive."

I took another drag on the cigarette and held my breath for a long moment, the tobacco burning deep in my chest. The gray of the smoke hung before us in the humid air, and it was dark out, not even a hint of moonlight reflecting off the wavy window glass now. It was impossible to see what lay beyond the skeleton branches, even just outside the window.

RAMBOUILLET, FRANCE
◆
THURSDAY, AUGUST 24, 1944

[T]hese Frenchmen were just going out of
their minds wanting to get to Paris, as we
all did . . . Finally the order came.
—Journalist Helen Kirkpatrick

A thunderstorm pelted the windows of the
inn's dining room the next morning. The dull
dawn light showed the curled corners of peeling
wallpaper, a crack across the marble fireplace
hearth, a thin layer of dust on the bronze woman
and the stone man and the cherubs in the dry
fountain. No tables pushed together to accommodate big groups. No one to tease us. No loud
Chicagoan. Only two other diners across the
room, and a limited menu: bread and apples and
pears. Even the yeasty smell wafting from the
kitchen didn't leave me hungry, but the food
came served on real china, and our hands were
soap-scrubbed clean.

"Jane," Liv started. "Fletcher." She fingered a
slice of crusty bread and tore it in two. "I was
thinking that—"

I watched the rain streaming down the

windows. I'd never imagined Allied troops marching into Paris in a downpour. A real frog wash, Mama would say.

"I'll go first," Fletcher said. "I'm thinking it's about to happen. As soon as tomorrow you two will be sending your photographs and stories off from Paris and the whole world will know your names." He raised his cup.

I took a sip of my coffee, an unfortunate barley-based drink. "*I'm* thinking this stuff they call coffee here is *nasty*," I said. "I'm thinking perhaps I'd do better with tea?"

Fletcher said, "The tea, I'm afraid, is no less beastly."

With lemon. That was how he took it back home, but there were no real lemons in France any more than there were real coffee beans.

Liv said, "I was thinking that if we left for Paris now, we'd be the first correspondents there."

Fletcher sat back, a mix of amusement and concern on his neatly shaved face.

She said, "We could photograph the troops coming into the city."

A gust of wind pushed the rain more violently against the windows, rattling the panes.

"Head-on," Liv said.

Fletcher cleared his throat. "You forget, I'm not a correspondent."

"The first *photographers* there."

Someone laughed at the table across the room.

Fletcher said, "Jane isn't a photographer."

"You're a military photographer, Fletcher," Liv insisted. "You *need* to get there now. You don't want to cover the liberation. You want to photograph the Germans defending a major city."

"I'll go alone then, shall I?" Fletcher responded. "I expect you two can find another lift."

"It was *your* idea. 'I imagine she intends to march in before the troops will have done!'— that's what you told the little girls at Trefoil."

He pushed back his plate, ran a hand over the back of his neck. "It's pouring out, Liv."

"We'd get the front page, the first pictures from Paris." To me, "You'd get the first story, Jane."

I glanced at the fountain, the bronze woman with the empty water jug. Again, laughter from the other table. Low, polite laughter.

Fletcher said, "It won't be the first photographs taken that will run in your newspapers, Livvie. It will be the first photographs to make it past the censors' shears and to the States."

"But we'd—"

"We'd get killed," he said softly but insistently, leaning forward as he spoke. "We would be politely introduced to the first German soldier we came across, and before we knew it, we would be begging to spill our guts about precisely how many forces would be attacking the city, and precisely when."

Liv lowered her gaze, fixing on Fletcher's

smooth chin, the skin there pale and vulnerable. "Full page," she said. "Full bleed."

And there was a part of me, too, that wanted to go, a part of me that minded the feather bed and the china teacup, the fresh bread and the porcelain tub, and my clean hands.

Liv and I emerged from our top-floor room not much later that morning, rucksacks and musette bags on our backs and our rain ponchos on over it all. We would *not* go into Paris ahead of the troops but there was no reason we had to wait in Rambouillet for a briefing to tell us where we were going. We knew where we were going. General Leclerc's men—the French Second Armored Division—were already on the road, waiting for the order to advance, as was Barton's US Fourth Infantry. There was no reason we ought not to be out there, as close to Paris as possible. That was where the stories would be. Where the photos would be.

Fletcher was waiting at the landing to the floor below ours, in his rain gear, too. Together, we headed down the main stairs for the lobby. We'd turned the corner for the final half flight of stairs when Fletcher stopped suddenly, muttering, "Hell."

A man at the reception desk spoke intently to the clerk. He wore a snowdrop helmet, gloves, and belt—unfathomably dry—and a thin mustache.

Fletcher silently urged Liv and me both backward up the stairs. "Your guardian angel, I'm afraid," he whispered as we hurried off toward the servants' stairs and the back door.

The damned jeep had no top to protect us from the downpour, or from the view of the MP who might emerge at any moment. Pale eyes, I thought, although we hadn't paused long enough to see, really. It wouldn't take him more than the moment of opening our rooms to realize we'd left, and he wouldn't have much doubt which direction we were headed. It was only a question of which road toward Paris we took.

We climbed into the jeep with our packs still on under our ponchos, Fletcher letting his seat all the way back with a single movement and still with almost no room between his body and the steering wheel. He threw the jeep into reverse. Backed out.

"Don't look now," he said.

Liv, in the backseat, turned and looked over her shoulder, and I did, too. The inn's door swung open.

The front tire was losing air again. The cracked windshield was a confusion of streaming raindrops as we sped off.

"The French will be the first into the city," Liv said. If she was afraid the major would catch up with us, it didn't show in her rain-drenched face, and there was nothing of the excitement that ought to have been in her voice at the prospect of being caught. The liberation of Paris might have been only an obstacle to her getting home to Charles.

"Right, we go in with the French," Fletcher agreed. The French forces would be too wrapped up in the liberation of Paris to mind two AWOL American journalists in their ranks.

Liv removed her pack from underneath her poncho and tucked it beneath the supply tarp. I helped Fletcher remove his while he drove, and heaved it beside Liv's, then took off my own.

NEAR CERNAY-LA-VILLE, FRANCE
◆
THURSDAY, AUGUST 24, 1944

[I]t was Helen Kirkpatrick who read the maps, charted our course, and drove the lead jeep. She loved to sail along so fast, however, that the Colonel was always in a dither, knowing that before the day was over her exuberant little jeep would disappear into the distance and leave the rest of our convoy far behind.

—Photojournalist Margaret Bourke-White

Fletcher eased our jeep in at the back of a column of tank-destroyer guns, the soldiers dressed in American army garb but wearing red berets and speaking French—some of Leclerc's French forces. The road was so thick with military vehicles and men and mud and rain that there was no way to continue. Still, when the column stopped and Fletcher stopped with it, Liv urged him on.

Fletcher threw the jeep into park and climbed out. "Why don't you drive, then?"

Liv climbed from the back into the driver's seat, shifted into gear and swung wide, off the road and into the mud.

"You coming, Fletcher?" she called back.

Fletcher caught up with us, flipped the windshield down flat against the hood, and climbed into the back.

Liv began to weave through the column, as often as not off the road. We broke free of the olive drab mass and moved up to a still-mobile column of troops. When that column halted we swung wide and surged ahead again. Liv drove swiftly, trying to avoid the worst of the mud and rubble, but with a wildness that was a little frightening.

The tire went again at Cernay-la-Ville, a village that was little more than a road intersection at an ancient stone church. Liv eased us to a stop beside a spire that had stood for centuries but remained as vulnerable to bombs as the ruin at Saint-Lô where they'd placed Major Howie.

"Roebuck Tire and Axle at your service," Fletcher said, the tension seeping out of him as the air seeped from the tire.

It had stopped raining, at least there was that, and the storm had broken the heat and humidity. We stripped off our ponchos, and Liv cut the patch and handed it to Fletcher, whose easy banter as he pressed the patch and held it to the damaged inner tube eased us all. While they worked, I made notes about the morning: the breakfast, the major in the lobby, the escape in the rain.

"Livvie," Fletcher said, "I believe there's a future

for you at the Brooklands racetrack—with a clear course and a pit crew."

She lit a cigarette and inhaled.

He said, "You wouldn't be dirtying your hands patching tires yourself."

Liv looked down at her hands, filthy again despite our bath just the night before. "It feels wrong to have clean hands in this damned war," she said.

I looked down at my own hands, remembering how Fletcher said Charles had described Liv, as a woman who photographed like a man but didn't smoke or curse.

We continued through Pecqueuse, Limours, and Forges-les-Bains, running parallel to the main German defensive line and forever approaching a medieval stone turret without ever reaching the thing. It was the castle keep at Montlhéry, one of the French soldiers told us. It had guarded the road to Paris from Orleans for centuries of war.

"The tower, it is where Alfred Cornu measured the speed of light," the French soldier said, as if the fact of its history gave it strength against the bombs. And perhaps it did. Orly airbase, not far beyond the tower, was seized by the Luftwaffe in '40, and we'd been bombing the hell out of it since late May, but the Montlhéry tower stood.

The soldier was from Montlhéry himself, and had meant to study physics at the Sorbonne, before the war. I suggested perhaps he would soon, although it was hard to see how any of us could take up the pieces of the lives we'd abandoned.

Off in a field to the left, French guns were firing, and word came down the line that their targets were German antitank guns and mortars. We continued up the road, past a twisted wreck of an antitank gun and a German tank engulfed in flames. Several of the townspeople, so thrilled to see Allied troops that they would not be persuaded to stay in their homes, were killed in the shelling, their bodies lying at the roadside, their expressions stunned.

"All that's left of the Battle of . . . where the devil are we anyway?" Fletcher said.

Liv consulted the map. "Longjumeau?" she said, mangling the French.

"Longjumeau," Fletcher said. " '*Long*' like 'long' in English—it has the same meaning. And '*jumeau*' means 'twin.' "

Evening came with the swishing sounds of shells lighting the starless sky and news that resistance fighters inside Paris had taken the police prefecture on the Île de la Cité. Charles Luizet, who'd been Leclerc's roommate at the French military academy, had managed to get a wireless message out that the resistance fighters were at the end of their resources, and Leclerc sent a small plane over the city to drop leaflets urging them to hold on.

"I'd hate to have been that pilot," I said.

"I'd hate to be in Paris, hoping for armies or at least arms, only to receive a bleeding leaflet," Fletcher said.

"I'd love to be in Paris," Liv said.

We declined beds offered us in a cottage that night, wanting to be ever ready. I slept sitting with my bedroll loosely around me in the passenger seat, dreaming I was eating peach ice cream, and woke in the darkness to staccato gunfire and the smell of smoke. Liv woke with a gasp, and I climbed into the small backseat, careful not to wake Fletcher, wedging myself in beside her. She'd been having a nightmare that she'd been arrested, that she was standing in front of a bare metal desk in a dank prison cell, with Mrs. Shipley cackling at her that women didn't belong in war zones, that she ought to be home tending children. "Then somehow Mrs. Shipley was Charles, and I was back at the field hospital again and Charles was there, hunched over the table under the apple tree, writing and writing. But there was something wrong about it. About the sound of his typewriter. The ding of the bell signaling the carriage return was missing. The zip of the carriage returning was missing as well."

It happened all at once then: A scream of rushing wind. Ducking low in the jeep. Covering our helmeted heads with our arms.

A boom. The ground trembling. The jeep shaking.

A sharp bite in my left arm.

Liv and Fletcher grabbed their cameras and climbed from the jeep, their shutters snapping at the smoke and the blackened earth just yards away, the remains of an 88mm shell in flames.

Fletcher turned back to me, saying, "Jane?" Then he was in the jeep beside me, pulling out his shirttail.

As calmly as anything, he called, "Livvie!"

I felt as if some part of me were floating up out of my body, hanging in the air just above the jeep.

Liv, barely visible in the light of the flames, turned toward us.

"There's an emergency medical kit mounted under the dash," Fletcher told her. "Get it right now please. Put down your camera and get it right now. The electric torch, too."

He tried to tear his shirttail. It wouldn't tear.

Liv climbed back into the jeep, on the driver's side, found the flashlight, and shone it in my eyes. With the blinding light, I was no longer floating. I thought I would vomit.

"The medical kit, Livvie," Fletcher said. "The tourniquet, please." Then to me, right in my face, looking into my eyes as if to climb inside me, "I'm here, Jane. I'm going to take care of you. You're going to be fine."

Liv dislodged the metal box that was the medical kit from under the jeep's dash and opened it. She found the tourniquet in a small cardboard box inside the metal one and handed it to Fletcher. He wrapped it around my arm almost at my shoulder and pulled it tight.

He took the flashlight from Liv and shone it over me, fingering my face, my neck, my chest, my hips. Mercifully, he didn't touch my arm, which burned like the second circle of hell.

"You've been hit in the arm, Jane," he said. "I don't see anything else. Do you hurt elsewhere?" He shone the flashlight on my arm again for a longer moment. He went back over the rest of me with the light, then handed it to Liv. She shone it right in my eyes.

"Her eyes look okay," she said to Fletcher. Then to me, "Your eyes look okay, Jane. Do you feel sick at all?"

She leaned over the seat and put the back of her hand to the bridge of my nose, just below my helmet, then to my cheek. She put two fingers to my neck, feeling my pulse. "She doesn't seem to be in shock," she said to Fletcher.

Fletcher said to me, "I believe you've taken on a bit of metal, Miss Tyler."

The sound of his voice soothing. Liv's touch soothing, too, like when she'd washed my hair.

Liv extracted another little cardboard box from the emergency kit, opened it, and handed Fletcher the scissors I'd used on his hair. He cut away the shredded khaki sleeve of my blouse.

I mustered a weakly voiced "Hey, that's from Saks."

Liv said, "Rest in peace, you gorgeous Saks Fifth Avenue blouse."

Fletcher examined my arm more closely in the beam of flashlight. A piece of metal not much wider than a typewriter ribbon guide protruded from my skin. I started to reach for it, thinking if I just pulled it out, it would stop hurting.

"Don't touch it, Jane!" Liv said. "Don't you touch it either, Fletcher. It could still be hot. It could burn you and then we'll be two men down."

She handed Fletcher my canteen, and told him to pour water over the wound. She held the flashlight again so he would have both hands free.

Fletcher tipped the canteen.

"Oh oh oh oh oh!" I said. But after he finished pouring the water, the sting of pain was less biting.

Fletcher said, "There you are, you crusty bugger."

He doused my arm again with the water from my canteen, and I gasped again.

"We ought to get you to an aid station, Jane," he said.

"You can pull out the shrapnel with forceps," Liv said.

"Shrapnel wounds get infected," Fletcher said.

Liv looked at the road ahead of us, the long line of troops. "How do you feel, Jane? Does it hurt a lot?" She focused on me again, intently, like the nurse promising Joey his peach ice cream. "And the pain isn't anywhere else, Jane? Just that one piece?"

I said, "If y'all keep repeating my name, I'm going to start thinking I'm dying."

Liv said, "If you say 'y'all' again, Jane, I'll *know* you're dying."

She shone the flashlight into the emergency kit and started extracting things from it: iodine, tweezers, gauze, bandages. She handed Fletcher a bottle of hydrogen peroxide, training the flashlight on me again.

"This is going to sting like hell," she said. "On three. One. Two. Three."

Fletcher poured some of the hydrogen peroxide over the wound.

"Mary, Mother of God!"

Liv handed Fletcher the tweezers. "On three again," she said, now with the tweezers.

"Wait!" I said. "Give me a minute."

I took a few deep breaths, then a few more. I told myself the doctors at the aid stations patched up soldiers in far worse shape than I was and sent them back to the front, but that didn't ease the pain.

"Liv," I said, stalling, "Liv, if you reload your

camera, you can shoot 'Operating Room by Flashlight Redux.'"

Liv said to Fletcher, "Don't listen to her, Fletcher. Jane is such a card." She smiled a little, and said to me, "Marie is probably back in the US now, with her 4F fiancé."

She said, "One."

"Sweet Jesus!" I said.

"You nasty little prat," Fletcher said to the shrapnel now at the end of the tweezers, a thing the size of a poker chip, perhaps, although I didn't really know; we'd played for cigarettes and gum.

"What happened to two and three?" I asked.

"I thought it best to have it done," Fletcher said.

Liv took the tweezers still with the shrapnel caught in its grasp, saying, "I'll tuck this little souvenir safely away for you, Jane. Someday you'll show it to your grandchildren."

She handed Fletcher a piece of gauze and told him to dab at the wound with it.

"It's hardly even bleeding," I said.

Fletcher said, "That, love, is the tourniquet. We need to get you to an aid station."

Liv said, "It doesn't look too bad, does it?" She put some hydrogen peroxide on a clean bit of gauze, handed it to Fletcher, and directed him to dab at the wound with it. "Gently."

Fletcher said, "Perhaps you ought to do this yourself, Livvie."

Liv handed the now-empty tweezers back to Fletcher, saying, "There's one more little piece, see it?" and pointing. "You can get it with the forceps."

He pulled it out without even a one-count warning.

Liv gave him the iodine and told him to swab around the wound but not in it.

Fletcher gave her a look.

Liv said, "It says so on the lid of the kit."

Fletcher started swabbing with the iodine.

Liv said, "Every Saturday night bar-brawl victim was brought to our door and laid out on the dining room table. I'm a decent assistant, but I pass out if I touch. Put a piece of gauze over it, though, Fletcher, and I can wrap a bandage as well as anyone."

Fletcher repeated to me, "We need to get you to an aid station."

Liv wrapped the bandage so it kept pressure on the gauze over the wound. It felt good, the pressure, as if everything that was meant to stay in my body might stay there after all.

I said, "I can't be showing my grandchildren a piece of metal no bigger than a thumbnail and saying this is why I missed the liberation of Paris."

"A thumbnail from a giant's thumb," Fletcher said.

Liv extracted another box from the emergency

kit and read the directions on it in the light of the flashlight. She opened the package and dumped out a handful of pills.

"All of these?" I asked.

"Sulfadiazine," she said. "They'll help keep the wound from getting infected."

She handed me her own canteen, since mine was now empty. "Drink as much water as you can with them, and every time you think of it, drink more."

The tourniquet needed to be released gradually, she said. Loosened just a little every ten minutes or so. I don't even remember the first adjustment. I don't remember Liv and Fletcher waking me to tip the canteen to my lips and make me drink. My sleep the rest of that night was exhausted, and mercifully dreamless.

OUTSIDE PARIS
◆
FRIDAY, AUGUST 25, 1944

I will never forget the next morning coming up over the hill and there below is Paris—white and shining in the sun.
—Journalist Helen Kirkpatrick

I arrived exhausted by my share of millions of handshakes—the embraces of grandmothers—of French sharpshooters and bevies of French girls. I was the "femme soldat"—small use to say I was just a journalist.
—*Vogue* photojournalist Lee Miller

The tourniquet that was on my arm when I fell asleep was no longer there when I woke to the sound of the jeep engine jumping to life, but the bandage was and the shirtsleeve wasn't, and the arm hurt like hell.

"While we were sleeping," Fletcher said, "some of Leclerc's men entered Paris."

"You're kidding!" Liv said.

"Word just came down the line. They got as far as the Hôtel de Ville. No press there, though."

He turned back to me. "How is the arm?"

"Drink some water, Jane," Liv said.

I kicked off my bedroll, feeling I ought to be doing something, saying something to mark the morning, but I could not get "good morning" from my lips. I pulled off my helmet, ran my fingers through my hair, pulled the helmet back on again. The arm didn't feel so bad, and it was my left arm—there was that.

It was just after dawn and the tanks were rumbling to a start. The air was thick with a white mist.

"You take the front seat, Jane," Liv said. "I can photograph better from the back. It's a little higher up."

With the windshield down she would have a better view in the front, but it was bumpier in the back; she wanted me to be comfortable.

Fletcher held a cigarette out to me, a Lucky Strike.

" 'Lucky Strike Means Fine Tobacco,' " I said.

I stuck it between my lips, and he lit it for me.

I asked Liv to hand me my Corona. I unfolded it—that did hurt—and rolled in a clean sheet of paper. I thought better of that and rolled the paper back out. Liv folded the typewriter up for me, and I pulled out a notepad and pen. Liv loaded new film in her Leica and carefully cleaned her lenses.

The troops began to move, and Fletcher cranked

the steering wheel, jockeying for position, weaving through the line. We turned onto a narrow side road not a mile from where we'd slept, heading north, reaching Gentilly before eight to find what must have been the entire population lining the street, crowding the military convoy, cheering.

Minutes later, as we approached the Porte de Gentilly, I turned to Liv and said, "Climb up here with us, Liv! I can't bear to beat you to Paris!" And she did, holding on to Fletcher's hand to steady herself so she wouldn't fall back or bump my arm.

The moment wasn't anything like I had imagined. The wall that had once marked the city's boundary and the city gate had been taken down after the last war. We might not have known we were in Paris if the soldiers ahead of us weren't cheering wildly as they entered the traffic circle. We couldn't see Notre Dame or the Louvre or even the tip of the Eiffel Tower. But the street overflowed with people. Children— all unbearably thin and unmistakably happy— danced everywhere, oblivious to the old men scurrying worriedly around them, warning of the continued presence of snipers. Women in bright dresses, flashy jewelry, and hair ribbons the blue, white, and red of the French flag waved and screamed and laughed and kissed everyone, climbing up onto jeeps and tanks, their pale white arms reaching up to take soldiers' cheeks in both hands. They kissed the French soldiers in their American helmets or leather tank helmets or French berets. They kissed Fletcher again and again, his cheeks becoming red with lipstick or with the constant pressing of lips on skin, or perhaps with the embarrassment of so much adoration. They kissed Liv and me, too, even as Liv tried to steady her camera and I tried to protect my bandaged arm. They kissed first one cheek and then the other, and I felt all they'd endured in the sharp bones of their half-starved shoulders.

Bicycles, bicycles. Everywhere, there were bicycles.

And flowers. Flowers thrown joyfully, bright red and yellow flowers strewn in the cobbled streets, landing on the military vehicles and in our jeep, their sweet fragrance blotting out the smell of gunfire.

The men slapped one another's and the soldiers' backs and shook hands and bellowed their joy, too, kissing the same double kisses the women did, their shoulders as bony or more so. And everywhere people were crying. Tears streamed down the hollow, stubbled cheeks of old men, the old and the sick brought out from the hospitals to greet freedom in the streets. Young women pulled their children tightly to their sinewy legs, watching for their children's fathers, hoping they might appear in a passing truck and wondering if they would recognize them. The crowds applauded and held babies high to see— undaunted by the sounds of the war continuing around them: the rattle of machine gun fire elsewhere in the city, the whine of shells, the low boom of explosions as the Germans tried to destroy the bridges over the Seine. *"Vive la France!"* and *"Vive la liberté!"* and simply *"Bravo!"* the Parisians shouted as Liv's shutter snapped and snapped.

Much of Paris had been liberated from within, by young men in FFI armbands taking control of the telephone network and the metro, Nobel Prize–winning scientists assembling Molotov cocktails, grandmothers and mothers heaping furniture and stoves and dustbins onto barricades of overturned trucks and downed branches and barbed wire—barricades often topped with Hitler's photo or a Nazi flag so that attacking Germans would have to fire on their own flag or, worse, their führer. Even young children participated, their bicycle baskets loaded with cobblestones hacked from the roads by older, stronger citizens to reinforce the barricades, or with food and drink to reinforce the men guarding them. After four years, the entire population had finally said no to German occupation, unaided by generals squabbling over who would govern after they were freed, or by journalists vying to be the first to capture the beginning of a liberation that had already begun.

As we passed Parc Montsouris, one of the Haussmann parks I'd seen in pictures in high school French class, the sound of war began blasting right in my ears again, that staccato rat-a-tat-a-tat. The crowd dove, clenched-fist salutes opening, grabbing for cover, unblown kisses left on hands scrambling for the ground, babies tucked up to their mother's chests, pressed between parental body and unyielding ground.

Fletcher grasped my torn sleeve, sending fresh pain through my arm as I tumbled from the jeep. He shoved the Webley into Liv's hand and shoved Liv and me both behind the jeep, telling us to stay down.

We crouched there, the fear in Liv's eyes mirrored in my cottony throat as shots rang out.

Liv peeked cautiously over the top of the hood, and despite Fletcher's admonition, I followed her lead to see Fletcher crouching low to the ground. The gunfire came from a stone tower, or from a house across the way, or from both. He moved carefully toward them as he shot photographs, recording the details of the places German soldiers sought refuge in a city under siege, and how and when they fought from the hiding spots they chose. He didn't even have a gun. He'd left that for Liv and me.

Leclerc's men fired on the tower and the rooftops with machine guns mounted on the trunks of vehicles, the stone flying into the air in sprays of white, sunlight reflecting off flying shards. When had the sun come out?

Liv rose just a little more and swung her Leica to catch several FFI men taking cover near the house, storming the door. A moment later, the bang of a grenade, and then silence.

The crowd surged again, pouring out of the buildings, leaving only a narrow lane for our convoy, which moved along the Boulevard Jourdan and up the Rue Saint-Jacques. We crested a hill as we crossed Boulevard Saint-Germain at the Sorbonne, and there was Paris stretched out before us: the Eiffel Tower and the Louvre, Notre Dame, the River Seine. As we rolled downhill and crossed a cast-iron bridge to the Île de la Cité, the sun was blinding, the light beautiful on the water and on the cathedral's square towers, on the barricades.

We crossed the Seine a second time, to the plaza at the Hôtel de Ville. The clock face in its tower read ten o'clock, although my watch read nine and was ticking; the Paris clocks had been advanced an hour, to German daylight savings time. Liv photographed a crowd celebrating at the intersection across from the Hôtel de Ville, people gathered around an old car in front of a barricade. The wheel of an upside-down wheelbarrow atop it spun behind them as an emaciated old woman handed what must have been her last tomato to a soldier, who handed it back to her. A curly-haired toddler threw flowers. An old, old man held up a baby, waving its little hand.

"They're my mother's eyes," Liv said.

It took me a moment to realize she was talking about a middle-aged woman standing atop the old car in front of the barricade, cheering with the crowd and yet not quite with them. The woman was just that little bit higher up on the car's roof, setting her apart. Thin, square shoulders in a thin, flowered dress, like so many of the Parisian women. Her hair was short and dark, like Liv's, but her nose was stronger and her mouth, too, her brow bone sharper under the perfectly arched brows. Blue-green irises against a sturdy, determined white unsoftened by her lashes, or that's the way those eyes seemed. Joyful, yes, but something else, too. Looking straight into Liv's camera as Liv photographed her, as if some answer she needed might be found in Liv's lens.

Imagine that, Livvie, I thought, and I wondered if Liv understood yet that this was what her mother meant for her to imagine. I imagined my own mother opening the newspaper in the morning and saying to herself, *My own Jane. Imagine that.*

The rip of gunfire cut through the air again, shots from the Notre Dame Cathedral tower behind us now across the Seine—a sound so loud that I couldn't hear Fletcher shouting. He grabbed my arm, thrust me on the raw road under the jeep, and Liv at the same time, Liv's camera scraping along the ground beside me under the jeep's metal undercarriage. Rat-a-tat-tat, rat-a-tat-a-tat. I made myself open my eyes, raised my head in the direction of the gunfire, banged the back of my skull on something metal and greasy and hard.

"Are you close enough yet, Liv?" I asked, gallows humor, but she couldn't hear me over the noise.

I wondered where Fletcher was. He'd given me the Webley this time. It had all happened so fast I hadn't even realized.

Beyond the jeep's tilted wheels, girls in Red Cross uniforms carried a stretcher out into the gunfire, waving a Red Cross flag. They laid their stretcher beside a wounded soldier and moved swiftly to attend to him as the bullets rang in the air around them. Liv focused her Leica as best she could and took the shot: the stretcher, the hands holding it, their feet, legs, hips, waists, and the Hôtel de Ville behind them. The gunfire continued for perhaps twenty minutes, and Liv shot what she could from the vantage point of the jeep underbelly. I didn't even try to take notes.

The gunfire sputtered, sputtered again, and a long silence descended, leaving only the wail of a child somewhere. I looked at Liv, so close beside me, the pupils of her eyes huge and dark. I scanned the square for Fletcher, found him just a few yards away, returning to us as we climbed out from under the jeep and the crowd swelled again.

A rumor rippled through the soldiers that Billotte had used the telephone network at the police prefect to reach von Choltitz and demand a German surrender, but the German general had refused. Our line of troops would be making their way toward German headquarters at the Hôtel Meurice.

Around the corner on Rue de Rivoli, a news kiosk displayed Nazi and collaborationist newspapers. The window of a bookshop read "*Buchhandlung*," the glass pockmarked with the star shatterings of bullet holes. Swastikas flew over the hotels everywhere, along with signs that read "*Soldatenheim*," "*Speiselokal*," and "*Lese Schreib und Spielzimmer.*" The ugly flags hung above the doors of stores now closed for the celebration, over playhouses where, when the city had become dangerously low on electricity, plays were put on by candlelight. Signs taped to *téléphone* booths and *vespasiennes*—the French public toilets—read "*Accés interdit aux juifs*," not to be used by Jews.

The German resistance grew even more intense as we approached the Louvre Museum and

German headquarters beyond it. The fighting in the Tuileries Garden was tree to tree, the only things separating us a high and highly permeable iron fence and the few hundred yards we stayed behind the front troops. At the Hôtel Meurice, two French officers, covered by machine gun fire, ran through the front arches and tossed in phosphorous grenades. Smoke billowed out the door and up to the Nazi flags hanging over it, driving out several German soldiers with their hands over their heads. Liv and Fletcher both took the shots: the French soldiers, the improbably tidy plaques on either side of the doorway, the German guards.

One of the French officers entered the hotel. We waited, watching for what seemed such a long time. Fletcher had turned his camera back to the soldiers in the garden, photographing through the gaps in the fence, when the French officer emerged from the hotel with the German general carrying a suitcase, as if headed for a weekend at Mont Saint-Michel.

"Von Choltitz," Liv said.

The general who might have set Paris burning instead lit nothing more than a cigar.

Men and women and even children surged toward von Choltitz, yelling curses and spitting. One woman rushed at him and smashed the cigar. The crowd cheered even as the French soldiers tried to protect him. A Red Cross nurse hurried them to a waiting car, leaving the crowd to spend the rest of its anger tearing his abandoned suitcase open and ripping its contents to pieces. And still, the gunfire rang out from the Tuileries, where Fletcher's camera remained focused.

I pulled out my Corona and rolled in a sheet of paper, and the words came spilling out despite the pain in my left arm as I typed, mostly one-handed. And while the jeep edged forward and Liv photographed it all—a toddler's hands grasping his mother's hair, a soldier weeping with joy, a frail old couple wrapped in a shawl of tricolor flag—I wrote my guts out. I wrote to get it down, to have a piece I might have time to edit, or might not.

The Place de la Concorde up ahead wore a thorny crown of barbed wire and logs at its base, an echo of the obstacles at Omaha Beach. We turned right before we reached it, heading north toward the Place de la Madeleine and l'Opéra and the hotel press camp, where journalists coming in with troops from the other directions might or might not have arrived before us. The opera building with its towering columns and great winged figures was almost dwarfed by the volume of traffic signs for branches of the German forces: "*General der Luftwaffe Paris*," "*Zentral-Kraft*," "*Zentral-Ersatzteillager*." Across the imposing stone building that might have withstood almost anything stretched the heavy letters KOMMANDANTUR, the great landmark reduced by German bureaucracy to a place where Frenchmen came to apply for requisite permits, or to file forms, or to do whatever else needed to be done to conduct routine business under the Nazi regime.

"Boulevard des Capucines," Liv called out, intent now on reaching the press headquarters before anyone else, while I wrote and wrote. "And there's the Scribe!"

I looked up from my typewriter. A block up on the avenue to the left, a six-story building wrapped around the corner as if not to be contained in a single block. Signs on the wrought iron railing at the base of the second floor and again higher up proclaimed it to be the Hôtel Scribe, the predesignated press headquarters in Paris—with a Nazi flag flying between the two signs. If the Germans, who used it as a propaganda office, hadn't been able to destroy their transmitters before they fled, Liv and I would send out our work in just minutes.

A beaming man welcomed us under the square awning over the entrance, announcing even before I could set aside my typewriter that he was Monsieur Louis Regamey, agent-general for the Canadian National Railway, which leased the building to the hotel. The hotel manager was there, too, and the head porter, both of them opening the doors of the filthy jeep and offering to take our bags as if we'd just arrived in a limousine. Our Allied uniforms served as the once-required jacket and tie, although just hours earlier only a German uniform would have sufficed.

"Scribe," Liv said. "What a perfect name for the press headquarters!"

"I'm afraid it's pronounced *'screeb,'* " Fletcher said.

I pulled the page from my typewriter, grabbed a pen, and climbed from the jeep. My piece was more typographical error than not and lacked a closing line, but a copyeditor could fix the former, and a piece that ended abruptly but might be the first out of Paris was better than a polished one that lagged.

"Mademoiselle, you are in need of a doctor?" Monsieur Regamey said, the note of alarm in his eyes carefully kept from his voice as he registered my bandaged arm. "I will call the doctor for you, yes?"

A thunder of cheering rose from behind us, and we turned to see a tank passing through the intersection at Avenue de l'Opéra and Boulevard des Capucines just a few yards away. Two French officers and one German one rode together in the tank, announcing something in French and in German that couldn't quite be understood over the cheers of the crowd. You didn't have to speak either language, though, to understand that they were announcing a cease-fire. And the people in the street were kissing again, and we were kissing, too. I was kissing a baby whose mother held him out to drool on my copy when another sound—a sound as antithetical to the sounds of gunfire as could be imagined—caused a silence to all over the crowded streets.

From behind us, the bells of Notre Dame clanged and clanged and clanged.

Other bells joined in, one after another after another, until the whole city juddered with the sound. The ringing was marked by the occasional boom of a heavy gun, the pop of rifles, but then the sound of voices joined in, the spontaneous singing of the "Marseillaise" in the streets: *"Allons enfants de la Patrie. Le jour de gloire est arrivé."* Everywhere, people were singing the same notes, the same French words: *The day of glory has arrived.* Paris was free.

HÔTEL SCRIBE, PARIS
◆
FRIDAY, AUGUST 25, 1944

The General said, "If you're fool enough to be here, I haven't seen you."
—AWOL journalist Martha Gellhorn

Fletcher said—for about the fifth time—that we needed to find a doctor for me, but I couldn't imagine another hour or two would matter for my arm and it certainly might for Liv's photos and my copy. Fletcher relented, and he offered to go into the Scribe to see about getting our work off for us.

"I don't care if they take me into custody now," Liv said, her blue-green eyes bright against her grime-streaked face, her unkempt hair, her wrinkled and muddy uniform. "I've gotten what I came for."

"Liv," Fletcher insisted.

But Liv had always spoken of getting to Paris. Fletcher was our ride to Paris, and here we were, and now she would go back to Charles. Had Fletcher really imagined anything else? Liv had done what she'd come to do, and so had I, even if I hadn't known it was what I'd come to do until I

273

met Liv. We were in Paris and the city was free, and soon the world would be free and we could return to the lives we'd left behind, mundane lives for which we now had a great appreciation. I would go home to Nashville, to Mama and the trolley to Belle Meade. There would be no place for newspaper girls after the men folded away their uniforms, and Mama couldn't wash dishes forever, and she had no one else to care for her.

I gathered myself and said, "We want to hear what excuse the army devises for excluding us now, Fletcher. Surely they can't stick with 'no ladies' latrines' in Paris."

Fletcher laughed in spite of himself. I could make him laugh.

"You underestimate the military mind," he said. "Or maybe you overestimate it."

He ushered us through the door into the hotel's Art Deco interior, the Baccarat crystal chandeliers bubbling light onto marble floors and deep wood paneling, heaps of khaki duffel bags and bedrolls, stray gas masks and mess kits, men in field clothes and mud-caked boots. Waiters hauled in champagne by the case and served it to journalists already sitting everywhere, their typewriters set up on tables in the lounge and on the registration counter and even the floor. British and Canadian press, but also Americans—damn! Still, the tapping of keys and the popping of corks together were glorious.

It wasn't something you could capture in a photograph: the ache of a soldier's voice asking you to talk American to him, the tapping out of the news, the joy that was every church bell in the city clanging as the people of Paris sang.

I put my foot on a metal heat register and tried to hold my copy steady on my knee with my left hand—yes, it did hurt—long enough to scribble a last line, trying to capture the bells and the voices, the cacophony of freedom, while at the same time scanning the room for the censors. The first floor was consigned to the press offices, with men setting up bare tables and lines forming (damn again!) although no censors had yet arrived.

"The mess is being set up in the basement," someone said. "Today's special: K rations, coffee, and champagne."

We turned to see the man shake Fletcher's hand enthusiastically, saying, "Fletcher Roebuck! Imagine seeing you after all this time!"

"Hell, I haven't seen you since we were in short trousers," Fletcher said. He was, I thought, grasping for the friend's name.

"These are my traveling companions, Jane Tyler and Liv Harper, Andrew," he said, pulling the name out of thin air. He hesitated—was the fellow's name Andrew?—but he wasn't corrected. "Andrew was a clarinet player," he said, "and good at maths."

"You're still rattling around the Continent, then," Andrew said to us. Then to me, "What did you do to your poor arm?"

The German cable setups and broadcasting studios were intact, Andrew assured us, but the censors were not even in Paris and wouldn't be for hours at best. I turned to my copy again, setting it on the registration counter this time. I struck through every line and word I could spare, distilling the piece to its most vivid images, a length of text that could be cabled. It always surprised me how tightening a piece to fit space restrictions could make it pop.

The hotel manager set a glass of champagne beside my copy. *"Pour mademoiselle la journaliste,"* he said, *"avec la reconnaissance de toute la ville de Paris." With the gratitude of all of Paris*—as if the pen with which I edited were as important as any weapon. *"Monsieur Regamey m'a demandé de vous dire que le médecin va arriver bientôt, pour s'occuper de votre bras."* A doctor was on his way to see about my arm.

He handed a second glass to Liv, saying, *"Et pour mademoiselle la photojournaliste."*

"Would you point me to the darkroom, please?" she said.

"We are converting the bathrooms to this purpose, Mademoiselle," he answered, "but I am told that we have not at the moment the warm watcr, and the temperature, it must be just so, yes?"

He offered to take her film, but she—perhaps thinking of Capa's D-Day shots—declined. She asked him if there was any way to get information about an American soldier, and he took her brother's name and said he would find out what he could.

Within moments we were incorporated into a large group of correspondents: a man whom Fletcher met in Caen; one he'd worked with years before, in London; a friend of his brother's who was saying how sorry he had been to hear about Edward and asking about Elizabeth Houck-Smythe. Already the competing claims over who had been first into Paris were beginning, everyone having come into the city from different directions with different forces. Sonia Tomara had some claim to being first, having ridden in on a weapons carrier. Bob Reuben of Reuters joked that Lee Carson wasn't sharing the honor even with her jeep mates.

"We were in the backseat while Lee here particularly chose the front," he said.

Carson hadn't been able to get a single story out while she was AWOL, which she still was, of course.

Catherine Coyne, Iris Carpenter, and Lee Miller, who'd been confined to the press building in Rennes until Paris was liberated, hadn't yet arrived, but *New Yorker* columnist Janet Flanner was there, dressed in an officer's uniform with a scarf made of parachute material at her heavy jaw. Ruth Cowan pulled me aside to ask how I'd gotten my roots done in the middle of a war zone; her first order of business after she got her work out was to find a beauty parlor, she said, so she would match her passport and credentials again.

"I'd gladly swap my hair for your credentials," I said.

Ruth said, "As long as I don't have to take your blouse in the bargain. Whatever happened to you, Jane?"

My own first order of business after I got my story out would be to change my blouse.

Someone said Charles Collingwood from CBS had prepared a draft report of the liberation of Paris—complete with street names and land-marks—and sent it to London the day before, marked "Hold for Release." It wasn't clear exactly what had happened in London, but somehow the story came to be read on the air a full twelve hours before the liberation. If that wasn't bad enough, King George of England, having heard the radio broadcast at Buckingham Palace, had announced the "liberation" over the BBC.

Fletcher was still laughing at the Collingwood story when I caught site of an MP across the lobby. Nearly colorless eyes. *You don't want to get close enough to him to see that,* Ernie Pyle had warned. As the man approached in long, swift steps, I scanned the room for the easiest exit. There was Lee Carson slipping out before she was seen. But it was too late for Liv and me. I folded my copy, meaning to sequester it next to the note from Mrs. Roosevelt in my brassiere, then thought instead to tuck it into Liv's musette bag and hand the bag to Fletcher, who accepted it as easily as we all accepted cigarettes from one another, without much thought. I hoped that when Liv and I were in custody he would realize what he had and get it out for us. I could rewrite my piece, but Liv's photos of the liberation would be held as evidence against her, never to see their way to the front pages or anywhere else.

The major said a polite hello to the gathered correspondents, introducing himself as Major Adam Jones almost as if he were one of us: dedicated, benign. A New Yorker, I thought as Fletcher stepped forward a little, imposing himself between the major and us. The major's accent like Liv's husband's, I supposed. His eyes the palest hazel.

"I have orders to apprehend Mrs. Olivia Harper and return her to London," the major said to Liv.

I braced myself for the sound of my own name as a murmur ran through the group. Others from the lobby turned to look.

The major lowered his voice and said, "I don't suppose any of you has seen Mrs. Harper?" He studied Liv. "You, ma'am, look rather like you fit her description."

When Liv started to respond, the major cut her off, saying, "Perhaps I could see your tags?"

Left with no option, Liv took her dog tags from around her neck and handed them to the major.

He looked at them—Olivia James Harper— then handed them back to her.

I scanned the room again, as if there must be a way out of this, but there wasn't. Lee Carson was gone and Ruth Cowan was accredited, and Liv and I were the charge of this Major Adam Jones.

"I saw the photographs this Mrs. Harper took at the Falaise gap," the major said. "They sort of made me proud to be the one chasing her down."

As Fletcher looked from the major to Liv putting her tags back around her graceful, gritty neck, I wondered whether the major meant the photograph of the Polish vodka toast or the others, the medics and the horses. If those photos had run in newspapers, they would have appeared without attribution beyond "AP" or, if they'd been transmitted, "U. S. Signal Corps Radio-telephoto," but I supposed any number of people might have identified them as likely Liv's. And the major would have been kept abreast of where Liv's photos and my writing were coming from, to track us down, whether or not our work had found its way into print.

"I was thinking, ma'am," the major said to Liv, "that you might want to get out of here before I mistake you for Mrs. Harper." He looked to Fletcher. "We have information that Mrs. Harper is traveling with a British military photographer named Fletcher Roebuck. You haven't seen him, I don't suppose?"

Fletcher tugged unconsciously on his ear. "No," he said. "No, I'm sure I haven't done, but if I see either of them I will certainly let them know you're looking for them."

Fletcher took Liv's arm to hurry her out the door before the man changed his mind, but she didn't budge.

"The photos," she said.

"Beastly hell," Fletcher muttered.

The major was disobeying orders for no apparent reason other than some odd combination of the goodwill of the moment and his admiration for Liv's work.

Liv linked her arm in mine. "We need to get our work out, sir," she said.

The major laughed, a big booming laugh from underneath the silly mustache and the pale hazel eyes.

Fletcher said, "Liv, you can't send your photographs uncensored, and no one has any idea when the censors will show."

· · ·

Safely outside the Scribe, we laughed even harder than the major had. When we'd stopped laughing enough to catch our breaths and get the words out, finally, Fletcher said there was a press wireless facility at Cherbourg, that if we could somehow get our work to Cherbourg, they could transmit directly to the United States.

"Cherbourg!" Liv exclaimed. The city was two hundred miles away, at the northernmost tip of the Cotentin Peninsula. But with the line already formed at the Scribe's unmanned censorship tables, our work would not be the first out from the Scribe.

Moments later we were in the jeep, heading for Orly airbase, Fletcher easing us through the throngs of people again, and the trucks and army cars and motorcycles clogging the road. Liv, in the front seat, set my typewriter in her lap. I took the scrawl of my piece out and read it aloud to her, editing as I did, and she typed as ferociously quickly as she could.

At Orly we found an American Piper Cub just about to depart for Cherbourg.

"I don't care who gets the credit, I don't want the credit, I only want the photos to get to the press pool, to be shared," Liv told the pilot.

"Don't be going all noble on us *now,* Livvie," Fletcher said. "We know you a damned sight better than that."

Three minutes later the plane was in the air, carrying a story banged out in road-bumpy typescript and a sack of film to deliver to the darkroom staff at Cherbourg along with instructions that if they worked quickly they could have a part in the first news of the liberation of Paris to reach the world.

"Now the arm, Jane," Fletcher said, and he asked around until he found a doctor at the airbase. The doctor unwrapped my bandage and had a look at the wound, and asked who in the world had dressed it. Fletcher allowed that he had, without fingering Liv for having put him up to it.

"The antibiotic, too?" the doctor said. "You'd make a fine medic, son, if you're ever inclined to set aside that camera." Then to me, "I might have put a few stitches in to save you a scar, but that's a fine job is what that is." He redressed the wound and said if I left the dressing in place for a few days, it should heal well enough. Then he excused himself, saying he'd best get along or they'd leave for London without him.

"London?" Fletcher said, and he joined the doctor long enough to arrange with the flight crew to get his film to British intelligence headquarters there.

Back in Paris, we checked for news of Liv's brother—nothing yet—and we set aside our work for the white and red Burgandies, the red Bordeaux, the champagne and brandy and cognac, rum, Calvados, Armagnac, all hidden from the Germans in anticipation of this day. We raised our glasses time and again, and we shouted with the crowds and sang when others sang, and we laughed and hugged and kissed. We kissed other correspondents at the zinc-topped bar in the Scribe basement, and strangers in the streets.

We were on the Pont des Arts between the Louvre and the beautiful Gare d'Orsay, and we had just finished singing the "Marseillaise" again when Fletcher wrapped his arms around Liv, scooped her up and spun her, her feet lifting from the bridge. He set her down again, and he kissed her—not a French double kiss but rather his mouth pressing hers, his lips surprisingly urgent, the stubble of his beard on her sun-touched skin.

I was as startled by the gesture as Liv was. I stared at the wooden slats of the bridge under my feet, at the light-jumpy Seine below, trying to think of something funny to say that might ease us out of the moment. The only words that came to mind, though, were those final words of the "Marseillaise," the call for the French to take up arms, to water the fields with blood.

Fletcher rubbed his upper arms as if trying to warm himself. He looked to the Eiffel Tower outlined in the distance. "It's rather incredible, isn't it?" he said. "To be here now, for this."

Liv looked at me as if just remembering me, and she reached up and wiped a tear from my cheek. "You're crying, Jane," she said.

"It is something. It is," I said, pressing the back of my hand to my cheek. "Liv," I said, despising my thought even as I voiced it, "don't you wish Charles were here?"

Liv was already turned back to Fletcher, though, and he was tipping a bottle of wine someone in the crowd had passed to him, filling Liv's glass. He poured carefully, but the deep red wine overflowed the rim, spilling onto Liv's dirty fingertips.

PARIS

◆

SUNDAY, AUGUST 27, 1944

Scoops depend on luck and quick transmission, and most of them don't mean
anything the day after they are published.
—Photojournalist Robert Capa

The celebrations of the liberation of Paris were
carried around the world by radio as they'd
happened, John McVane of NBC sharing the
actual sounds of the bells of Notre Dame I'd
only written about, and all the world hearing de
Gaulle proclaim "Víve Paris!" from the Hôtel de
Ville. Even before that, while we'd waited on the
fringes of the city with no facts from inside to
report, the AP's Don Whitehead had telephoned
the US embassy and spoken to a caretaker who,
from a window overlooking the Place de la
Concorde, gave him detail enough to write a full
piece. It had run in the American newspaper
Saturday morning editions, scooping those of us
who'd never imagined the telephones still
worked, much less thought to call. The first
photos from the liberation, though, had to wait
for the photo-journalists to take them and get

them to the United States. They ran in the Saturday late editions, and so we crowded around the Scribe's registration desk with everyone else Sunday morning to wait for the papers, to see whose photographs had run.

"Perhaps you would like to see the last registration card that was signed before you arrived?" the manager offered for entertainment. "Look at the name: 'Joachim Hugo Klapper, Gestapo.' All the Gestapo stayed here."

This particular German officer had checked out only hours before we'd arrived, but now the hotel's walls were decorated with Allied maps and plans of operations. The heaps of khaki bags and gas masks had been cleared and the ground floor was full of the stuff of Allied news: radio and telegraphy equipment, broadcasting studios, typewriters. Censors reviewed copy at the tables while maids scurried to clear the endless paper tape produced by the telex machines. Bathroom space was difficult to find, many of the loos having been taken over for film developing. And a transportation room off to one side doubled as a mail room, the beds with their red eiderdown quilts piled high with V-mail envelopes— including the letters Liv and I had written in the weeks we'd been AWOL—and pushed against the wall to make room for stacked jerry cans of gasoline.

It seemed every journalist in France lounged in

the lobby that morning, or crowded into the basement bar, eyeing the double magnum of champagne and the demijohn of Armagnac that were as much decoration as was the charcoal drawing of Charles de Gaulle. Floyd Davis of *Life* had sketched a colored-pencil cartoon of the bar scene: a brutish Ernest Hemingway, Janet Flanner, and William Shirer of CBS at the front table while Lee Miller and others partied in the background and Robert Capa, in battle dress, observed. Miller, finally released from confinement, had settled her Baby Hermes typewriter in room 412 along with a dozen jerry cans of gas on her balcony. She was in the lobby that morning, entertaining us with a roster of fictional military personnel she'd invented to command the Scribe—Captain Calamity, Corporal Sanction, and General Nuisance among them—when a courier dropped the bundles of newspapers on the reception counter.

The courier was trying to escape through the crush of journalists already pulling off the strings when I caught a glimpse of the *New York Times* front photo, above the fold: a crowd celebrating around an old car in Paris, captioned "Parisians Celebrate Arrival of Allies."

The photo was not full page. It was not full bleed. The headline on the paper already read "Allies Sweep to Troyes, Nazi Rout Grows." And the photo was attributed only to "U. S. Signal

Corps Radiotelephoto." But it was Liv's photograph of the crowd celebrating in front of the barricade: the dark-haired woman atop the old car, among them and yet not quite, somehow; the wheelbarrow spinning behind her; the eyes that Liv had said were her mother's eyes, although you couldn't tell much about them in the grainy black and white of newsprint.

Fletcher began grabbing papers from the hands of other journalists, looking at them and holding them up for Liv to see her photograph in a dozen papers, saying to the gathered journalists, "It's Liv's shot." And all around her now our fellow journalists were thumping her on the back and offering to buy her champagne, saying, "It couldn't have happened to a nicer *fellow*," with no sign of the envy that was welling up in me.

I touched her arm at the elbow and whispered, "Your mama and daddy are looking down on you now, Livvie, busting every button on their angel wings."

I looked at the photo in one paper and in another, fingering the bandage on my arm underneath my clean, untattered blouse. It was such a moving photo, all champagne and toasts and the bells of Notre Dame.

Fletcher plucked one of the newspapers from the front desk and rolled it into a tube in his hands, his eyes looking back at Liv full of joy but with something troubled underneath.

"How does it feel to be the photographer of the moment?" he asked.

Liv looked at the papers spread across the dark wood of the front desk as if it couldn't be her photo, as if someone else must have taken a shot of the same moment—the same camera angle, the same light—and seen something entirely different than she'd seen.

"I don't know, Fletcher," she said.

She eyed the banners spread out on the desk: the *New York Times* late city edition, the *Chicago Tribune*, the *San Francisco Chronicle*.

"Where's the *Daily Press*?" she asked, her words slipping out quietly.

Fletcher stuck the newspaper in his hands behind his back and started to say something, then faltered, his eyes filled with what looked like pity.

"Where is it?" Liv repeated.

He handed her the rolled newspaper, Charles's *New York Daily Press*. Its front page offered a photo of the chaotic shooting in the plaza of the Hôtel de Ville. In the foreground a rifleman aimed for the sniper in one of the spires of Notre Dame while the crowd sank back from their celebration, some turning to run or seeking refuge in doorways and under cars while, already, the Red Cross stretcher-bearers moved into the photo at one edge, headed for a soldier who lay dead on the plaza. That soldier's face was blurred out, but you wouldn't notice if you didn't know to look. It was a powerful shot—one that couldn't have been taken from Liv's and my position underneath the jeep.

"Perhaps Charles never saw your photographs," Fletcher said, but the hand reaching up to tug on his ear told the truth his words denied: Liv's photo could only have been so widely distributed through the press pool. It was made available to everyone.

Liv set the *Daily Press* on the front desk, the gray-white of the paper stark against the deep brown of the wood. She carefully tore the top half of the front page from the paper and folded the half page—the banner and the headline and the photograph that wasn't hers—into a rectangle. She was tucking it into the pocket where she kept that last letter from her brother when I became aware of the quietly insistent words of a reception clerk.

"*Vous êtes Madame Harper? Madame Olivia Harper? Nous avons un télégramme pour vous.*"

Liv looked up at the clerk, a surge of hope surfacing. "Yes," she said. "Yes, I'm Olivia Harper." Fearing the clerk might not understand her, she said, "*Oui.* Yes, I am. Yes, that's me."

The clerk smiled, and several of the journalists laughed warmly. One speculated that the telegram was from *Life* magazine, begging Liv to come on staff. Another said it was no doubt from Mrs. Roosevelt, offering her congratulations on the photo, and I thought of the note in my pocket, and "Operating Room by Flashlight." Had I written my Paris piece carefully enough?

Liv took the thin envelope from the desk clerk and eased the glued flap open slowly lest her own carelessness undo whatever good might be inside. Prisms of sunlight splashed down on her from the chandeliers. Other journalists prattled on around us and began to fall away in twos and threes, this telegram of no interest to them. Liv pulled out the thin sheet and read it silently, then refolded the fragile paper, put it back in the envelope, pressed the flap against the other edge. She looked up at Fletcher—at his clean-shaven cheeks nicked at the corner of his mouth, tender from being under the growth of beard for days again, protected by the stubble.

"Congratulations from Charles," she said. "He's arranging my passage home."

Outside the hotel, the square was again filled with still-ecstatic French men, with women walking arm in arm with men in uniforms, and everywhere children untethered from their parents, running free. The German signs that had dominated the square were gone, the swastikas replaced with the Tricolor, the blue and white and red. The Opera, stripped of its KOMMANDANTUR sign, cast sharp shadows in the bright sunlight. The clocks had been reset.

Liv, looking up to the intricately carved winged creatures atop the Opera, said, "What am I doing here?" her words sinking into the crowd in the square, the women and men and children, everywhere the children.

Fletcher reached down, touched a strand of dark hair at her forehead, longer now than it had been when I first met her.

"They forget to tell you the only way to photograph this war," he said, "is to stand up like a bleeding idiot and point your camera when anyone with any sense has his head tucked low in a trench, praying to any god who might listen."

Liv shook her head slowly, wanting to make him understand what she didn't understand herself. "Not that," she said. "Even if I didn't care about dying—"

A small redheaded boy bolted past us, jostling Liv. He kept running, a second child close on his heels, a little sister with the same strawberry blond hair. The girl was gone before we even saw her expression, her thin legs and square shoulders and flying red hair disappearing into the crowd.

"Sometimes I think I have one small piece of this," Liv said, "that some photograph I've taken has captured some truth about this war, but . . ."

She looked again to the Opera building—a

building that could be photographed as a monolithic whole or in small bits of intricately carved detail, neither of which did it justice. That was the way it was, covering war. The little bits of detail you could get on paper or on film were just that, little bits that didn't tell the whole story. And you couldn't possibly capture the whole of it no matter how far back you stepped.

PARIS
◆
SUNDAY, AUGUST 27, 1944

I want to stick it out until I get to Berlin.
—*St. Louis Post-Dispatch* journalist
Virginia Irwin in a cable to her editors,
who had offered to relieve her

Liv insisted on setting off from Paris late that same afternoon, despite Fletcher's cajoling and arguing and practically pleading for her to wait until morning, to give the idea a decent night's sleep in a decent bed in a decent hotel.

"Every bleeding journalist here is marinating in champagne for at least a few days," he said.

"Jane isn't bleeding anymore," Liv said.

"I do have a lovely scab, though, thank you very much," I agreed.

The fact was I couldn't bear to stay in Paris any more than Liv could. I'd gotten my liberation piece off and I'd gotten my letters on their way to my mother, and I'd even gone to mass that morning, and there was nothing more for me in Paris.

"Read the headlines," Liv said. " 'Allies Sweep to Troyes, Nazi Rout Grows.' "

I said, "The troops are already in Reims."

There was no war left to cover here, and the longer we waited, the farther we got from it. It seemed preposterous, how anxious we were to leave the clean sheets and soft mattresses, the fresh baguettes and champagne. But the comfort was oddly discomfiting. Nothing I would write in Paris could save boys like Joey dying in the field hospitals, boys like the one with the blurred face in the photograph Charles had run.

"Stay here with Hemingway if you want, Fletcher," Liv said. "Jane and I are going to cover the war."

Before we packed, Liv unwrapped my bandage to check my wound, which she declared "much better" before redressing it with clean gauze and a smaller bandage we'd taken from the emergency kit. I put my untorn blouse back on, and she turned to packing her gear, pulling the red gown and gloves from the bottom of her rucksack to refold them.

I said, "You didn't get a chance to wear them."

She hesitated, then continued folding. "No dancing shoes," she said.

I said, "And dancing barefoot on the streets of Paris in these crowds . . ."

I finished buttoning my blouse and turned to my own packing.

"They were my mother's," Liv said. "The gown. The gloves."

The second wedding ring. The love of photographs.

She said, "I took them from her wardrobe after she died."

I considered this: what it meant to have a mother who wore fancy gowns, who settled her gloved right hand in her husband's left to dance to a live orchestra. To lose a mother like that, or any mother. To have a father to lose.

She tucked the gown and gloves back into her rucksack, then held my pack steady as I eased my bandaged arm through the strap.

I nearly tripped over Fletcher sitting on his own pack outside our door. I would have tripped over him had he not reached out and grabbed my arm.

"Ouch!" I cried out.

"Sorry," Fletcher said. "Sorry." Then to Liv, "Whom do we join, then?"

Liv's eyes under her dark brows were clouded with a doubt I hadn't seen before.

Fletcher stood and hoisted his pack, swinging it hard up against his shoulder. "We do need to get out of town before that MP chap changes his mind, in any event."

"You were staying here with your old pal Hemingway," I said. "But we're happy to have your company."

"My jeep. You're happy to have my jeep," he joked.

Liv's and my plan had been to hitch rides wherever we could. Not much of a plan, but that's how we'd gotten to Fletcher.

"My jeep and my tent," Fletcher said.

"You have a tent now?" Liv said. Then to me, "He has a tent now, or so he says." As if this were a deciding factor, as if we might not let him take us in his jeep if not for the tent.

"Not much of a tent," Fletcher admitted. "Just a little pup tent."

"He's suddenly looking more attractive, isn't he?" I said to Liv.

"The shaved chin?" Liv said.

"I think it makes his ears look a little smaller, doesn't it?"

"The shaved chin does?"

"The fact that he has a tent."

Liv and I set off, and Fletcher fell in with us. We pushed through the lobby and out the door, onto the walk.

"I understand Iris Carpenter and Lee Carson are likely to be assigned to the First Army press corps despite their numerous acts of insubordination," Fletcher said. "Whether that means SHAEF is giving up or we're too far from Washington or too close to the end of the war for anyone to care, I'm not certain, but it seems likely we're to be left alone if we—"

"*Jane and I* are to be left alone," Liv said with a little pop of anger even she didn't seem to have expected. "And SHAEF? 'SHAEF' is just an acronym. 'Strategic Headquarters.' It isn't a damned acronym getting in Iris's and Lee's and our way. Don't depersonalize the bastards who are trying to keep us from what we need to do."

I flinched at the word "bastards," at the word "need," remembering again Charles's description of her as a gal who photographed like a man but didn't smoke and didn't curse. Still, the major had let us go when we were right there, when he knew we were right there, and it wasn't like Liv to swear, to use a word like "bastard." It wasn't like her to *need* anything—or to admit to a need, anyway. Though there had been that moment at the Dives River, Liv and Fletcher floating together in the green water, their fingers intertwined.

Liv heaved her pack into the jeep. It landed with a heavy thunk that seemed to shut off argument. Fletcher threw his in beside hers, then took mine and threw it in, too. He climbed into the jeep. She climbed into the back, saying I should take the front; it was less bumpy and I would be more comfortable.

She said, "The US First Army is already headed northwest of here."

"Having declined to stay for the champagne, as I understand it," I said. "Not a Hemingway among them."

Fletcher grinned despite himself. "Right," he said. "Yes, well, the Canadians and my fine countrymen, Dempsey's men, are farthest north. Perhaps we join them? They'll head for Le Havre and . . ."

"And Dieppe," Liv continued for him. "Then probably to Dunkirk."

"To Dunkirk," Fletcher said almost under his breath. His brother had been evacuated from Dunkirk to spend two more years at war, to father a child who would never be born, to spend his last moments at Dieppe climbing over the dead bodies of men he'd called friends, only to be killed himself.

Patton's men were south of us, Liv said, headed southeast to hook up with the Americans and French heading up from Marseille, assuming they took Marseille. Operation Dragoon—the Champagne Campaign, people were calling it. They had taken all but the port cities, which were expected to fall any minute. "Light casualties, I heard," Liv said. "The Jerries in full retreat. Nothing much interesting there."

Fletcher slipped the key into the ignition, his expression full of the sadness of Dunkirk and Dieppe, of Edward.

Liv squared her camera between her feet. "I vote we find the US First," she said. "They'll head through northeastern France and into Belgium and Holland. They'll likely be the first into Holland."

Fletcher glanced at her in the rearview mirror,

302

relieved that somehow she hadn't chosen the path to Dieppe or Dunkirk with the Canadians or the British, who were more likely to look the other way at two AWOL American women. I tried to think of something flip to say about Liv's preference for non-champagne-drinking American boys, but came up empty.

I said, "I suppose we might be mistaken for Iris and Lee as long as we don't all four show up at once"—never mind the improbability of me passing either for Iris Carpenter, who was the daughter of a British movie magnate and looked like she ought to be one of his stars, or Lee Carson, whom *Newsweek* had dubbed America's best-looking journalist.

"You'll have to hide your camera, Liv," I said, "since Iris and Lee are both journalists, not photographers."

Fletcher turned the key and the jeep engine kicked alive with a rattle. "Shall we head toward Compiègne, then?" he said, no more able than I was to yank back the curtain of cigarettes and "bastards" and "damns" to expose Liv.

"We'll be the first to report from Germany," I suggested wryly, wondering if we hadn't known on some level even on the morning we left the field hospital that Germany was our real destination. Wondering if Paris hadn't been an illusion all along. And trying to sort out why Liv didn't want to follow Patton. Why, if we were willing to risk joining American troops, weren't we setting the more direct course for Berlin? Belgium wasn't front-page news. Belgium was not the photographs the papers would run. Was that *why* Liv wanted to go to Belgium?

Fletcher eased the jeep through streets cluttered with the detritus of war: white flags still hanging from the windows, barricades not yet cleared, bullet-pocked storefronts that would be left for some time as proof that the Germans had been in Paris but in the end had lost.

"Liv," I said, "you don't think we ought to hook up with Patton's—"

"The First Army," she insisted.

And it was only after we'd driven in silence through the streets of Paris and on into the countryside that I thought of Liv's brother. Perhaps Geoff was with the First Army? I turned around to say something about him, to ask Liv if she thought her brother was in Belgium, sure suddenly that she was looking for him. Her eyes were such an empty, emotionless blue, though, that my voice caught in my throat.

She was looking for Geoff, I supposed, just as I might be looking for Tommy if he hadn't gone off and married another girl, just as Fletcher might have looked for Edward if he hadn't died at Dieppe.

"Two months," Liv said, turning to the windshield, to the road ahead. "Two months ago, he flew all the way from New York to London just to see me."

I tried to make sense of what she was saying: her brother had flown to London to see her?

"Two months ago," she said, "we were at your country house in Chichester, Fletcher, talking about having a family together, a girl and a boy, one of each."

We pitched Fletcher's pup tent in a field that night, not sure where we were and too tired to consult the map, but certain from the distant sounds that we were not yet at the front. Liv disappeared into the tent almost the moment it was up, as if she meant for me to have some time alone with Fletcher. He laid his bedroll out on the ground beside the jeep, and the two of us sat on it, leaning back on the jeep's hard metal. A fog began to settle low. The damp ground smelled earthy and close.

"A bite of pudding?" Fletcher said, and he offered me the chocolate bar from his pocket.

"We call it dessert," I said.

"Yes. We consider that barbaric," he said.

"The barbarians being . . . ?"

"Anyone who can't trace their lineage back to Alfred the Great."

I unwrapped the chocolate and took a small bite, then handed it back. "It's hard to believe anyone would give up this 'pudding,' even for a nice clean table back at the Scribe in Paris," I said.

He took a bite himself, and chewed it, and swallowed. "Only the finest for you, Jane."

He offered me the chocolate bar again, and I held his hand to steady it as I took a second bite, and I let my hand linger on his as long as I could without feeling foolish.

"It's Sunday night," he said. "Back home, the mums will have headed back to London. The girls will be so sad."

"Maybe Mrs. Serle will have made them a 'pudding,'" I said.

He laughed, and he said, "Yes, I suppose she will have done. The berries will be in, and the first of the figs."

"My mother makes a berry cobbler that will make you want to hit your mama," I said. I swatted a mosquito, thinking of the no-see-ums even in the daytime at home. It was Sunday afternoon in Nashville. Mama used to make cobblers on Sunday afternoons, which she served with milk poured from her special pitcher.

"The peaches will be ripe now," I said. "Mama's peach cobbler is the best."

Fletcher offered me the rest of the chocolate bar and, when I declined, wrapped it back up.

"Fletcher," I said, "what do we do if ever you don't come back? When you go off by yourself, I mean."

He tucked the chocolate into the pocket where he kept the photograph of Elizabeth. "You leave my bedroll and my pack wherever you are, in case I can get back to it, and you take the jeep and the Webley, and you carry on."

"Without you?"

He took out a cigarette, but didn't light it. "Do you suppose Charles knows you and Liv are traveling together?" he asked.

"Does Charles know?" He might not, I supposed. She'd written her husband just as I'd written my mother, but we'd only mailed them from Paris; they wouldn't have received them yet.

"I don't know what Charles knows," I said. "I suppose he will have heard, though."

"The MP only asked about Liv," Fletcher said.

"The MP?"

"That Major Adam Jones. The man asked if Liv was Liv before letting her go. He said he had orders to apprehend Mrs. Olivia James Harper and return her to London."

If the MP had been looking for a Miss Jane Tyler, he hadn't mentioned it.

But I didn't want to think about Liv and Charles. I didn't want to worry whether the MPs would continue to pursue us now, whether the reprieve Major Adam Jones with his snowdrop hat had granted us would extend beyond those few moments of celebration.

I said, "Look at the moon, Fletcher."

In the mist, it glowed eerie and haunting. The dampness tamped down the sounds of the countryside, too: the chirping of night frogs, the hum of crickets, the more distant booms and rattles of war.

I turned to Fletcher, thinking I would just kiss him.

"Well then, we ought to get some rest," he said, and he stood and offered a hand to help me up.

Liv lay in her bedroll in the low little tent that night, but her breathing wasn't the easy, even breath of sleep. She didn't speak at first, and I didn't either. I climbed into my bedroll and lay with my eyes closed, exhausted but awake. I focused on making my breath slow and easy, as if I'd fallen asleep.

After a few moments, she whispered, "Charles sees the truth. He believes in sparing the public their breakfast stomachs, but he won't print anything but the truth."

The darkness so reminded me of the darkness of our tent in the field hospital that first night, when we'd talked so easily, but I didn't say anything.

"He thought the liberation of Paris would be the moment of the century, but he looked at the photos," she said. "The other papers, they've all run what they expected the liberation to be, what we all wanted it to be, what I photographed. But Charles looked at the photos and he saw what was actually happening here, and that's the photograph he ran."

Not the kisses and the flowers and the cheers, the singing of the "Marseillaise," but wartime written on the face of one ordinary person who was afraid or angry or exhausted, still at war even as the crowds around him celebrated what we all wanted to be the war's end, but was not.

"One soldier shooting in the midst of the cele-bration," Liv said. "Another dead."

The Red Cross stretcher-bearers moving into the frame, toward the dead boy whose face was blurred out. Would the photograph have been any more powerful if it had shown his face?

"It's as if I've boiled the whole war down to this one moment in Paris that isn't at all the war," Liv said. "That shows the war less, even, than my shots of that operation by flashlight back at the field hospital. Less than the story you wrote about that night."

I knew she needed me to say something, to deny what she was saying or even just to acknowledge that she was right. But it was late and I was tired and freshly rejected, and the jealousy nibbling at the edge of our friendship left me unable to do anything but pretend sleep.

OUTSIDE COMPIÈGNE, FRANCE
◆
SUNDAY, AUGUST 27, 1944

It was a nerve-shattering experience. We "ran off" the map and had to navigate by guess.
—*St. Louis Post-Dispatch* correspondent Virginia Irwin, from "A Giant Whirlpool of Destruction" in the May 9, 1945, issue

Fletcher didn't know how long he lay in his bedroll—fifteen minutes or fifty or more—but the moon had almost disappeared entirely into the mist when the flap of the tent opened and Liv emerged out of the darkness, dragging her bedroll. She wore not the gray undershirt and gray long johns she always slept in, but rather a long, fancy thing that left the white of her neckline and arms so bare and ghostlike that for a moment he thought he was dreaming her. For that moment, he expected to see Charles join them, the red tip of his cigar cutting through the fog.

"Fletcher?" she whispered.

He hesitated, finding his voice. "I'm here, Livvie," he said finally. "Right here."

She arranged her bedroll beside his and lay down on top of it. White skin. Red gown.

She curled up to him, shivering at his side, and he unzipped his own bedroll and slid his arm around her, pulled her to him almost like he sometimes did with the little girls at his country house when they were missing their mums and their fathers and their modest little homes, when they were not understanding the cost of this war to them.

"Fletcher," she said, her breath slightly ripe with the late hour, her eyes shadowed in the mist, the dreamworld light.

He hated to touch the red silk of the gown with his rough, dirty hands.

"Fletcher, was Charles the one who started the rumor?" Her voice so faint that it, too, seemed to belong to a dreamworld.

He stared up at the starless sky, at the dim glow of moon behind the cloud cover now. He wanted to ask which rumor, but he didn't want her to have to answer.

"The rumor that I was pregnant," she whispered.

Fletcher inhaled the damp air deeply, blew his breath out in a long sigh.

She turned toward the dim glow of the moon. "To keep me from getting security clearance or to get me sent home after I'd gotten here. To keep me from getting myself killed."

Fletcher turned toward her, and she snuggled

more deeply into him. He smoothed a wrinkle in the gown with his thumb.

"He was the one who told me I should come," she said, not so much with accusation as with regret.

Fletcher stroked her hair, as silky as the gown, trying to attend to her words, trying to think of something to say other than that she would be fine, that everything would be fine. Then her lips were pressing his, softly parted. Her tongue pressing into his mouth. He tried to resist, told himself he had to resist, that this was her grief speaking, that she would regret this and he would, too. But her breath was warm on his skin and the night was cold and bombs sounded in the distance, muted but real, very real, and the drone of the planes and, occasionally, the hazy light of a flare flashing dimly, glowing with the moon. And the touch of her fingers on his cheek was achingly soft, the slide of her fingers over his chest, his ribs. And even softer, the skin of her neck against his fingertips, his cheeks, his lips. The sharp line of her ribs and her surprisingly full breast, the sharp hip bone, the softer belly. And he had wanted her for so long without allowing himself to want her, had wanted her since the night in the barn when he'd dreamed of her, since the moment he'd seen her in that first shock of Saint-Lô, since even before that, since he'd poured wine into her glass at Trefoil, with Charles sitting by her side. Since the day in Charles's office when she'd eyed him so coolly, when all he'd done was ask her to fetch him tea. Of course he'd known—even then, he'd known—that she was no office girl. He'd seen the way she captured so much of a person in a photograph, without even a slant of light, and he'd wanted to be known that way. Even before he met her, before he saw how beautiful she was—that naive kind of beauty that somehow didn't recognize itself—he'd wanted to be known by her, and to know her. But she had been Charles's girl even then, and he'd been reduced to pretending he thought her no more than an office girl; he'd been reduced to asking her to bring him tea with lemon just to see the rise it brought in her, the spark in her flame-blue eyes.

Fletcher awoke to the dull light of dawn, and peered through slit eyes to see Liv already loading her things into the jeep.

"Liv," he said softly.

Her back was to him, her dark hair just-awake messy. He sat up slowly, repeating, "Liv?"

"We're almost out of gas," she said. "Do we have anything we can trade for gas?"

"Liv," he whispered.

She pulled a map from the jeep, unfolded it, refolded it to expose the area northeast of Paris.

He stood, pulled on his trousers, and came up behind her. "Liv," he said. "I—"

"We're almost to Compiègne," she said. "Charles and I drank a bottle of wine from Compiègne the first night of our honeymoon."

He shoved his hands into his pockets, then pulled them out, ran them through his hair. Reached for his undershirt and pulled it on, inhaling the smell of it, the smell of her. Wine from Compiègne? There was no bloody such thing. Or if there was, there shouldn't be.

"Petrol," he said, grabbing onto the buoy of the practical need. "This damn war would be over but for the shortage of bloody damn petrol." He buttoned his shirt, the blasted tiny buttons. "How many rations have we left?" he asked irritably. "We can trade rations. We can trade our damned fags."

She turned with a guarded, defiant look. *I'm a photojournalist,* she'd said that first time they'd met. *I don't fetch tea. But if you're bringing yourself a cup, I take mine with just a drop of milk.*

Yes, he wanted to say now. *Yes, it was Charles who started the rumor that you were pregnant, Liv.* The rumor Fletcher had heard was that Charles had received a letter from Liv herself—from England or from Normandy, the accounts varied—that she was pregnant. Who could have started that rumor but Charles himself? Why would the MP have asked only for Liv's identification unless Charles had something to do

315

with tracking her down to be sent home? But if Fletcher told Liv that, she would hate him for having told her.

He closed his eyes and tried to picture Elizabeth Houck-Smythe. He pictured her in his brother's arms, dancing.

OUTSIDE COMPIÈGNE, FRANCE
◆
MONDAY, AUGUST 28, 1944

> It is not a woman's place. There's no question about it. There's only one other species on earth for whom a war zone is no place, and that's men.
> —Photojournalist Dickey Chapelle

It seemed I waited forever that morning, imprisoned in the tent to save Liv and Fletcher an awkwardness I didn't really want to spare them, or to spare myself something I didn't understand. Maybe it was my own fault, for not having listened to Liv, or not having responded.

I heard quiet movement, finally, and Fletcher speaking in a low voice, words I couldn't make out. I peeked through the tent flap to see Liv bent over the map.

"You don't have any smutty photographs?" she asked Fletcher—a question, but in a tone of disapproval. Photographs of scantily clad women, or women clad in nothing at all. They were easy to carry and brought a high value in trade with the troops. Rumor had it you could get five gallons of gas for a single long-legged blond.

We loaded the jeep and headed down roads everywhere under construction, men in uniform repairing the bomb damage so supplies could be moved to the front. We crossed pontoon bridges straddling rivers and drove through forests stripped of their leaves, and often of limbs, too. Old men and women and children walked with their possessions neatly stacked in wheelbarrows or baby buggies, making their way to whatever was left of their homes. Fletcher stopped the jeep again and again—at farms and villages—trying to trade for gasoline. Petrol, he called it, which I'd always found charming, but the word now grated. There was none to be found—not in trade for cigarettes or for food or for smutty photographs.

At a stone cottage with a steep red roof at the edge of a cemetery, a woman with four boys and a single girl looking out from behind her, all thin and gaunt, said in rapid French, *"Les Américains . . . pas de . . . Non."* The same story we'd heard everywhere: whatever gasoline the Germans hadn't taken, the Allied forces moving through had. And still there were military vehicles abandoned at the side of the road, always with their gas tanks empty. There were abandoned jerry cans everywhere, each one smelling of gasoline but offering none.

I went to the jeep, dug out a dozen ration tins, ones still with the biscuits, and five extra chocolate bars, and I took them back to the woman and thanked her anyway. We climbed into the jeep, and Fletcher turned the key. The jeep did not start. We sat there, looking to the cemetery, crosses paired back to back as if to protect one another. It was daylight, but still it seemed so clearly a cemetery unblessed by the moon.

The little girl emerged from the cottage, chocolate rimming her mouth, her pinafore worn but clean. She glanced back to the door, as if uncertain of the task she'd been put to or worried about being caught doing some forbidden thing. I found myself ridiculously wanting the girl to come to me rather than to Liv.

"Maman m'a dit de vous dire qu'il y aura un peu d'essence dans le hangar pres du cimetière," she said, chirping like a little bird as she nodded in the direction of all those crosses she looked out at every day.

I pointed to the shack at the far edge of the cemetery. *"Cette petite . . ."* Not able to call up the word she'd just used. There would be gas in a . . . hanger? I was so tired.

"Maman dit si vous n'avez pas besoin de tout cela, laissez ce que vous pouvez." She glanced back at her mother, now watching through the narrow strip between the front door and the jamb. *"S'il vous plaît,"* the little girl said earnestly. *"Maman dit s'il vous plaît laissez ce que vous pouvez." Please take only as much gas as you need. Please.* Her mother emphasizing that her

daughter must be polite in the same way my own mother would have.

"*Comment vous appelez-vous, ma jeune amie?*" I asked the girl.

"*Je m'appelle Ange.*"

Yes, of course you are, I thought. *Angel.* Someday, if I had a little girl, perhaps I would name her Angel, too.

"*Ange, s'il vous plaît, dites à votre mère que nous allons prendre juste assez pour nous rendre à la ville voisine,*" I said. *Tell your mother we will take only the gas we need to get to the next town.* This family wouldn't need the gasoline to flee as long as the Allied advance continued, but we couldn't guarantee them that.

"*Merci, Ange,*" I said, remembering my own manners.

I pulled out a handful of vanilla caramels and handed them to her, and kissed the top of her head. She disappeared back into the house, the door closing behind her as we set off on foot over the graves to find a ten-liter can of gas, labeled in French—gasoline someone had hoarded since the Germans took over northern France. We poured half of it into the gas tank and returned the rest to the cemetery shed.

Smoke on the horizon not long before dusk was thick in our lungs and gritty in our mouths by the time we reached the next village. Several houses were on fire and the town was deserted—no people, no animals, nothing but the heat and crackle of flames. At a crossroads a minute later, we nearly hit an ambulance careering around the corner. We followed it toward a sudden loud sound, a gunshot maybe. The world grew louder: shots, yes, and the crank of machine gears, trucks, and then voices shouting.

We were stopped some distance from a château by an American soldier who told us the Germans who'd occupied the village were holding the townspeople captive inside. Allied soldiers surrounded the château, and the Germans had just sent out a French girl with an offer of surrender. The Civil Affairs scouts were already there, organizing a hospital and food. One was trying to determine if any townspeople had escaped being rounded up and might now help identify conspirators and Germans among those who would emerge from the château.

"The lousy bastards always surrender at dusk," the soldier told Fletcher, addressing him as if Liv and I weren't there. "So's they can slip out in the dim light, mixed in with the townspeople, pretending to be the fucking French. And they always tell us there's less townspeople than there is, so we'll be short-handed, so's we won't have enough soldiers to sort out the phonies." The soldier spit at the ground. "Goddamn Krauts."

Riflemen lined the road to the château, and people began emerging through the heavy front doors. The sick and the injured came first, some bandaged already, some bleeding raw and wounded from Allied fire or German abuse or both. After the wounded came the children, little sisters and brothers gripping tightly to one another's hands, stumbling, followed by mothers carrying babies or bundles, or pushing carriages piled high with possessions. They wore the same numb expressions as did the men shuffling behind them, exhausted and dazed. Only the nuns—three nuns walking together, their chins raised—looked undefeated. They walked side by side but not touching, their bodies isolated, their habits and winged coronets improbably white among the bundle-carrying crowd, against the smoke drifting across the sky.

Liv watched the procession with a hopefulness that made me ache. Looking for her brother, I could see that. I wondered if she could see it herself.

Fletcher photographed the château where the Germans had chosen to hole up. I uncapped my pen, the familiar motion soothing, and began with the soldier's words. I didn't suppose any publication would run the word "bastards," but I wanted to record the truth of it.

A French teenager identified to the Civil Affairs scouts as a patriot now stood among several soldiers at the far side of the road, scanning the emerging townspeople. He pointed to a middle-aged man and said something, and a soldier pulled the man from the line, frisked him for weapons, and led him off the road at gunpoint. Liv caught the sequence with a long lens as I described it in the best words I could find. A second man—a pathetic-looking, stoop-backed old Frenchman in a dark beret—was pulled from the crowd, too, and a younger woman with a toddler in a rabbit coat. The child did not want for soap and warm water, I thought as Liv's shutter clicked. The child ate candy and beef.

I avoided Fletcher's gaze as he, too, watched the toddler.

She had beautiful silken hair against the pure white fur, the girl did. The mother held her hand. How did you lay the responsibility for what would happen to them on the shoulders of a schoolboy who ought to be thinking about soccer balls and girls' breasts? How did you blame a mother for what she did to protect her child?

The injured were helped to the side of the road, loaded on stretchers, and whisked off in ambulances. There were tears and hugs, and there were skirmishes, too, angry words and sometimes blows exchanged before, almost inevitably, one of the group would be pulled from the crowd and escorted off at gunpoint. An old woman somehow found the energy to spit on one—a

German soldier trying to blend in or a collaborator, I wasn't sure which. Liv raised her camera just in time to catch the spittle coming from her pursed lips.

I watched the nuns: the coronets, the heavy crosses at their chests, the rosaries hanging at their waists. The taller one reminded me of Sister Mary Alice, who taught me in the third grade. She'd once said of my father that he was in God's hands, that I had to pray for him—maybe God would listen to me. I'd imagined my father in heaven, but I saw as I stood watching those nuns that she'd meant that my father, whoever he was, was a sinner. Sister Mary Alice would think Liv's father a sinner, too, in limbo at best. People who killed themselves didn't go to heaven. "Thou shalt not kill." And yet in war, if you didn't kill you were court-martialed. You were a coward. You were shamed.

A boy was pulled from the line, his civilian shirt far too small, his civilian slacks too short and baggy for his gawky-thin frame. He had pale, smooth cheeks and a prominent Adam's apple, and his eyes were wide-set and sunken, like the German from the woods, the boy Liv had commanded to find her brother in words he couldn't understand.

"Do you suppose there is a god anywhere who listens to any of us?" I asked.

Liv photographed the boy straight on to capture

the shame in his eyes. She lowered the camera and took in the scene unaided by the lens.

"I don't know," she said.

I looked to the jeep with its empty driver's seat, my bedroll in the back where I'd stuffed it that morning after waking up to Fletcher and Liv entwined.

Several overly young, overly indignant French resistance fighters looked to be badgering the pathetic old Frenchman in the beret. They raised their long rifles and pointed at his chest, and he climbed reluctantly into a jeep that motored away. Liv took off, running after them despite the American guard's protests, and Fletcher took off after her. I felt too dispirited to do anything but lope along well behind them.

At the other side of the road, the jeep with the old man was nowhere to be seen.

Fletcher grabbed an American soldier who was halfheartedly guarding the road. "Where did they go?" he demanded, loud enough for me to hear from yards away.

The soldier shrugged.

"Which way!"

"He's a German spy, that's what they told me," the soldier said, and he nodded toward the back of the château.

Fletcher said, "But they'll—"

"Been ratting on his own neighbors, that's what they said."

Liv was already sprinting toward the back of the château. Fletcher followed, calling, "Liv! No!" His camera in its case thumping at his hip.

Behind us, a line of surrendering Germans marched with hands overhead in one direction as Allied soldiers marched in the other, rifles at the ready and grenades hanging from their lapels. The mother and toddler were being escorted by soldiers to a building already swept for mines, to answer questions or perhaps to refuse to answer. Which would be safer for the child now? For the mother to tell the truth or to lie or to say nothing at all while the girl sat alone in the next room, sucking on a red Life Saver from the pocket of her rabbit coat?

When I rounded the corner of the château, finally, the old man was standing before a stone garden wall in the distance, beret in hand, with the Frenchmen lined up several yards away, rifles raised and aimed. Liv was rushing toward them, meaning to stop the firing squad or simply to get the photograph—I couldn't tell.

Fletcher, twenty paces behind her, called out, "Liv!"

"Liv!" I called, too. "Liv, no!"

She raised her camera, her hands working the focus as she kept running, her camera swinging toward the lust in the Frenchmen, the blankly staring eyes of the collaborator.

"Feu!"

The rifles fired, the bitter smell of cordite filling the air.

"I got the photo," Liv said in the canvas-musty darkness of the pup tent that night—proudly and sadly and irritably all at once. She and Fletcher had argued the whole evening about it: Liv insisting she'd photographed exactly what he was forever demanding she shoot—the old man's face just before he was executed, and just afterward—and Fletcher saying if Liv rushed into gunfire like that again he would personally escort her to the nearest MP.

"I got the photo," she repeated. "What does Fletcher want from me?"

When I didn't reply, she asked, "Jane, are you okay?"

"I'm fine," I said, stuffing down all the things I wanted to say, starting with the ridiculousness of anyone being okay just hours after we'd watched an old man being stood against a garden wall and shot by his neighbors.

"Does your arm hurt? Maybe I should unwrap it and have a look?"

"My arm is fine."

We lay there for a long time, listening to the quiet sounds of Fletcher cleaning his lenses in the dark.

"I was the one who found my father, Jane," Liv

said finally. "I took a cup of coffee up to his room, but his bed was empty. I can still see the pattern of the coffee spill on the basement stairs as clearly as I can see my father's face."

I turned toward her, taking her hand, saying, "Oh, Liv," embarrassed at my anger.

She said, "His eyes were just at the level of mine as I came down the basement stairs, calling for him."

The newspapers had said she and Geoff went down to the basement together, but in truth she alone had found their father, she said. The old photo of him the newspapers had run left the impression that he looked in death as he had always looked, that his eyes were the same kind eyes that had greeted his patients, and his shoulders were still broad and square, and the only difference was that where he usually had a tie and a stethoscope, he'd chosen instead to wear a rope.

Charles is wrong about not showing the faces, Fletcher had insisted. *It's the faces that make the deaths real.*

The face Liv had photographed that day, though—the man killed by the firing squad— wasn't a hero. I wondered if she realized that. The man was charged with betrayal, like my own father had betrayed me by never claiming me as his daughter, like Liv's father had betrayed her by putting his own grief before hers and Geoff's.

328

Liv's grief leaked around the edges when she talked about photographs—*Imagine that, Livvie*—and she was not able to understand how much her mother must have loved her, how hard it must have been for her mother to die before her children were grown, how much she must have wanted to leave Liv with something to carry her through her grief.

They were her mother's eyes—that was what Liv had said about the woman celebrating atop the old car in Paris. Her mother's eyes, and Liv's camera trained on them looking directly back at her, as if by stripping away all the light and shadow Liv might understand what it was that her mother meant for her.

COMPIÈGNE, FRANCE
◆
WEDNESDAY, AUGUST 30, 1944

I took a last picture of those feet still in their muddy boots and with the boy's own rifle between them, where it served as a splint for a crushed leg. I knew I was getting dramatic pictures. If these men had to go through so much suffering, I was glad, at least, I was there to record it.
—Photojournalist Margaret Bourke-White

The last days of August brought a collapse of the German defenses. We moved with the Fifth Corps of the US First Army as it took Compiègne, while the Third Army entered the Argonne Forest not far from the German border and the British sealed off the German forces on the Channel coast, neutralizing their robot bombs. Rumors flew that General Bradley had ordered the winter uniforms coming in at Le Havre stored, expecting the Third Reich to collapse entirely before harsh weather came. The Germans fled so quickly they left behind field bakeries full of bread, depots stocked with millions of pounds of frozen and tinned meat, grain and rice and flour, sugar. They abandoned staff headquarters rich with cheese and sausages and fruits and wine, and train cars filled with coal and with other more interesting if less useful fare: ladies' lingerie, lipstick, perfume. All of it found its way into our poker games with the soldiers, games in which our betting chips were photographs to be taken by Liv and Fletcher. This was worth more than one might have imagined: a chance at immortality when mortality had you by the throat.

Liv enjoyed the games as much as ever—the men scooting over to make room for us, the spirited banter, their eagerness to win a chance to be photographed by her. We both won for the most part. Perhaps they let us. "Liberated items": a ring setting missing its gemstone, a tin of caviar Liv couldn't stomach, Belgian chocolates so creamy that we ate them all in one sitting without saying a word lest we break the spell. Fletcher shared Liv's Saint-Lô–Périers road nickname with the soldiers, Pitiless Livvie, but they thought it was only right that Liv and I had all the luck, "being dames and all."

Crazy Livvie, Fletcher started calling her, because unlike in Normandy, where Liv and I had stayed back when Fletcher went out on patrol with the soldiers, Liv now insisted on going. The patrols generally went at night because daylight brought the added danger of visibility now that the weather had improved, and nighttime photographs invariably came out grainy and flat, the low light bleaching contrast to a muddy gray. Still, Liv seemed unable to get enough of the patrols.

"It's absurd," Fletcher told me. "Even the soldiers don't go every night. They go when it's their turn in the rotation to do so, and are relieved to return."

He had slept with Liv, and now he couldn't look at her without thinking of that, and he couldn't not look at her. He watched her through the lens, achieving with that barrier the same false sense of security he felt looking through it at a German, as if the lens isolated him from everything. He saved his talk of Liv for his late-night conversations with me, as if I were just the one to understand. We split chocolate bars and he talked about Liv as if he'd never cared for Elizabeth Houck-Smythe. Not that he ever said he'd slept with Liv. He was a gentleman. He talked about what she should be doing but wasn't, what she was doing but should not. And he talked about Charles, too—Charles who was his friend, who'd saved his life.

Liv talked to me about Fletcher, too. "I slept with him, I don't even know why," she told me late one night as she put on her woolens to go out on patrol, a night after a day spent like all the days: interviewing men who were not obvious heroes, taking sympathetic portraits of them washing socks and underwear in their helmets, eating unenthusiastic bites of pork-and-apple-and-carrot mix, stirring lemon powder into water with wooden spoons. I supposed she was looking for me to say I understood, that what she'd done was forgivable, perhaps that Charles need never be told. She repeated the words again later, as we settled into our bedrolls—Liv so overwhelmingly tired that I worried for her even more than for myself. Still, I offered no words of comfort. I left her to her nightmares: little girls with big eyes looking mutely up at her, refusing to tell her their names; Charles somehow not Charles, with the little girls around him, their laughter all the same dry cackle as Fletcher demanded she fetch tea.

The entire Fifth Corps ground to a halt on the second of September, unable to go beyond Cambrai for lack of gas. The Allied armies were outrunning the supply line. The French railway east of Paris had been bombed to rubble, and the pipeline extension to move gasoline under the ocean and on to Chartres wasn't operational yet. Some six thousand Red Ball Express trucks were carting gasoline from the ports to the front—a fifty-hour round trip, and none of the drivers slept until after they returned—but even operating twenty-four hours a day, they couldn't cart enough five-gallon cans across Europe to sustain the advance. We began to hear rumors of a squabble between Montgomery and Patton,

Patton raging that his men could eat their goddamned belts but his tanks had to have gas.

Patrols continued to go out on foot each night, though, or sometimes just before dawn, and each time the soldiers readied to go out, Liv loaded her film. Because she did, Fletcher and I, too, pulled on our woolens, cursing the damp and the cold, and Fletcher checked his Webley. The war was nearly over, and we had no intention of dying in the final days.

The morning after we won a second box of Belgian chocolates, we awoke before dawn to the sound of gunshots. Fletcher was already out of his bedroll, sprinting. We caught up to him at the edge of an open field not far ahead, where a number of soldiers huddled together behind a stone fence, peering out into the white air of the morning. The patrol was made up of new recruits—that had been how Fletcher had talked Liv out of joining it. New recruits bunched up rather than spreading apart, making them easy targets. They couldn't help talking. They even lit cigarettes. Their inexperience left them far more likely to return from patrol in body bags—as was anyone who went with them—than men who'd been at the front for any time at all. You learned quickly at the front, or you lost all opportunity to learn.

My eyes adjusted to the dim light, catching

movement out in the field: the shadow body of a soldier making his way across.

"He's one of us?" Fletcher asked, and one of the soldiers confirmed this.

"Why do I have the feeling this is *too* close?" I whispered to Liv, trying to calm myself with my words.

The soldiers watched silently, breathing warmly into the mist as the single figure made his way across the field.

"Why is he going alone?" Liv whispered.

No one answered at first. Then a voice— Fletcher's voice?—said, "He shouldn't be going alone."

"Frigging war's almost over," another voice answered. "You want to go, go ahead. Say hello to those Germans for me."

"How many?" I asked.

"Quiet," said the first voice—not Fletcher's voice after all, not even British. But a familiar voice, someone who sounded like someone I must once have known.

Another shot rang out, a single report. The shadow in the field lurched up, then crumpled.

A second figure sprinted forward, seemingly out of nowhere, crossing the open field, shouting, "Medic! Medic! Don't shoot!"

I raised up from my squat a little, scanned the field for the fallen soldier. At the horizon, where the rolling earth met the lightening purple-black of the sky, were the Germans I couldn't see.

The medic hurried in a low crouch across the field toward the fallen man, the bright red cross hand-painted on the white square on his helmet visible even in the early-morning mist.

German fire cracked out again.

The medic put himself squarely between the wounded man and the Germans and began to tend to him. Liv focused her camera, took the first distant photograph—a shot that would be washed out in the dim light and the mist.

"It's Hank," she said. "It's Hank Bend."

I nodded, remembering the familiar voice that had spoken, although I couldn't make out the round face and round glasses of the ambulance driver from Colorado Springs who'd driven us from the field hospital to Saint-Lô.

The other soldiers remained behind with us, their attention fixed on the medic and the wounded man but their feet as unmoving as my own.

"Can't you help him?" Liv pleaded to them as she took a second, no better photograph.

"He's a medic," someone answered. "He's protected."

More shots rang out.

Liv screamed over the rattle of the gunshots, then, for the soldiers to help him, to help Hank help the wounded man. She swore—anger, frustration, hopelessness—and she sprang forward as if her body were moving of its own will. She tugged away from Fletcher's hand on her sleeve and raced across the field, not all the distance to Hank and the wounded man, but closer, to a fallen tree trunk in the field halfway to them.

The medic used a pair of scissors tied to one of his wrists with a shoestring to cut away the wounded man's shirt. Liv took the photographs: the medic grabbing the bottom hem of his own raincoat and slicing off a strip of it, slapping it onto the man's chest where the skin was torn open, a sucking chest wound, and covering it with a compress. Not Hank Bend after all, but a boy who looked impossibly young, as if the pack he wore on his back ought to be filled with school-books and baseball cards. He looked like his first kiss must be in his future. His eyes were the bright white of a young man who grew up on carrots and Brussels sprouts, who built snowmen in the front yard without once imagining he would never see them melt.

She focused in more closely on the medic: the hem of his raincoat tattered as a result of dressing so many similar wounds; his eyes behind his glasses intent on the soldier, oblivious to her. Her shots would be no good; she knew that. There was simply not enough contrast, not enough light to capture the quick, sure movements from that distance.

Shots rang out again, more shots from the Germans across the field as the American soldiers continued to do nothing. Liv froze for a moment, paralyzed by the pop of a bullet near her left ear. But her camera found the wounded man again, his clear eyes looking up at the medic with an utterly unbearable hope. And she was already moving forward again despite the German fire.

Fletcher's voice rang out, then, his words indistinguishable, guttural. Liv swung her camera to photograph him charging. In his hands, he held not his camera but the Webley that had been his brother's gun. He sprinted past Liv, ahead of her, ahead of the medic and the wounded man, shots ringing from the Webley while, not far behind him, the soldiers, too, finally charged. They were too bunched together, but Fletcher started yelling for them to spread out, and by some miracle they did; they spread out as they ran past Liv toward the Germans, with their rifles aimed.

NEAR CAMBRAI, FRANCE
◆
TUESDAY, SEPTEMBER 5, 1944

We decided, like millions of other people, that we were most heartily sick of war; what we really wanted to do was borrow a sled and go coasting.
—Journalist Martha Gellhorn, from "The Battle of the Bulge," *Collier's*, January 1945

There was no talk at the poker game that afternoon of the German soldiers taken prisoner, no talk of the American soldier with the sucking chest wound who'd still been alive when they'd carried him from the field. There was only spirited banter and men betting everything they had, and laughing when they lost. Fletcher alone was subdued—Fletcher who'd led the men, who'd saved the soldier tended by the medic who was not Hank Bend. The word that came to mind from Fletcher's quiet expressionlessness was "ashamed."

One of the poker gang tossed a Luger into the pot, the futuristic revolver carried by German officers that was the favorite war souvenir of all the soldiers; none doubted that the very luck of having such a trophy could save your life. And this one *had* saved its owner's life that morning. He'd been hit by German fire, but the bullet struck the Luger and he was unharmed.

He lost the gun with two pair to Liv's three of a kind.

The poor boy looked devastated by the loss, but still, I was surprised to see Liv pick the gun from the pot and hand it back, saying, "You keep it. I'd have no idea how to shoot it anyway."

It wasn't like Liv to give up her winnings.

The boy caressed the gun. "It will bring me luck for sure now, Mrs. Harper," he said, "because you owned it, because it was a gift from you."

When he said he wanted to give her something in return, another of the players suggested the biscuit from his ration tin. In response to the looks given him, he said sheepishly, "It's all Mrs. Harper seems to eat."

"The only other thing I got is a bicycle," the soldier with the Luger said to Liv. "Not much of a bicycle, but I'd be proud for you to have it."

"A bicycle?" Liv asked.

Fletcher pulled a pack of Chesterfields ("Milder—Cooler—Better Taste") from the netting of his helmet, and lit one with the Zippo. "Have you any idea where we might find two more bicycles?" he asked the boy.

The Parisians, when they'd had no gasoline, the

Parisians had gotten where they needed to go by bicycle.

Fletcher said, "We have a perfectly good jeep we can give in trade."

"With a cracked windshield," I pointed out.

"With a cracked windshield," Fletcher allowed.

"A propensity to flat tires," Liv said.

"And not a drop of gasoline in the tank," I said.

Fletcher said, "If there were a drop of petrol to be had anywhere this side of Paris, we wouldn't be offering to trade a perfectly serviceable jeep and a fine Luger for three bicycles with rusty handlebars and bent frames."

It took the better part of the day to round up two more "liberated" bicycles, arranging a complicated series of liberated item trades. They were slightly smaller than the mangled-handlebar thing Liv got from the boy with the Luger (which took some substantial balance just to ride straight), but they all had sturdy chains and front baskets and back wire carriers, and they required no gasoline.

Fletcher asked me to cut his hair again that night. I followed him to collect the scissors from the emergency kit in the jeep, and we sat at the edge of his foxhole, his legs dangling into it. I ran a hand through his hair and said it didn't look bad to me. He patted the ground next to him for me to sit, too, and he pulled out a chocolate bar, fine chocolate the Germans had left behind for him to win in a poker game. He peeled the wrapper back, and I put my hand to his, to hold it steady while I bit off a piece. His fingers were warm against mine.

I said, "Delicious dessert."

" 'Pudding,' " Fletcher said. "I hear it can't hold a candle to your mum's berry cobbler."

"It's her peach cobbler that's best," I said.

"Yes, I remember," Fletcher said.

He peeled back the chocolate wrapper and held it for me again. It was a quiet night, with the Germans cleared out in the morning foray. Only the occasional trickle of quiet conversation. The moon was up, and the stars. Another patrol would be going out soon.

"It was brave, what Liv did this morning," I said. "What you both did."

"It was foolish, what Liv did. It was bloody foolish and it left me no choice but to follow her."

I let the chocolate sit on my tongue as I considered the possibility that Liv's running out to the medic might have put others in danger.

"Your following her was brave, anyway," I said. "Your brother would have been proud."

He pulled his feet up and put his arms around his knees, easy with his body. "Bravery is merely another form of cowardice. You fight because you don't want to humiliate yourself."

His brother's words that he'd shared weeks

ago, the day of the German boy in the woods. I'd never told Fletcher about that, and I didn't imagine Liv had either.

"I thought that was courage," I said.

"Aren't bravery and courage the same thing?"

He unwrapped the last of the chocolate, confirmed that I truly didn't want it, and popped it in his mouth.

I said, "If what your brother described is courage—that you fight to keep from humiliating yourself when you don't really believe you'll die—then maybe bravery is acting even when you know you'll be killed, or believe you likely will."

Fletcher had rushed out after Liv, expecting to be killed. The only protection against death he imagined was whatever his dead brother might have provided, a superstition that I supposed had more to do with an afterlife in which Edward waited for him than with any defense from death.

He said, "I'm not sure Liv would survive this war without you, Jane."

I said, "And you think she'll survive it with me?" And I laughed, because I wanted him to laugh.

He did laugh, too, and I remembered, then, the play we'd put on for the Fourth of July back at the field hospital, the lovely sound of an audience laughing because I'd written words to make them laugh.

"I think she couldn't bear to do nothing," I said.

"Sometimes nothing is the best thing you can do."

I crossed my arms, feeling chilled, wondering if he was right, if the bravest thing to do sometimes might be nothing at all.

"You're shivering, Jane," Fletcher said, and he gave me his jacket, and he scooted up right beside me and put his arm around me.

He said, "I'm not sure how *I'd* survive this war without you."

We sat together like that for a long time, with our feet dangling into the foxhole and the taste of chocolate on our tongues, the quiet between us comfortable.

Before the mist burned off Wednesday morning, Fletcher was leaning down into the foxhole Liv and I shared, and I was saying good morning and tapping Liv's shoulder, then shaking it lightly.

"Okay, I'm awake," she said without opening her eyes.

Fletcher took four rations out and set them around the edge of the foxhole.

Liv turned onto her back and opened her eyes. I hoisted myself up to sit at the edge of the foxhole, took one of the rations, and set to breakfast, such as it was. Fletcher handed Liv his biscuit, which she ate in three swift bites while lying on her bedroll in the trench. She sat up, shook off the bedroll and adjusted her helmet, then hoisted herself up beside me. Fletcher opened first one ration, then another, and set them back on the ground beside her. She picked one up and extracted the salt tablet.

"How can you chew those things when you won't touch a normal meal?" he said.

"Normal meal?" She eyed the lovely variety he'd hoped would entice her to eat before we set off on what might be a very long bicycle ride. "But I am ravenous enough to eat almost anything this morning."

He offered her a second biscuit, but she waved it aside and reached for a K ration tin of chopped ham and eggs. She downed it in a few oversized bites.

He offered her the last tin, a C ration meat-and-vegetable stew she'd pronounced "the most revolting muck she'd ever seen" just days before.

She wrinkled her nose at the sludge in the tin. "Amazing what we get used to here."

Fletcher watched as she made her way through the second tin in slow, steady bites. "Liv," he said finally, his voice low, serious, "that was stupid as hell, what you did."

"Well, Fletcher," Liv said, "I thought that poor boy needed his Luger more than I did."

"Liv," Fletcher said.

She ate a last bite of the stew and set the

empty tin down. She ate the salt tablet, then asked Fletcher if he wasn't going to eat his, and ate that one, too.

"Thank you for coming after me," she said to him.

"The medic was already helping the boy, Liv," Fletcher insisted.

Liv said, "He didn't have a camera, I don't believe."

She unwrapped the chocolate bar from the ration and took a bite, then another.

"Yes, but—"

Liv cut him off with just a look. Not the I-don't-fetch-tea look, but one that left him holding back his admonition not to run toward firing squads or German soldiers, not even for a Pulitzer.

Where did you draw the line between photographs important enough to put lives at risk and those that ought to be left untaken? Could you even know until you saw what showed up in the film?

We stripped down to the barest essentials in the rucksacks we wore on our backs, and we strapped our bedrolls to the back carriers and loaded our cameras and typewriter into the front baskets. Our plan was to pedal along until we found a Red Ball Express convoy, and to hitch a ride with it to wherever it delivered gasoline. As we pedaled off, I let go my handlebars, stretched my arms out like wings, and called out, "Look!"

and when Liv and Fletcher did look, I lifted my feet, too. "No hands!" I said. "No feet!"

We biked all morning, our only company coal-black crows, jackdaws, magpies with their long shiny-dark tail feathers. We stopped for lunch under the shade of a scrappy tree, then pedaled on only to see, at the next intersection, a line of trucks disappearing in the distance, a convoy we might have connected with if we hadn't stopped. We consulted the map, Liv determining that we ought to head for a small hamlet on the other side of a long, narrow woods. Fletcher worried the copse and town both might be in German hands, and Liv didn't want to go through the trees any more than I did after that. We decided, finally, to stay put, since we knew convoys passed here, and we were tired of biking. Fletcher pulled out a package of Lucky Strikes ("Lucky Strike Means Fine Tobacco") and we smoked and talked and sat in silence together, waiting. If this was a main supply road for gas to get to the troops, the Allied effort was in trouble.

When darkness fell, we ate dinner from tins and rolled out our bedrolls, Liv and me on one side of a privacy screen of bicycle frames, thin rubber tires, and even thinner spokes, and Fletcher on the other.

I woke with the dawn light to Liv sleeping beside me but Fletcher nowhere in sight. The Webley rested on the ground between Liv and me, the safety on.

"Liv," I whispered, "Fletcher's gone."

Something appeared on the horizon. I checked the Webley to make sure it was loaded, but already the something was taking shape as a long line of six-by-six, two-and-a-half-ton Jimmies flying down the dead middle of the bumpy road—sixty miles an hour at least, although the speed limit for Allied vehicles in Europe was twenty-five and the trucks were all equipped with speed guards that had to be disabled to go faster, a court-martialable offense.

The crack of a branch in the woods startled me, and I turned and aimed, the pistol's cold metal evoking Fletcher's admonition not to aim too low so that I raised the gun slightly as I shot, and shot again.

"Jane!" a voice exclaimed. "It's me! It's Fletcher!"

He waited until I lowered the pistol before reappearing from behind a tree, coming to us, and taking the pistol. He put the safety on.

"Bleeding hell, Jane, if you'd aimed an inch or two lower, I'd be dead!"

Perhaps my queasiness at that registered on my face because he put his hands on my arms, and he looked at me as closely as he had when I'd taken the shrapnel hit, and he said lightly, as if this were just another shooting lesson, "Jane, for someone who so obviously loves the feel of a gun in your hand, it's sad that you're such a bloody lousy shot."

We laughed and laughed then. Gallows humor. I laughed so hard I began crying, and then I was crying without laughing at all, and I was thinking I couldn't cry, I was a war correspondent, and if I couldn't do my job without crying they would send someone to replace me, and Fletcher was holding me, saying, "I know. I know, Jane. I know."

Liv, with a gentle touch on my arm, said, "The drivers are all Negro. Have you ever seen a photo of a Negro soldier, Jane?" She hurried to the side of the road, where the trucks whizzed by without even slowing, and she waved her arms high over her head lest we be left behind again.

I pulled myself together as one of the last trucks slowed for Liv. It didn't stop, but Liv raised her camera in salute to the next truck, one that looked like the farm trucks back in Tennessee, but with military letters and numbers painted in white on the front bumper and the hood. It pulled to a stop just up the road.

The driver leaned out the window. "You look like you need a lift," he said, his lovely deep voice surprising me, his *t* as perfectly pronounced as Fletcher's always were.

Liv asked if she could take his photograph. She

didn't say she wanted to take it because he was Negro. Neither of us had ever seen a photo of a Negro soldier in any newspaper, not in all the years of the war we'd spent in the States. I thought of the black maids on the trolley back in Nashville, always at the back. "Segregate"—a word I'd once offered Mama on the way home. "To set apart." It was in the dictionary between "seethe" and "segue," words I also meant to offer Mama that evening, but she'd begun singing without asking me to define anything.

We strapped our bicycles to the top of the truck and crowded in beside the driver, who set off again, going even faster now to catch up to his convoy. He didn't slow to read the signs warning vehicles to stay to the middle of the road in uncleared areas, or for the minesweepers off to the sides, or even for the MPs directing the trucks which way to go on the one-way roads. He slowed only once—as we crested a hill in the mostly flat terrain—and only slightly, only long enough to scan the horizon, alert to the possibility of German planes.

Not much later, Liv and Fletcher and I stood with our bicycles atop another hill, where the 743rd Tank Battalion of the American Second Armored Division and the Thirtieth Infantry Division, "Old Hickory," overlooked the ruins of Tournai, Belgium, bombed to almost nothing by the Germans early in the war.

The gas cans were still being unloaded from the trucks when Fletcher was summoned to see the commanding officer, a dark-haired major general named Hobbs.

"I've heard about the work you're doing, Roebuck, the look you're giving us at the Germans," Hobbs told Fletcher. "I'm pleased to have you in our neck of the woods, I don't mind telling you that."

"Thank you, sir."

"You have pictures to get out? Anything else you need?"

Fletcher said he'd get what he needed to send out to Hobbs's aide, and that he could use some food and film.

"Welcome to my war," Hobbs said. "We'd have this thing won if we could get supplies. But what's ours is yours."

"Thank you, sir," Fletcher said. "I could use a typewriter ribbon as well, and paper."

"Could you, now?" Hobbs called to his aide, "Do you have a spare typewriter ribbon for Mr. Roebuck here?"

"What kind of typewriter?" the aide asked.

When Fletcher didn't answer, Hobbs said, "I don't give a good goddamn who you're traveling with, Roebuck. If those ladies want to get themselves killed, that's their business. But if they endanger my men or my mission, I'll have them out of here faster than you can cap your lens."

Fletcher said, "I assure you, sir, Miss Tyler and—"

"Like I said," Hobbs said, "I appreciate what you do for us, the intelligence you gather. And I understand we're allowing lady journalists in these parts now, accredited ones, that's fine. If your traveling companions don't happen to have their papers in order, well then, I'm sure you'll have the good sense to keep that to yourselves. Are we clear?"

Fletcher assured him we were, indeed, clear as a well-polished lens.

"You let my aide know about that typewriter ribbon," Hobbs said. "And you tell your friends I expect them to do my men justice."

"Yes, sir," Fletcher said.

We made sixty-five miles the next day, over a gray world dotted with coalfields and slag heaps that reminded Fletcher of Wales. We camped south of Brussels, and made another twenty-five miles on the eighth before again running out of gas. The wait lasted only a day, though. By the tenth of September we were at Fort Eben-Emael, near the border with the Netherlands, hearing rumors of a frantic and confused German retreat, with soldiers as well as Dutch, Belgian, and French Nazi civilians fleeing in trucks and armored vehicles and even a horse-drawn hearse, and on stolen bicycles and children's scooters. The roads were reportedly thronged with dazed and disoriented Panzer troops in their black battle suits but without their tanks, with Luftwaffe airmen and Wehrmacht soldiers and even Waffen-SS troops. Trains heading for Germany and barges sailing up the Rhine were crammed to capacity, luggage left behind on station platforms. There were runs on banks all over Holland, and German soldiers were trading weapons for civilian clothes in which to avoid the Allied forces and their own military police.

On the eleventh of September, American patrols crossed the German border near Aachen.

THE NETHERLANDS
◆
WEDNESDAY, SEPTEMBER 13, 1944

I lose my friends and complexion in my devotion to the rites of flagellating a typewriter—and although the use of everything I send is madly satisfactory in the end, I've had time to be depressed to unproductivity, near suicide, or a change of career . . . I want more than anything, to be able to follow this war to the finish over here.

—*Vogue* photojournalist Lee Miller, in a December 1944 letter

By the thirteenth of September, when we moved with Old Hickory over a bridge thrown up across the Maas River to the rolling hills of Holland, I'd come to recognize the hope in Liv's eyes every time the country was mentioned; she was convinced Holland was where her brother's mission had taken him. As we drove into Holland, the Fourth Division east of Saint-Vith in the Ardennes drove right through the Siegfried Line—the three-mile-deep band of concrete pillboxes, troop shelters, command posts, and pyramidal concrete "dragon's teeth" antitank projections that stretched along the border of Germany and through Holland and Switzerland. They found machine gun emplacements with cement walls a meter thick and roofs three or four times that, all empty. Old Hickory, though, encountered resistance through the fields of wheat and sugar beets we slogged across, and into Eijsden and Gronsveld and the suburbs of Maastricht. Panzer shells disabled three Sherman tanks in our platoon, and those still firing were immobilized, again out of gas. Somehow, the German officers had taken the terrified, fleeing German soldiers and lined them back up.

"The Germans are defending themselves again," Liv said.

I didn't correct her. I didn't say that if they'd meant to defend themselves, they'd have fought in eastern France. We weren't twenty miles from the German border. What the Germans were defending now were their wives and mothers and children.

I said, "Why are you so sure he's here, Liv?"

Liv said, "Hobbs is giving Fletcher a courier to run our work back to the nearest press camp. Do you have your piece ready?"

"Your brother," I said.

She began pulling condom-wrapped film canisters from her bag for the courier. "His last letter, the postscript about the doll. It was a baby doll, a cloth one that I never played with. He said he used the missing shoe as a fishing bobber. I suppose it must have been made of wood. I suppose he was trying to tell me he was going to Holland in a way that would get past the censors and wouldn't mean anything to anyone else."

Liv was dealing cards early that evening when Hobbs's aide came for Fletcher, saying there was someone the major general wanted him to meet, and a task he had for him if he was willing. Liv and I slipped with them back to the abandoned farmhouse to find Hobbs in intense conversation with two members of the Dutch underground, big men in underfed bodies from a small town on the Geul River a few miles away. No one gave names—it was safer that way—but I silently filled the void with nicknames: Stewart for the one who was as tall and stoop-shouldered as the movie star Jimmy Stewart, and Bird for his companion with the fluttering hands.

I took notes while Liv photographed their pale, gaunt faces straight on in the dim light of the farmhouse. Fletcher listened but spent no film.

The two resistance fighters conversed in Dutch, their language sharper-edged than the French we'd become used to, more Germanic—as was their appearance. Stewart then addressed Hobbs in English, leaving me wondering where he had learned it, and how Hobbs knew he could trust these two, or if he did.

The town of Valkenburg was nearly empty of Dutch citizens, Stewart said. When the artillery fighting in the woods began and the first bridges were blown, most of the townspeople had moved to safety in caves outside the town. Only a handful of German soldiers watched over the last bridge not yet blown.

I knew I ought to be paying closer attention to the talk of the city and the bridge, the German soldiers, but my attention was fixed on the townspeople living in caves. The caves I'd seen back home, just over the Kentucky border, were as dark as the inside of a cow.

Hobbs nodded at Fletcher and at Captain Sixberry, with whom we'd shared a bit of jenever, a Dutch liquor something like gin, the night efore. The three of them stepped aside to confer for a moment.

I asked the Dutchmen if they would tell us about the caves.

Stewart said, "These caves, they are from the marlstone, the castle stone. Many miles of these caves, yes?"

"But the people," I said. "They live underground?"

Back home, miners wore helmets with carbide lamps on them, helmets that offered little protection when a mine collapsed.

Stewart looked to the remaining men as if trying to understand what to make of me.

"I'm Jane Tyler," I said. "I write for a newspaper in the United States. And this is Olivia Harper. She's a photojournalist." Talking over Bird when the man interrupted.

"Not the names," Stewart insisted. "We want not the names."

Bird took my measure, and Stewart watched him, and when Bird nodded almost imperceptibly, Stewart returned his attention to me and spoke slowly, intent on my understanding what he said.

"If you are from Valkenburg, then you live in these caves for days, yes?" he said. "Since the shooting is first, and then the freedom. The freedom, it is no good if you are shot dead."

"No. No, of course not," I agreed.

He told us whole families lived hidden in an extensive network of underground caves. When the Germans insisted the mine's owner take them through it, the owner led them into an unstable section and poked his walking stick at the ceiling so that part of it came down and the Germans turned back.

"If you are American *pilot*," Stewart said, using his hand and his voice to suggest an airplane crashing, "then you are in these caves for months, *misschien*."

"A crashed American plane?" Liv said, focusing

intently on Stewart. She extracted the photograph of her brother from her pocket and showed it to them. "It's my brother," she said.

Bird frowned at her and muttered something to Stewart, the words in his low voice disconcertingly Germanic.

"Geoffrey James," Liv said. "You could find out if he's hiding in the caves?"

"*Not* the names," Stewart said. "*Begrijp je mij*? The names, they make more danger."

"*Vertel haar over de Joodse mensen*," Bird said to Stewart—sharp, guttural sounds that suggested Stewart took direction from Bird. "*Vertel haar dat de Joodse mensen hier al jaren hebben ondergedoken.*"

"You are Jew?" Stewart asked Liv.

She shook her head, and he turned to me.

"No," I said, a fear creeping in: *Holy Mary, Mother of God.*

"If you are Jew," Stewart said, "you hide in these caves for long time, yes? More than four years."

"Will you take us to the caves?" I said. "Tonight. After it's dark. I would write about the people living there."

"You will write the story?" Stewart asked.

He looked to Bird, who nodded slightly just as Fletcher and Hobbs and Captain Sixberry rejoined us, Fletcher asking Stewart where he'd learned to speak English with a note of suspicion in his voice. Bird spoke to Stewart before Stewart could answer. Bird had understood Fletcher's question but didn't want us to know it, or didn't want Stewart to answer, or both.

Hobbs arranged with Stewart and Bird for an American patrol to move into the city early the next morning using the password "Steeplechase" to connect with the Dutch resistance. Steeplechase, as if this were some course to be run by beautiful horses, where one had only to sit in the saddle and hang on.

Liv started to insist on being included, but Fletcher shot her a warning glance. He meant to take us along somehow, and he didn't want to give Hobbs an opportunity to forbid it.

OUTSIDE VALKENBURG, THE NETHERLANDS
◆
WEDNESDAY, SEPTEMBER 13, 1944

In wartime, truth is so precious that she should always be attended by a bodyguard of lies.

—Prime Minister Winston Churchill

"As a child, I loathed the dark, and I've grown no fonder of it since the war began," Fletcher said as Liv and I gathered our gear later that night, to be ready when Stewart and Bird returned to take us to the caves. I'd always liked the dark: its protective cloak, its heightened sense of sound and smell, touch and taste. Summer nights with my bare arms humid-damp against the seat of the Chrysler.

Liv said, "You ought to have stayed back in Paris, Fletcher, in your warm bed."

"With Hemingway," I said.

"There will be a real war to photograph come sunrise," Fletcher said, "and there will be no light by which to take photographs in these caves."

Liv slung the Leica strap over her head, then put on her helmet.

"Anything the two of you get will be censored,"

Fletcher insisted. "Forever caught up in Washington red tape. We'll be beyond the front, in German-controlled territory."

I tightened my chin strap and the lace of my left boot. Maybe Fletcher was right. Maybe nothing we did tonight would make it into print. But what if these people didn't survive?

"I'm a photojournalist," Liv said. "This is my job and I'm damned well going to do it. You don't have to come, Fletcher. I'm not asking either of you to come."

"Going to the caves tonight was *my* idea," I said. It was the kind of story that could make a difference, the kind of vivid story that would lodge in people's imaginations.

But of course Liv was thinking of her brother.

"I don't even need the kind of light you two do to work," I said.

"You stay behind if you want, Fletcher," Liv said. "Jane and I are fine."

Fletcher muttered an obscenity and went to fetch his gear, to my relief. Everything felt safer with Fletcher. And when Stewart and Bird returned—searching us for weapons before leading us off—Fletcher waded along with us through the fields outside Valkenburg.

Stewart led and Bird followed as we made our way by the light of a hazy moon in a starless sky to a hillside entrance hidden in the brush, like the machine gun emplacements of the Siegfried

Line. Within a minute, the world around us was pitch-black and I was creeping uneasily behind Liv, groping for the sides of the cave. They were gritty cold, but anchoring, and slightly less frightening than the smell of the damp stone and the taste of underground air and the quiet crunch of steps that might be ours alone, or might not.

"Did I tell you how much I loathe the dark?" Fletcher whispered behind me.

I wondered again how Hobbs knew he could trust these two Dutchmen, or if he did. I wondered why Stewart hadn't answered Fletcher's question about where he had learned English. I wondered what Stewart's and Bird's real names were. I wondered if they were even Dutch.

Stewart lit a dull flashlight, and I was just able to distinguish the outline of Liv a few steps ahead of me, and then the shadow of Stewart. A faint circle of light bobbed on the path ahead of him as we made our way forward and down—for thirty minutes or perhaps more.

A wail sounded in the distance—high-pitched and animalistic. Liv stopped and I did, too, leaving Fletcher bumping into me, his front warm on my back for that short moment, a strand of my hair catching in the stubble of his chin.

I reached for the cold, gritty cave wall. It was utterly dark, even Stewart's dull flashlight extinguished.

Human. The wail was human, I thought as it

sounded again. Someone being tortured. But I wasn't sure.

Fletcher's hand touched my shoulder gently, and he stepped in front of me, and in front of Liv.

"It is fine," Stewart said, clicking his flashlight back on. He offered no explanation for the cry, nor did he sound surprised or troubled by it.

After another minute or two, the Dutchman stopped and said a few words, not in English, and a voice—male, elderly, suspicious—answered, more guttural foreign words that tingled at the back of my neck.

A workman's boots were caught in the dull circle cast by Stewart's flashlight.

A few more words were exchanged, and the elderly voice called back to someone behind him, the hard foreign words more brutal in the louder tone.

I inhaled the stink of human sweat over the damp-stone smell and a fainter, more unpleasant smell, too. Urine. Excrement.

A moment later footsteps sounded, coming from deeper inside the cave.

A bright light flashed onto Fletcher, who instinctively raised one hand to shield himself, reaching back with his other hand to protect Liv and me.

The click of a gun being readied to fire.

"*Nee!*" two voices said at once, Stewart ahead of us and Bird behind.

Several less frantic Dutch words followed as Fletcher lowered his arm, still shielding Liv behind him, all of us blinking into the sudden brightness. A stooped old man lowered a pistol, the cave passageway now lit by a bright beam of flashlight trained directly at us, casting frightening shadows back across the old man.

"*Hij moet de vrouwen zien*," Stewart said to Fletcher. "He must see the others."

Fletcher stepped aside slowly, and the light beam fell on Liv. She raised her hands slightly: empty. The light moved on to me.

Again, a few words in Dutch, Stewart's stooped shoulders relaxing as he gave a curt explanation to the old man. I made some sense of a few words I could pick out: "*fotograaf*" and "*camera*" and "*journalist.*" He did not use our names.

The old man tucked his pistol into the waistband of his trousers and turned and began down the passageway, the single beam of his brighter flashlight lighting sharply cut stone walls—a mine rather than a natural cave, or a cave that had been mined. After a moment, we came to a narrow passageway marked with a black arrow and black letters painted on the stone: VERBLYF VOOR 53 PERSONEN.

"There are fifty-three people living here?" I whispered.

"In this . . . in Dutch, one says '*grot*,' yes?" Stewart answered. "This room, and others."

"Fifty-three in this cavern and others?" I said, trying to imagine fifty-three people living underground together, even in separate caverns.

"In some larger *grot*, two hundred, yes? In some smaller, ten."

In another moment, the old man's flashlight splashed out over a stone chamber. A group of women sitting together blinked into the light, moving their arms protectively over children sleeping stretched out on blankets on the ground beside them. Everywhere, people slept, and those who didn't were impossibly silent. Fifty-three in one cavern.

The old man called out a few quiet words.

A hushed murmur of relief exhaled from those who were awake, a sound that echoed off the stone. Several of the children stirred.

The single beam of light splashed over an entrance to another cavern across the way. The entrance—marked in the same black writing, VERBLYF VOOR 8 PERSONEN, with the same black arrow—was framed with wood beams, and there were posts supporting the ceiling in both this first room and the far one. I followed Liv's gaze to a mother with a child, hardly more than a baby, in front of the sign. A faint light seemed to linger behind them even after the old man's flashlight fell back onto the stone at our feet.

The child might be half German, but the war had come suddenly to this part of the Netherlands, in early 1940 before anyone could even believe what Hitler was doing; there were young men here who had come of age under almost five years of German occupation, who never had a chance to join an army. Stewart himself. Stewart couldn't be much more than twenty. The mother might be Jewish, too. She might have been living in this cave with her husband for the entire war.

"This is where the people, they wait," Stewart said to us. "The soldiers, they use the dynamite. It is to fire *de huizen en de stad*—Valkenburg, yes?—but what do these Germans care? They leave Valkenburg and nothing left, yes?"

I wondered if he'd learned English from the American pilot hiding here.

"We have the ration cards, yes? *Gestolen.* Not for us, but we take. Now we can get no more the ration cards. Now the children, they eat first."

Fletcher, his eyes fixed on the dark shadow of the mother and child, felt in his fatigue pockets for something, but left his hands there.

It was surprisingly temperate in the cavern, warmer than the chill passageways, the body heat of the cave's inhabitants warming the air. The warmth accentuated the stench of human life lived without access to fresh air or sewage drains.

Another wail filled the air—this time distinctly a woman's voice, long and high. It came from beyond one of the other entrances, from another chamber. Everyone turned toward the noise, but no one looked startled or even troubled.

Several of the children again stirred, but none woke.

Stewart said something to a stout woman sitting with several others just inside the cave, and she answered with a pleasant smile and a few words.

"*Zij is voor het eerst moeder, yes?*" Stewart said. "She have no baby, but this one, he will be born tonight. Tomorrow, *misschien.*"

"Someone is giving birth here?" Liv asked.

Stewart's grin revealed bucked front teeth. He looked so kind, suddenly. "The babies, what do they know?" he said. "It is the time to be born even if it is the war."

Liv, camera in hand now, scanned the room. "May I take photographs?"

"This is why we come," Stewart answered. "One man, he dies here already. Not dies from the war but dies only from the being old. It is no place to die, yes? In this cave with only the fear."

I said, "Perhaps we could . . . The mother? If we wouldn't be too intrusive?"

"The photograph of the child is being born," Stewart said, "it will make the difference for the Americans?" He nodded, and he spoke a few words to the old man, who uttered a single syllable and disappeared in the direction of the entrance to the eight-person cavern, the light bobbing along beside him. A moment later, he reappeared, signaling with a wave of his free hand to follow him.

A short passageway led to another cavern, this one marked in the same black arrow and writing, VERBLYF VOOR 5 PERSONEN, and dimly lit by a single candle. A woman lay stretched out on a thick layer of blankets on the ground, panting, her knees up and her legs open. Fletcher averted his gaze, and I knew he was thinking of Elizabeth Houck-Smythe then, and his brother's baby.

Two older women tended the birthing mother, one running a damp cloth over her forehead, the other at her feet. A fourth woman—a woman almost as pregnant as the one giving birth—busied herself with something off to the side. She was fair and blond and big-boned. She might have passed for the sister I never had.

The birthing woman wailed, a raw sound.

Liv stood staring, wide-eyed, her camera limp at her side, a single graceful hand touching her own stomach as if trying to absorb some of that pain herself.

"The photograph, it is permitted," Stewart said. "She say is fine."

"Okay, then, on three," Fletcher said to Liv, raising his camera, not looking through his lens but only pointing his flash unit in the right direction.

The pale skin of Liv's neck flexed and her

delicate fingers moved to her chest, her camera untouched.

"Liv?" Fletcher said.

She looked to him, and he nodded at her camera and indicated his.

"If we coordinate the flashes," he said, "there might be light enough."

Liv looked down at her Speed Graphic. "Yes," she said. "Yes, of course."

"On three," Fletcher said. "One. Two. Three."

The light fell back again into the glow of the single candle and the flashlight, barely making a dent in the darkness.

Liv looked at her flash as if it might somehow be coaxed to do more. Even with the larger-format film of the Speed Graphic, the light wasn't enough.

She opened her musette bag, extracted something, and set it on the floor, not too close to anyone—the ground flare she'd traded a whole box of French cigarettes for earlier that evening, after the Dutchmen had left and before they'd returned for us. The transport truck driver she'd made the exchange with said she could just have it, but she didn't like to take it from him without giving him something in return.

"It was what Margaret Bourke-White used to light the Otis Steel Mill; it's how she made her career," Liv said. "Hers was magnesium. Bright white. I have no idea what this is."

She flipped the dark slide over and pulled, flipped, and reinserted the film holder to ready the second shot.

I offered to light the flare, so she could focus on the photographs, and I extracted from my slacks' pocket the Zippo lighter Fletcher had given us at the inn in Rambouillet.

Stewart explained to the women about the flare so they wouldn't be startled, his Dutch words sounding rounder now, less threatening.

When the next contraction started, I flicked the lighter and set it to the fuse.

In the longer, brighter light of the flare: the woman's contorted face, the mucous red of the blood, the twist of hair at the crown of the head that surged just the slightest as she groaned. Liv took shot after shot—images I couldn't imagine ever being in print anywhere, but maybe I could couch the moment in words that would go down well enough with breakfast even if a photo might not.

Fletcher patted his shirt pocket for cigarettes, then shoved his hand into the pocket of his fatigues where he kept his last chocolate bar. He'd lost his nerve. He turned to the other woman, the pregnant one, and met her brown-eyed gaze, and he pulled the chocolate bar from his pocket and offered it to her.

Liv, watching the exchange through her lens, became so still that she seemed to be her own tripod.

She lowered her camera and stared at the pregnant woman.

The woman shook her head, saying something about the chocolate to Fletcher, declining it although her expression made plain her hunger.

"She wishes for you give this to the children," Stewart translated.

"I want her to have it," Fletcher said. "She should have it herself."

Elizabeth Houck-Smythe had craved chocolate when she was pregnant, he'd told me.

Again Stewart translated. Again the woman shook her head. Again, the birthing woman began to groan, and Fletcher looked uneasy. Stewart smiled slightly. "I think you will like to give this chocolate to the children yourself. Then you can continue on, yes?"

Liv let her camera hang from its strap and began fishing in her pockets. She pulled out a chocolate bar and handed it to Fletcher. She opened her musette bag and fished from it a second candy bar, pausing for a moment, looking from her bag to the pregnant woman. She pulled out two more chocolate bars and handed them, too, to Fletcher, her eyes fixed on the woman, the skin pale in the slant of light.

"Go ahead, Fletcher," she said. "Jane and I will follow in a minute."

Fletcher looked to Bird. Bird nodded at Stewart and said a few Dutch words to Fletcher that I took to mean "follow me" or "this way," that only in retrospect would I realize included "Valkenburg" and *de brug over de rivier.*

As I listened to the sound of receding footsteps, Liv stared at the pregnant woman who had declined the chocolate. The woman stared back with brown eyes, like mine.

Liv moved her musette bag from her side to her front, her belly.

When the sound of Fletcher's steps was distant, Liv looked into her bag again and extracted something. She held out a closed fist that was pale and yet steadier, more certain. With only the quickest glance at me, she opened her palm to the woman.

A single salt tablet rested there.

"Salt," Liv explained.

The woman stared.

Liv turned to Stewart. "Tell her it's salt."

Stewart said, *"Zout,"* and the woman smiled slightly, the light from the flare reflecting in her eyes.

Liv nodded. *"Zout,"* she repeated.

The woman reached out with slender fingers, and in the light of the waning flare, she took the salt tablet and set it in her mouth.

Fletcher was nowhere to be found when we emerged from the smaller cavern into the larger one. Stewart, after a heated exchange in Dutch with Bird, told us they would see us back to the camp. Liv and I protested again and again that we wouldn't leave without Fletcher, but Bird, his hands fluttering nervously near a pistol holstered at his waist, ignored us, demanding of Stewart, *"Begrijp je mij? Begrijp je mij?"*

Stewart said to Liv and me, "Yes, you will follow me now."

OUTSIDE VALKENBURG, THE NETHERLANDS

◆

THURSDAY, SEPTEMBER 14, 1944

I know it will be a long time before I want to go with any attack to take pictures again.

—Photojournalist Robert Capa

Liv slept beside me in our foxhole perhaps four hours later, only half covered with her bedroll despite the predawn cold. I lay on my back with my helmet off to better hear, listening as I had all night. Still, I was startled half to death when Fletcher peered down at me.

"Showtime," he whispered.

"Fletcher," I said, working hard not to cry with relief as I climbed from the foxhole.

He hugged me for a long moment, saying, "You and Liv put me in a devil of a spot. I hadn't meant to take a detour to visit bloody caves on my way into town, but I sure as hell couldn't let you two go alone."

"You went into *Valkenburg*?" I said.

When Liv and I had returned from the caves, we'd gone to Hobbs about Fletcher's disappearance, only to have the major general appoint a soldier to escort us to our foxhole and keep an eye on us—punishment for having left the camp without Hobbs's knowledge, we thought. Now I saw it was Fletcher's safety that had been his concern, that Hobbs had known where Fletcher was. From the caves, Fletcher had snuck into town to assess the position of the Germans before this morning's assault on the bridge began. What he would capture on film during the planned attack in the coming day—how the Germans guarded the bridge and the positions of their snipers, their explosives—would be helpful for the future, but it wouldn't help Hobbs's men this morning. That was why Fletcher had been so reluctant to go to the caves, because Hobbs had needed him to suss out the situation in Valkenburg.

"I'm sorry I wasn't able to see you safely back to camp," Fletcher said, "but my gut told me the chaps from the underground could be trusted. And it was safer for you to have no idea where I was."

Around us, men were stirring, gathering their gear and speaking quietly in the darkness. I sat at the edge of the foxhole, shivering in the damp chill. Liv didn't wake.

"Lordy, I want a cigarette as badly as a preacher wants to cuss," I said.

Fletcher leaned into the foxhole and rustled

Liv's shoulder. She hooked an arm over her helmet as if to shield herself from him. She was wearing gloves—a good thing. She never dressed warmly enough. She said she was too warm even when I was cold.

Fletcher lifted her arm—heavy with sleep—and patted her gloved hand vigorously, the leather all scrunched together at her wrists.

"Come on, Livvie," he said. "Time to go to Valkenburg."

She rolled over onto her back and looked up. "You're ill?" I said.

"No," she said. "No, I'm just not sure I can—"

"Liv, we're almost to Germany!" Fletcher said, his voice far too loud. Everyone turned. Why not just light that cigarette? Why not send up a flare to announce to the Germans that we're here, right here?

Fletcher reached behind him for the ration tins and cranked open a chopped ham and eggs, her favorite. "Eat," he said in a more controlled tone. "You'll feel better after you eat."

Liv climbed out of the foxhole and removed her helmet, her hair sticking out at odd angles. She ran gloved fingers through it and set the helmet back on and tightened the chin strap. She loosened the fingers of the glove on her left hand and pulled it off, revealing the two wedding rings. She pulled the other glove off as carefully, folded them, and returned them to her pack, with the red gown.

Fletcher said, "You two will stay back with the troops until the rendezvous is complete," and he laid out for us what he had arranged for the morning: He would go with the small patrol that was to protect Captain Sixberry during the rendezvous. We would wait up the road with the rest. If the rendezvous was successful, Fletcher would ride in our jeep for the assault on the bridge.

Major General Hobbs didn't know Liv and I were going, and Captain Sixberry didn't know we hadn't been invited; Fletcher meant to keep it that way.

Liv didn't object.

"The child was a girl," Fletcher said. "The baby born in the cave. I heard earlier this morning."

Liv and I smiled at the thought.

The mother had died giving birth, but Fletcher didn't have the heart to tell us.

I looked around, at the boys girding themselves as best they could against the planned foray into the city. I met Fletcher's gaze, his green-brown eyes, and I wondered if his brother had had those same eyes, those same generous ears, and if his brother's baby would have had them had he or she lived. I wondered if that was when Fletcher had gone gray, when he'd lost his brother, or if that had happened after Poland with Charles.

Fletcher found and opened another ration, and

we ate silently but quickly: chopped ham and eggs, all of our biscuits, powdered coffee mixed in cold water—I didn't even care, didn't even add my box of sugar, just drank it thin and gritty, unsweetened, most of the grounds at the bottom. When I finished, Liv, too, had eaten everything, even the caramels. Fletcher handed her his salt tablet without her even asking. Liv took it, and she began to gather her gear.

I turned to her then, and I whispered, "You don't have to do this, Liv," thinking I ought to tell Fletcher about the salt. Fletcher hadn't seen that in the cave; he'd already gone to give the chocolate to the sleeping children. I understood in that moment that the salt meant something, although it seemed impossible that it could mean what it must. That Liv was pregnant. That she'd realized it herself as she'd watched the child being born. That was why she offered the pregnant woman the thing she could never get enough of, the salt. Why she hesitated now. Why she didn't insist on going to see the rendezvous.

How could she not have known she was pregnant, though? How could I not have seen it even if she didn't realize it herself? But it can be impossible to see what's right in front of you when it doesn't make sense, and so many things get muffled in the fog of war.

Or maybe Liv *had* known? Maybe seeing the birth in the cave had only made her own child more real? She'd kept the telegram about her brother secret even after we'd watched the boy die by flashlight in the operating room. *Don't tell anyone,* she'd insisted after she set free the German soldier in the woods. *Not even Fletcher. I couldn't bear for anyone else to know.*

"You don't have to do this, Liv," I repeated, thinking they were impossible, the choices. The mother sending little Ange out to tell us about the gasoline in the cemetery shed, offering us their only means of escape if the Germans returned. My own mother watching as my train left Union Station. The mother pulled from the refugee line outside Compiègne, who'd sold her whole future for a few red Life Savers, for a child's rabbit coat.

Liv wiped the lens of her Leica carefully with a cloth. She capped the lens and looped the camera strap over her neck and shoulder, and began loading film canisters into her pockets, along with a handful of condoms. When she was ready, she took the red gown from the bottom of her pack and pressed her face to it for just a moment, as if something of her mother might be left in the silk.

"This is all I can do," she whispered. "Shutter speeds, *f*-stops, angles of light."

VALKENBURG, THE NETHERLANDS
◆
THURSDAY, SEPTEMBER 14, 1944

The war correspondent has his stake—his life—in his own hands, and he can put it on this horse or that horse, or he can put it back in his pocket at the very last minute.
—Photojournalist Robert Capa

Fletcher hid in the brush on a bank near the rendezvous area with several soldiers from the patrol as Captain Sixberry sat coolly waiting on a bench near the entrance to a coal mine. The early morning was eerily quiet as a Dutchman in civilian clothes appeared some distance down the Daalhemerweg street. The Dutchman approached the bench cautiously, his eyes darting from the captain to a limestone sign painted with black letters—*"Daelhemer-Berg Steenkolenmijn"*—to the building to the right of the mine entrance and the stone stairway leading up to woods behind it, where anyone might hide. He glanced back to the crumbling walls of an old castle and the town beyond it, too. He was older than Fletcher expected, considerably older than Fletcher himself. Perhaps in his forties.

The captain, watching the approaching Dutchman, grinned and said, "Hey there, you want a cigarette?"

The tension in Fletcher's fingers on his camera made them ache. He'd agreed to take no photos until after the contact was made, and these were not the photos he needed in any event, but he longed for the distraction of his camera, the excuse to hide his fear behind his lens. He'd been farther than this the night before, but he'd been alone. So often, it was safer being alone.

"I like Steeplechase," the Dutchman responded to Captain Sixberry, and he introduced himself as Paul Simons, saying the name with conviction.

Fletcher wondered what his real name was.

Captain Sixberry asked the man how many German soldiers remained in the town and where they were. He spread an ordnance map across his lap, and Paul Simons studied it.

No one was left on this side of the Geul, Simons said.

"This bridge by the Den Halder Castle," he said, indicating a point on the map, "is the only bridge now, but it is mined and it is guarded from the Hotel Oda, over there."

There might be Germans left in the casino dance hall, he said, and there was German traffic from Meerssen through Houthem to Valkenburg, traffic heading on through Heerlen to Germany.

A few of the soldiers with Fletcher emerged

from the brush, one of them already speaking into his walkie-talkie, passing along the information. Simons watched, wide-eyed. Fletcher was sure the Dutchman must be used to men emerging from hiding after this much time spent under German occupation. It must be the walkie-talkie that fascinated him.

Fletcher stood.

A squawking voice replied over the walkie-talkie, directing the platoon to try to take the bridge over the Geul in a pincer movement. Deploy the soldiers in two separate groups, the voice directed. Position them to allow snipers to surprise the Germans, to prevent them from blowing the bridge. "We need that bridge. Don't let it blow."

Paul Simons turned down the road and waved, beckoning someone.

Fletcher held himself perfectly still.

A single, younger Dutchman emerged from hiding and approached—Stewart.

L'Istelle, he said his name was now, and perhaps it was.

The two Dutchmen deliberated for a moment in their language before Simons nodded to the captain. The captain said Simons would come with his platoon, and Stewart would go with the other.

"Okay, let's go," the captain said.

VALKENBURG, THE NETHERLANDS
◆
THURSDAY, SEPTEMBER 14, 1944

I'm never sure what I am going to do, or
sometimes even aware of what I do—only
that I want that picture.
—Photojournalist Margaret Bourke-White

Around the bend up the road where the rest of the
patrol waited—Liv and I with them—the driver of
the lead jeep signaled. The drivers released their
brakes, and the queue of open jeeps, machine
guns fixed to some of their hoods, began rolling
silently down the steep incline. Partway down
the hill Fletcher leapt into our jeep. Farther along,
the lead jeep pulled to a stop at the bench and
Captain Sixberry and two soldiers at the
rendezvous with the Dutchmen jumped in. The
captain directed Simons to climb up onto the
hood and Stewart to the same post on a second
jeep. The captain didn't trust them.

We rolled on downhill along the Daalhemerweg
street, past a crumble of ancient castle wall to our
right, a perfect perch for snipers. The morning
was still, only the roll of the jeep wheels on the
road.

At the square, a small cluster of people awaited us. The older Dutchman sent them quietly off to warn the few townspeople who hadn't fled to the caves to be silent, not to start celebrating the arrival of the Allies as was so often done. The town remained mute, the houses and shops appearing abandoned but for a drape moving here and there behind closed windows.

Liv seemed to hesitate as we piled out of the jeeps. She still looked so pale that I wanted to tell her it wasn't too late to turn back, that I would turn back with her if she wanted to. I said nothing, though, as we followed the soldiers into the narrow lane.

They split into two platoons.

We went with Captain Sixberry and Paul Simons, headed for a position from which to observe the bridge. We passed through an ancient stone archway, an old castle gate as high as the two-story buildings crowding the lane's edge, with a statue of the Virgin Mary looking down on us from a recess between two windows. *Holy Mary, Mother of God, pray for us sinners, now and at the hour of our death.*

From the street beyond the archway, we slipped into the Hotel Smeets-Huynen. Inside, an older lady gasped at the sight of us, but the family stayed otherwise silent, leaving only their expressions to betray their fear.

The rest of our patrol would be pushing two of

the jeeps forward, the heavy machine guns fixed, the engines switched off. They would station the guns between two other hotels, the Neerlandia and the Bleesers. From there a small group of soldiers would follow Stewart along the back sides of the houses to the Protestant church, through some gardens and on to another hotel, the Prince Hendrik. Others would try to reach the banks of the Geul through the school yard.

We slipped out the back door of the hotel as silently as we'd entered. Liv seemed to hesitate as she crossed the threshold back into the open air, as if she would just as soon hide in the basement with Mrs. Smeets-Huynen until the Germans left. But she took a photograph: several of our soldiers with their machine guns, ascending a church tower from which they could cover the bridge. A little color seemed to return to her cheeks.

Fletcher did not use his camera. It was the positions of the Germans, how they defended the bridge, that British intelligence would want.

Paul Simons led us to a nearby building that smelled of yeast, a brewery. My mouth was dry, but I hadn't brought a canteen. Fletcher's hung from his utility belt, clipped to the holes in the canvas alongside his extra film, but I couldn't have managed to open the canteen to drink even if I could have gotten it from him without making any noise.

We made it to the spot that was to be our observation point, and Captain Sixberry fished a periscope from his pocket. A castle wall obstructed the view of the bridge, though. This castle, unlike the one up by the coal mine, was more or less intact.

Simons indicated another location with a gesture, and the captain nodded.

Silently, we slipped along the castle wall to a lower wall on the Geul River. The wall offered so little protection.

Captain Sixberry again raised his periscope.

"Jerry on the bridge," he mouthed.

He beckoned Simons to look through the periscope. The Dutchman watched for a moment, frowning.

"He sees something," Simons whispered. "He is stopped. He is looking toward the Hotel Prince Hendrik."

That was where the other patrol was meant to be.

"He is looking now to the dance hall."

There might be lookouts at the dance hall, he'd warned.

The captain took the periscope, and looked, and whispered, "He's seen someone from the other platoon."

Liv looked to me, her hand on her camera, as if she needed to take the shot but could not.

I thought, *Are you close enough now, Liv?* I thought, *You don't have to do this, Liv.*

She began to rise from her crouch, and I was sure she was going to run; she was going to take off back in the direction of the hotel, and I watched as if in slow motion, wanting her to run and wanting to run with her, and wanting not to want to run.

She lifted her camera and turned toward the bridge.

"Liv, *don't*," I mouthed, but she was already looking over the wall, her eyes taking it in through the lens. I rose, too, then, not like Liv but just enough to peer over the edge of the wall.

Just a single man—one German soldier—stood on a small stone bridge.

That was what everyone was afraid of, a single young man who must be far more terrified than we were, standing over a river so narrow you could almost step across it if the years of water flow hadn't cut so deeply into the earth. A single man standing out in the open where anyone might shoot him, while we hid in the shadowed protection of the wall. He was young; his body as he turned to flee the bridge moved with the fluid ease of a boy, his uniform jacket stretched across his narrow shoulders, his rifle following the movement of his arms. He glanced back, and Liv took the shot: a soldier in a battle helmet, his jacket buttoned to the top. Maybe my age or

Liv's, not a boy like the German in the woods, but still with women to love and children to have.

He shouted.

He's German, I reminded myself. He's the enemy.

I tried to capture the scene in my mind as Liv shot the photo: the man's deep-set eyes under his helmet, his mouth shouting German words I didn't understand. He was just a man on a bridge, a man trying to do his job like Tommy or Fletcher or Charles or Geoff or any man any of us had ever known. A man who did not want to end up like the soldiers Liv and I had watched the nurses clear from the field back in Normandy, who'd lost their legs and then their lives or, if they were lucky, everything at once.

The world filled with such a loud noise then, and the bridge was exploding and I was diving for cover, a reflex, as the explosion enveloped me, everything fire and flying debris. And Liv was not there for a moment, for maybe longer, maybe less. The world was perfectly quiet and Liv was not there, Liv was not anywhere or I wasn't, and there was no pain, I felt nothing at all.

I needed to crawl away, but I could not lift my arm.

Then Fletcher was dropping his camera and shouting, his words coming to me as if through water, "Jane! Jane!" And Liv was nearby, her face pressed to the cobblestones, and the sound was all around me again, but muted now, as if someone had known the world was too loud for me and had turned the volume down. A voice was humming, too. A soft, beautiful voice. "Tell me a word I don't know, Janie," the voice said. Was I home? I wanted a blanket and I wanted to tell Mama a new word, but no words came.

VALKENBURG, THE NETHERLANDS
◆
THURSDAY, SEPTEMBER 14, 1944

No one ever understood disaster until it
came.

—Journalist Josephine Herbst

The explosion was still overwhelming Fletcher,
the shrapnel and earth and the stone of the
bridge improbably filling the air as he shouted,
"Jane! Jane!" Then, "We need a medic here!"

Something hit his bare hand, stinging like a
bullet. He fell sideways with the force of it, and
there was Liv, too. "Liv!" he said. "Oh, Livvie."

He crouched beside Liv, his hand dripping
blood on her helmet as he cried, "Medic! We
need a medic here!"

Blood soaked the arm of her blouse.

He pulled out his shirttail, tried to tear it for a
tourniquet. The damned fabric wouldn't tear.

He unbuckled his utility belt. Yanked it off. It
fell to the ground with the weight of the things
clipped to it.

A soldier beside him, staying low to the ground
as shots rang out, said, "Jesus."

Fletcher tried to rip the things from the belt. He

threw it aside and pulled off the belt securing his trousers. Wrapped it around Liv's arm almost at the shoulder. Pulled it tight.

"Liv," he said. "It's okay, Livvie, I'm here, I'm going to take care of you, you're going to be fine."

He secured the belt as tightly as he could, but the bleeding didn't stop.

His camera lay on the ground by the wall. Liv's was closer, half under her leg. He grabbed it and wrapped the thin leather of the camera strap above the belt on her arm, a double strap because that was quicker than trying to unhook it from the camera. He pulled it much tighter than the belt.

"You're going to be fine, Liv," he said again.

He turned her slightly toward him so he could see the right side of her face. "Are you okay? Does that hurt too much? Can I turn you over? Can we get you back to the wall?"

One eye fluttered open and looked up at him, the shocking blue iris tucked into the corner, the lash blinking.

He touched her shoulder, eased her gently onto her back.

The soldier beside him gasped.

Fletcher took in the blood-covered front of Liv. Some part of her that ought to have been inside her was not.

"Get a fucking medic," he said in a low voice to the soldier.

The soldier just stood there, staring.

"Get a medic! Get a bloody fucking stretcher!"

The boy ran off in the direction of the archway.

Liv looked up with both eyes—a vague, faraway stare.

"Don't worry, Liv," Fletcher said, focusing on her face framed by the helmet, unable to look at the rest of her.

"You're going to be fine, Liv," he said. "We're getting you help."

"Fletcher," she said.

"Shhh, Livvie, shhh," he said. "Look at me, Livvie. Don't talk. Save your strength."

He slid his hands under her and lifted her, trying to ignore her gasp.

She seemed to weigh almost nothing, to almost not exist.

He ran with her in his arms, crouching along the low wall, the damned camera dangling from her arm where the strap was tied hammering his shin. He carried her into the hotel, the family not anywhere in sight, hidden in the safety of the basement. He pushed out backward through the front door of the hotel and under the archway.

The medic came, finally, a medic in a raincoat, rushing toward them, reaching them just on the other side of the archway, where there was a little more protection from the gunfire that continued in the wake of the bridge explosion. The medic came with a stretcher, which he set on the cobblestones.

Fletcher lay Liv down on the stretcher.

The medic cut a big slice of his raincoat and laid it over her gut. He administered a shot of morphine. He and Fletcher covered her with a blanket. Lifted the stretcher. Loaded Liv into an ambulance-jeep.

"We're getting you back to the aid station," Fletcher said. Then to the driver, "What the hell are you waiting for?"

The driver nodded in the direction of the archway. "There's one more coming, sir."

VALKENBURG, THE NETHERLANDS
◆
THURSDAY, SEPTEMBER 14, 1944

It is awful to die at the end of the summer when you are young and have fought a long time . . . and when you know the war is won anyhow.
—Journalist Martha Gellhorn

Fletcher loomed above me. I tried to hold on to that: the moss-brown eyes, the gray hair. The movement of clouds above him nauseated me and I wanted to vomit, and I didn't want him to see me vomit but there was nothing I could do.

"Raphs," a voice said, not Fletcher's voice. Liv lying beside me.

"Shhh," Fletcher said. "Don't talk, Livvie. We're getting you to the aid station. Just hold on. We're almost there."

I wanted to help her. I wanted to say she was trying to tell Fletcher about the photographs. She was worried about losing the photographs. Of course she was. But I had no words, no voice.

"Fletch," she said as I struggled to keep my focus on the reality of Fletcher's eyes.

"Shhh," he said, to her or to me or to both of us. "Shhh."

I felt the tingling beginnings of relief.

"Raphs," Liv repeated.

"Shhh," he said to her. "Shhh. There's an army regulation against . . ."

Dying. There was an army regulation against dying if you made it alive to an aid station.

He leaned closer to her, tears clearing paths down his dirty cheeks.

I couldn't feel one of my own hands at all, and the other felt weighted down with concrete, sunk in a mucky mire far from my waist.

"Renny," Liv whispered.

Fletcher leaned even closer to Liv, to her closed eyelids, the little bump on her nose. "You're going to be fine, Liv," he said forcefully, as if the power of his will could save her. He moved the camera tied to her arm out of the way so he could get closer to her. "You're going to be fine."

I wondered if my own skin was that pale, my own lips that blue.

"Where is the bloody aid station?" Fletcher said to the driver or to Liv or to no one at all. "Why is it taking so damned long to get there?"

He circled his arm around the top of Liv's head and stroked her hair as he must have done that one starless night outside Paris.

"It's okay. You're going to be fine, Livvie," he said again, his voice pleading now.

Liv, still with her eyes closed, whispered, ". . . so cold, Daddy." Her face some colorlessness paler than white. ". . . so cold."

HÔTEL DE VILLE, PARIS
◆
SATURDAY, AUGUST 20, 1994

I am pushing against the wall which is fog and therefore gives and swallows and cannot be pushed. For I am trapped with the puzzle of overcoming war. Dimly, I see my direction, but cannot see the footing, and so far am faltering, and marking time, and bluffing—and failing.
    —Photojournalist W. Eugene Smith

Britt's hand settles on my arm as Fletcher heads toward us, his tie tied just a little too precisely, as if he's pulled it from a field pack and ironed it into submission—or close enough to submission that a precise tying might finish the job.

"You're here!" he says, kissing first Britt and then me. "Sorry, the flight was beastly late." He borrows Britt's champagne long enough to clink the glass to mine. "To *Pushing Against the Fog: The Photographs of Olivia James Harper.*"

The book has gotten this far, through the miles of red tape to retrieve the censored photos— most of Liv's photos—from the American government, and through meetings with dozens of publishers before persuading one to take on the book. Without the promise of this splashy launch, there might have been no *Pushing Against the Fog*. Liv's photographs are incredible, yes, the publisher had said, but no one has heard of Olivia Harper in years. If it weren't for the one photo that became so well known—the Paris liberation shot, which wasn't attributed to Liv until after the war was over—there might have been no book even with Fletcher's influence, his introductions. Liv's death in the fall of 1944, "unfortunate as it was," made it off the obituary page only in the newspaper her husband ran.

I can almost forgive Charles, for having at least allowed Liv that dignity.

I wonder if church bells rang at her funeral. Neither Fletcher nor I had been there. I was in the hospital, and Fletcher was in the Netherlands, or perhaps in Germany by then, improbably carrying on. Charles alone had buried Liv—Charles who is approaching us now in the exhibit hall, a sad old tuxedo hanging crookedly from his uneven shoulders, one lower than the other as if he's carried the weight of everything he's endured in that one hand. The publicist told me he planned to come, and yet I'm surprised he has.

Charles greets Fletcher as if they are old friends, as if they last spoke only days ago rather than going on fifty years.

Fletcher sighs, and smiles, and says, "Charles,"

and I can see in his tired eyes that he's pushing back the urge to bash in Charles's nose as surely as I'm pushing back the nagging idea that a scene here between the septuagenarian widowed husband and the man Liv was traveling with at the time of her death might gain the book a trove of publicity. Liv, though, would never have forgiven anyone for gaining her publicity like that.

"So how have you been, old man?" Charles says to Fletcher.

"Charles, you know Jane," Fletcher says, although in fact Charles and I have never met; we've only communicated through lawyers for the requisite permissions from the estate of Olivia James Harper, trusteed by the widowed Charles.

He's never remarried, Charles hasn't.

"And this is our Britt," Fletcher says—our Britt, because calling her our granddaughter belies the fact that we raised her.

As Britt shakes Charles's hand, Fletcher looks away, to the book on the stand, the jacket cover photo of the woman celebrating atop the car in front of the barricade, her face looking straight into the camera, not angled even an inch. Charles was wrong in not running that photograph in his paper. Liv was wrong in thinking she'd not captured the truth of the liberation of Paris, the truth of the war. The thin shoulders in the flowered dress. The sharp brow bone and dark brows and blue-green irises—an intense color

407

suggested even in the black and white photograph—against the determined white of the woman's clear eyes. Eyes that are full of tossed flowers and double kisses and champagne, babies held high to witness, yes. But eyes bathed, too, in loss. It's a plain, beautiful face haunted with the truth of what one person will do to another with only the excuse of war. It seems a different photograph than the one I first saw in the newspapers at the Hôtel Scribe. Perhaps I hadn't looked closely enough that morning, or perhaps something had been lost in the transfer from film to newspaper print.

"Charles," Fletcher says again, unable to cough out the words he surely knows he ought to say: how good it is to see him after all this time or some similar drivel.

But Charles is already saying the words himself, and two other men are joining us, one my age and one Britt's.

Charles is saying to Fletcher and me, "You haven't met Geoffrey, have you?"

The eyes—Liv's eyes—meet mine.

"Geoffrey James, Olivia's brother," Charles is saying as I try to absorb the shock of seeing those eyes again.

"You have your sister's eyes," Fletcher stammers, placing his hand lightly on Britt's back as if to support her, although it's himself he soothes with the touch.

I set my champagne down and extend my good hand to Geoff, saying, "Your sister spoke so often of you."

I think to say something about being sorry to have missed Liv's funeral all those years ago, but this twin brother of Liv's missed it, too. He'd slipped into the Netherlands in July to prepare the way for Operation Market Garden and been captured. He wasn't known to be alive until Russian soldiers liberated his camp days before the end of the war. We'd tracked down his story after the peace. Fletcher had meant to write him, to share with him something of his sister's last days. It was what one of Edward's war buddies had done for Fletcher. But I had been the one to compose that letter, with Mama writing the words I couldn't write with my own hand. That had been at Trefoil Hall.

Charles introduces the younger man as Geoff's grandson Jeremy, then says to Jeremy, "This is Fletcher's granddaughter, Britt, the one . . ." Charles takes his glasses off and wipes them clean on the pleats of his tuxedo shirt, then puts them back on. "The one who took the photo I showed you at dinner," he says.

With that gesture, I blink against the tears welling in my eyes, the prick of pride at my granddaughter's talent mingling with the memory of Liv's voice as we'd looked out from that hayloft into one of so many nights unblessed by the moon. Liv describing how Charles would take off his glasses and clean them, how she lived for the approval he delivered in that simple gesture, the judgment that her photos were good. I hear Liv saying Fletcher had two mistresses—two that Charles *knew* of—although of course Charles had been mistaken, or worse. Fletcher was loyal to Elizabeth until he met Liv. He might have remained loyal to Elizabeth even then if Liv hadn't come to him. I think he might have remained loyal to Elizabeth after the war, too, but she chose a new love and new memories over holding on to the past with a man whose brother she'd loved.

Geoff's grandson Jeremy takes Britt's hand and holds it a moment longer than you might expect, as if he knows my granddaughter through the single photograph of hers Charles has shown him.

"Jeremy James?" Britt says in her warm, easy voice, and she says she read a piece about him not long ago. He's of the young computer-whiz variety, apparently, but with the decency to wear proper shoes.

"The piece reminded me of Grandma Jane's writing," she says in a tone that conveys admiration for the writer, if perhaps not for Jeremy himself—words that take me aback a little. When has Britt read my writing? I lost the use of my right hand at Valkenburg and never wrote again, not until Britt brought me a small cassette Dictaphone like the one she uses to document her photos. "Record your stories, Grandma," she said. "I know you don't want to, I know you never talk about what the war was like, but would you do it for me?"

No one but my typist and my editorial team has read any of the little bits I recorded, this book of Liv's photos in mind even when I started. Not until today. Britt has been overseas for her own work, and I don't suppose Fletcher will ever read what I've written for this book. I don't suppose he'll ever look at Liv's photographs beyond the ones he can't avoid seeing tonight. He does like that one photo of me learning to shoot, the bloody-lousy-with-a-gun photograph. But he says he prefers to look to the future, and I say I under-stand, which I do, somehow.

Still, Fletcher picks up the book and runs a hand over it as if he might touch Liv that way, touch the woman who took that photograph. He turns to the back cover, to the photo of Liv standing in Hank Bend's ambulance-jeep with her Speed Graphic in her hands and her Leica hanging from a camera strap, Liv watching as Major Howie's flag-draped corpse on the door stretcher was placed on the pile of cathedral rubble at Saint-Lô. Fletcher had taken this shot of Liv before we'd seen him on that day we went AWOL. Just the single shot. Then he'd removed the roll from his camera and carried it with him, undeveloped, all the way to Berlin.

"She was Mutt to your Jeff, that's what Liv told me," I say to Geoffrey.

He smiles at this little bit of memory of his sister. "No, she didn't much like to be called Mutt."

She chose Holland over Germany because of you, I want to say but don't.

I'm so sorry, I want to say.

Fletcher says, "Your sister was one of the most incredible women I've ever met."

Geoffrey's gaze drops to the parquet wood floor, and he smiles sadly. Nods to me. "I appreciate what you've done here, Jane, getting her photographs . . . this book . . ."

The sounds of the crowd in the next room mingle with our silence: a lady's titter, a man's more forceful laugh, the tink of glass with glass. I look to Liv's brother, wanting to see those eyes again. Wanting to tell him that the photograph I'd wanted for the cover was the last one she'd taken, in Valkenburg. A photograph of a German boy alerting his fellow soldiers to blow the bridge he himself was still on, turning back to try to identify the source of the danger even as he moved to flee. A photograph of a single Nazi soldier, his gaze caught straight on, with no shadow. An impossibly young man doing what was expected of him so that he could go home to a mundane life, to his mother, perhaps to a wife and children. A boy doing his job with courage, or perhaps with bravery, photographed by Liv doing her job in the same way, in the moment before they both died.

Geoffrey looks up, finally. Clears his throat. "Jane, could I . . . May I ask you one thing?"

The striking eyes cut to Charles standing silently beside us.

"Who was Renny?" Geoffrey asks.

To Renny. So simple, and not.

Fletcher fixes his gaze on the frescoed ceiling: a woman floating in white, playing a violin among others floating around her, all surrounded by cherubs in red. I did tell him about the dedication. He listened and nodded the way he does when he doesn't want to face a thing, the more quickly to have it done.

Geoffrey says, "She's my sister, you know, and she's gone and all she left are these photographs, and I don't have any idea who Renny was."

He extends a hand to Fletcher, who relinquishes the book to him. Geoffrey opens it to the dedication page as if he needs to show me what I've done.

I stare at the ink on the page in Geoffrey's hand, at the graceful fingers holding the book, both familiar and not.

Charles's hand goes to his glasses, adjusts them on his narrow face, and I fear he is going to cry. I imagine trying to tell him, just as I imagined trying to tell Fletcher in the days and months after the war. Liv's baby would have been Charles's daughter or son, not Fletcher's; I'd found some awful relief in that.

For a moment, I imagine assuring Charles and Geoffrey both that the book is dedicated to Fletcher's and my daughter. Had it been Fletcher's idea or mine to name our daughter Renny? I don't even remember anymore. What I remember is Mama appearing at my hospital bedside in England; the letter from Fletcher offering us a place at Trefoil Hall for my recuperation; Fletcher returning in the spring, after the evacuee girls had gone back to London and Elizabeth had gone off with her new love. What I remember is the long conversations Fletcher and I had in the summer and fall and winter after the peace, with Larkins and Serle and Mama caring for me at Trefoil Hall, and caring for Fletcher, too. Fletcher's wounds not physical, but the wounds of what he saw in Berlin and Buchenwald added to the rest. What I remember is the void we tried to fill with a child neither of us could bear to name Olivia, our Renata who grew beyond the burdens of her birth to be her own person.

But this isn't my book; this is Liv's book that I've put together, her photographs with my words only to put them in context. The Renny to whom the book is dedicated isn't ours.

Charles takes the book from Liv's brother and runs his finger over the printed name, a caress, almost the way I used to touch Renny's hair when she was sleeping, the way I used to remove her thumb from her mouth and, later, Britt's.

"Renata was a dream," he says, "something Olivia thought she wanted, a way she imagined herself." He sighs, his eyes through the eyeglasses shrunken, uncertain. "But what Olivia wanted was to take photographs."

I look to the first photo in the exhibit again, Fletcher teaching me to shoot. I remember Liv aiming the Webley at the cigarette butt on the road. Liv floating in the murky water of the Dives. Scooping up her poker winnings, handing the Luger back to the American boy with the bike. Watching the blackened airman falling through the sky, the horses, the woman having her head shaved. Hank Bend in his raincoat. The child born in the cave, who was Britt's mother, the child Fletcher and I went back to find after the war, in the spring of 1946. The child who helped us mend our hearts, only to break them again the day Britt was born. Our daughter, like her mother, did not survive the birth of her child.

I remember Liv asleep in our foxhole on that last morning outside Valkenburg, the day our daughter's first mother died, and Liv died, too. Liv's slender fingers lost in gloves of a red leather as soft as the silk of the gown Fletcher found in Liv's rucksack that night, after the world had changed. The gown and the gloves that Fletcher quietly kept when Liv's things were returned to

Charles, that he tucked beside the single shot of Liv in the bottom of his own pack, and took with him to his brother's grave when at last the war was done, and kept all the years of our marriage until, finally, he gave the gown to Britt. Only the gown, not the gloves. Somehow, neither of us can part with Liv's gloves.

I run a hand over the book myself, wanting to say something to ease Charles's loss the way putting this book together has eased mine, the way all the years of my loving Fletcher have eased my husband's pain and allowed him to return my love. But I don't say anything. I slip my hand into Britt's, wanting the warmth of my granddaughter's touch, the certainty.

Liv was close enough, after all. I was close enough, too, because I went with her. But I can't speak for Liv any more than Charles can. Any more than Fletcher or Geoff. None of us can know, really, who Liv's Renny might have become, or what Liv knew or wanted or why she made the choice she did to go into Valkenburg that morning; whether she would have chosen differently if she'd had more time to consider what she was risking, or if she'd had all the time she needed, if she'd been making that choice every morning of the war. All we can do is let Liv's photos speak for her now, and for us, too. Her faces looking straight into ours. Shades of gray. Of black. Of a misty, unforgettable white.

ACKNOWLEDGMENTS

Although Jane, Liv, and Fletcher are all fictional characters and this novel is a work of fiction, I have relied heavily on actual experiences of journalists and others for inspiration and for many of the book's details. The novel perhaps was born the moment I read about "Patricia," the imaginary daughter to whom Margaret Bourke-White and Erskine Caldwell dedicated *You Have Seen Their Faces.* The "Operating Room by Flashlight" scene was inspired by a short passage in Bourke-White's *Portrait of Myself* about a night at a field hospital in Italy; thanks to the Vanderbilt University library for allowing me to spend so many hours there reading it, and to the late Dr. Phillip Davidson for arranging that.

My apologies to the unnamed photographer whose photograph ran on so many front pages of American newspapers on August 25, 1944, for conscripting the photo, modifying it to fit my purposes, and moving it across the Seine.

The late Annette Roberts Tyler's personal recollections of her time "over there" inspired the character Jane, who, as might be expected of a character inspired by my aunt, refused to be left behind when Liv left the field hospital, and so charmed her way into a much bigger role than I meant for her.

Julia Edwards's *Women of the World: The Great Foreign Correspondents* was a terrific introduction to the real-life women who inspired this story. Nancy Caldwell Sorel's *The Women Who Wrote the War* not only was a fascinating read, but also led me to many other sources, including Catherine Coyne's "Miss Coyne Joins WACs in Invasion" from the July 12, 1944, *Boston Herald*. Other early sources of inspiration included Robert Capa's *Images of War* and John MacVane's *On the Air in World War II* (an incredible first-hand account of the liberation of Paris from a correspondent's view). Cornelius Ryan's *Collier's* article titled "The Major of St. Lô" and Andy Rooney's *My War* account of the same moment were indispensible for the Saint-Lô scene, as was Ernie Pyle's reporting from the Saint-Lô–Périers road—"A Ghastly Relentlessness," "The Universe Became Filled with a Gigantic Rattling," and "Anybody Makes Mistakes"—for the short-bombing scenes.

The details of the blowing of the bridge in Valkenburg come from a piece I found online, *"Verzet van Pierre Schunck en de zijnen"* ("The Resistance of Pierre Schunck and His People") by Arnold Schunck, whose father, Pierre Schunck, operated in the Dutch resistance under the pseudonym "Paul Simons"; from early e-mails with Sheila Knight and Laury Watervoort, who were kind enough to answer my questions; and from my visit to Valkenburg and the caves, which Tihana made much easier by the simple act of holding our bags.

Thanks to James Hamel at the Vouilly Château (once a World War II press camp, now a delightful inn) for his hospitality, knowledge, and photography skills. The staff at the Hôtel Scribe in Paris allowed me to poke around in the hotel of today, and helped flesh out my journey through their past with Pierre-André Hélène's *L'Hôtel Scribe: une légende au coeur de Paris*. There has never been a better tire-patch gang than Barney Rickman and Don Vantrease. And thanks to Jean Kwok and Erwin Kluwer for help with my Dutch, Ben Lanail with my French, and my brother David with my German.

I was also helped by Anne Kasper's April 3, 1990, interview of Helen Kirkpatrick; Peter Prichard's "Front Lines and Deadlines: A View from the War Zones" interview of Martha Gellhorn; Virginia Cowles's *Looking for Trouble*; Stephen Ambrose's *Citizen Soldiers*; the Smithsonian's *Reporting the War: The Journalistic Coverage of World War II*; *The Second World War: Original Recordings from the BBC Archives*; Shelley Saywell's *Women in War*; Martin Blumenson's *Liberation*; Sean Callahan's *The Photographs of Margaret Bourke-*

White; Larry Collins and Dominique Lapierre's *Is Paris Burning?*; Max Hastings and George Stevens's *Victory in Europe*; Judy Barrett Litoff and David C. Smith's *We're in This War, Too: World War II Letters from American Women in Uniform*; Peter Maslowski's *Armed with Cameras: The American Military Photographs of World War II*; Susan D. Moeller's *Shooting War: Photography and the American Experience of Combat*; Jonathan Silverman's *For the World to See: The Life of Margaret Bourke-White*; James Tobin's *Ernie Pyle's War*; Vicki Goldberg's *Margaret Bourke-White*; Antony Penrose's *The Lives of Lee Miller*; Caroline Moorehead's *Gellhorn: A Twentieth-Century Life* and *Selected Letters of Martha Gellhorn*; A. J. Liebling's "Letter from France" series from *The New Yorker*; Andrew Mollo's *The Armed Forces of World War II: Uniforms, Insignia and Organization*; and the *New York Times* archives, especially those from the summer of 1944. Sources I came to late in the writing, but which also proved helpful, include Carolyn Burke's *Lee Miller* and Michael Neiberg's *The Blood of Free Men*. I hate to think how many sources I turned to that I have failed to mention.

Tatjana Soli and her stunning *The Lotus Eaters* inspired me to persist. Ilsa Brink worked her web miracles yet again. Other friends and family who provided much-needed comfort and relief in less writerly ways include the extended Waite and Clayton gangs (special thanks to Ashley for all she does for me, to Emma for the pencil case that makes me smile every time I pull out a pen or pencil, and to Sadie for hanging out at bookstores with me); Fred, Laird, and the Santa Barbara gang; my WOMBA and poker pals; Grace; Gayley; Eric and Elaine; Camilla and Dave; Debby and Curtis; John and Sherry; Darby and Sheri; and last, but certainly not least, Jenn, Mom and Dad, and Chris and Nick. Without their good company, good humor, and the occasional much-needed good meal, I would long ago have taken Fletcher's Webley and shot the hell out of this manuscript.

Friends and teachers who read this manuscript over the many years I have been working on it include Madeleine Mysko, Leslie Lytle, Dan Levin, Ellen Sussman, Kate Brady, and Anna Waite. Tim O'Brien will long ago have forgotten the early encouragement that I won't ever forget. And Mac Clayton and Brenda Rickman Vantrease read draft after draft of this one, over more than a decade, and never wavered in their enthusiasm. Mac doubled as my intrepid traveling companion; it would be a much poorer story but for his questioning, his willingness to stray well off the usual tourist routes, his ten-mile-plus walking range, and his *excellent* driving skills.

The ever-amazing Marly Rusoff became a

convert when I might finally have given up on this one, and helped me find the gumption to stick by it. I am truly forever in her debt, and in Michael Radulescu's, too.

Hannah Wood, Katie O'Callahan, Rachel Elinsky, and Mary Beth Constant are lovely to work with, as is everyone at HarperCollins. Thanks also to Alison Forner for the stunning cover, and Bill Ruoto for the gorgeous internal design. And Claire Wachtel gave this book life, and so much more. Through her gentle questioning, her extraordinary wisdom, her unwavering expectation that this book could be even better and that I was up to the task, and her blessedly stubborn refusal to accept less than the best I could do, this is so much stronger a book than it would have been. I've grown immensely as a writer in the time I've had the privilege of working with her.

Claire and Marly, I wish I could come up with some more brilliant way to say thank you; this book has been close to my heart for a long, long time, and I am so very grateful for this chance it may have to find its way into readers' hearts as well.

ABOUT THE AUTHOR

MEG WAITE CLAYTON is the *New York Times* bestselling author of four novels: *The Four Ms. Bradwells*; *The Wednesday Sisters*; *The Language of Light*, a finalist for the Bellwether Prize; and *The Wednesday Daughters*. She's written for the *Los Angeles Times*, the *New York Times*, the *Washington Post*, the *San Francisco Chronicle*, the *San Jose Mercury News*, *Forbes*, *Runner's World*, and public radio. A graduate of the University of Michigan Law School, she lives in Palo Alto, California.

Center Point Large Print
600 Brooks Road / PO Box 1
Thorndike, ME 04986-0001 USA

(207) 568-3717

US & Canada:
1 800 929-9108
www.centerpointlargeprint.com